LETTING GO OF YESTERDAY

THE CORNISH BAY COLLECTION

JO BARTLETT

Boldwood

First published in Great Britain in 2025 by Boldwood Books Ltd.

Copyright © Jo Bartlett, 2025

Cover Design by Lizzie Gardiner

Cover Images: Adobe Stock and Shutterstock

A CIP catalogue record for this book is available from the British Library.

Paperback ISBN 978-1-83678-136-3

Large Print ISBN 978-1-83678-137-0

Hardback ISBN 978-1-83678-135-6

Trade Paperback ISBN 978-1-80656-053-0

Ebook ISBN 978-1-83678-138-7

Kindle ISBN 978-1-83678-139-4

Audio CD ISBN

MP3 CD ISBN

Digital audio download ISBN

This book is printed on certified sustainable paper. Boldwood Books is dedicated to putting sustainability at the heart of our business. For more information please visit https://www.boldwoodbooks.com/about-us/sustainability/

Boldwood Books Ltd, 23 Bowerdean Street, London, SW6 3TN

www.boldwoodbooks.com

For Viv and Richard, who let go of yesterday and found a love story they wanted to hold on to forever xx

1

Laughter drifted down from the end of the wood-panelled corridor that led from Rowan's office to the staffroom. Lessons had finished almost two hours earlier, but the school was still a hive of activity. She glanced out of one of the windows as she continued towards the staffroom. Outside some of the girls on the all-weather pitch were whizzing hockey balls at a goalkeeper, whose protective gear made it look like she'd been wrapped in a duvet. Voices carried up from the hockey practice, and beyond that from the rugby pitches where the first and second teams were training for an upcoming tournament. Membory Grange was never quiet in term time. There were more than two hundred boarders on site seven days a week, and a further seven hundred day pupils, as well as the large team of staff who took care of them. Even if all of them had teamed up, Rowan still wasn't sure they'd be able to drown out the raucous laughter emanating from the staffroom.

'Okay what am I missing out on, because it sounds worth hearing?' Smiling, she looked at the two women sitting side by side on a dark green sofa in front of an oak coffee table, strewn with magazines. They were the only people in the staffroom, which was typical by this time on a Friday evening. It was why a debrief of the week, over a cup of coffee, was a regular date for the three of them.

'Ooh watch out, the head's here. We better stop having fun.' Odette West, the school's head of modern languages mimed putting a finger to her lips and then gave another hearty laugh. Rowan might technically be the boss of the other women, but first and foremost she was their friend and, after the day she'd had, she badly needed to know what was so funny. The tension must have shown in her face, as Odette stopped laughing and tilted her head to one side. 'Why don't you sit down, Rowan. I'll make you a drink and Pippa can tell you what's she's just told me.'

'It's okay, I don't mind making the drinks.' Rowan was conscious of her friends treating her slightly differently since she'd become headteacher. Thankfully it hadn't been a huge change, they were her closest friends after all and she would have hated to lose that bond as a result of her promotion, but there had been a subtle shift. Before they'd have taken it in turns to make the drinks if they met up in the staffroom, but now Odette was jumping to her feet and waving away Rowan's offer, as if the idea of the headteacher making the coffee was absurd.

'No, I'll get them.' Odette gestured towards the seat she'd just vacated. 'You're going to want to sit down for this anyway.'

'Will I need something stronger than coffee?' Rowan looked from Odette to Pippa, who was already laughing again.

'I think you might.'

'And once you've heard it, you're never going to stop imagining what might be going on behind the doors of Keeper's Lodge either.' Odette grinned. 'I thought we were all the same – living this quiet, boring life – and then bam, you get hit with something like this. It just goes to show that you never know who your neighbours are.'

'Okay, now I'm not even sure I want you to tell me.' Keeper's Lodge was one of eight staff houses in the grounds of Membory Grange. Rowan lived in the largest of the properties, with her husband, James, the school's chaplain, and their two children. It was a four-bedroomed detached cottage somewhat unimaginatively called Head's House. The bursar lived next door and beyond that was Elderberry Cottage, where Odette lived with her family. In addition to their teaching responsibilities, Odette and her husband were house parents taking care of some of the boarders. Pippa, who taught English, was also a house parent and lived in Keeper's Lodge with her husband Daniel, who ran the school's farm. They were almost like any other neighbours in a suburban cul-de-sac, except that they lived in the magnificent 250-acre grounds of an exclusive private school, as sheltered from the realities of the real world as their pupils were.

It could easily have been a nightmare living in such close proximity to people she had to work with too, but from the moment Rowan had started at Membory Grange, nine years earlier, when her daughter Bella had been less than a year old, it had been like finding her tribe. She'd bonded with Odette and Pippa quickly, and both of them were godmother to Theo, her youngest child, who was now almost seven. She felt blessed to be raising her children in a place like Membory Grange, but clearly something had been going on at Keeper's Lodge.

'If you don't want to hear it, I'd better just show you.' Pippa pressed play as she passed her phone to Rowan, and a video of her husband Daniel appeared on the screen. He was wearing a dinner suit and could have been dressed for any one of the events the school regularly hosted, where formal attire was a must, but then suddenly the strains of 'You Can Leave Your Hat On' started playing. Daniel turned his back to the screen, flicked up the tails of his jacket, looked over his shoulder and wiggled his bottom like a part-time stripper who should definitely have stuck to the day job. Pippa's distinctive laugh could be heard in the background of the video and suddenly it was in stereo, as she started laughing again, watching Daniel attempting to remove his jacket in what Rowan assumed was supposed to be a sexy way. Unfortunately, his arm got stuck in the sleeve and his attempts to flick the jacket off ended up with it wrapped around his head. When Daniel finally emerged, he was laughing too and had abandoned any attempt to take his strip tease seriously. He was lip-synching to the words and pulling ridiculous faces, as he slid his belt out of the loops of his trousers and lassoed it around his head.

'Oh my God.' Rowan started laughing long before Daniel undid the top four buttons of his shirt and pretended to tease his 'audience' by sliding it off one shoulder and up again. By that point he was laughing too and the camera was shaking badly, Pippa clearly having lost the battle to hold it steady. The laughter already felt like it had done Rowan some good, but she couldn't help feeling a tiny bit guilty. 'Does he know you're showing this to people?'

'He gave me permission to show you two and don't worry, it doesn't go any further than a little hint of shoulder. We were both laughing too much, but it still gets funnier every time I watch it.'

'Poor Daniel, there he was trying to be sexy and all you could do was laugh.' Rowan tried to keep a straight face, but it was impossible.

'Oh, don't worry, Daniel knew *exactly* what he was doing. He knew his sense of humour was what made me fall for him in the first place, and being funny is always going to do it for me.' Pippa put down her phone. 'If he'd done a striptease with serious intentions I'd be running for the hills. Thank God it was supposed to be funny and let's just say he got what he was hoping for.'

'You've got to give Daniel his due.' Odette set the coffee cup down on the table. 'Seb is about as subtle as a sledgehammer, grabbing my bum when he walks past, or pressing up against me while I'm trying to make the kids' dinner or unload the dishwasher. Why is it that men never seem to grow out of acting like sex-obsessed teenagers? Sometimes I just want to fall asleep in front of the TV, without getting pestered, but men are just always bloody well up for it, aren't they?'

'I think it's wired into their DNA.' Pippa rolled her eyes. 'At least Daniel seems to have realised he needs to make an effort over the course of the day if he's going to stand a chance by the time we get into bed, although the dance was a whole new level of effort.'

'What about James? Does he whip his cassock off for you the moment he gets through the door? Or dance for you in just his dog collar.' Odette wiggled her eyebrows suggestively and Rowan gave a non-committal smile.

'Ooh look, she's gone quiet, you know what that means. It's always the quiet ones you've got to watch.' Pippa grinned and Rowan shrugged, grateful that her friend's imagination had let her off the hook. She could have told them the truth, and a big part of her desperately wanted to confide in someone, but she just couldn't do it. How was she supposed to admit to her two closest friends that she couldn't remember the last time she'd had sex with her husband? And that when she tried to reach out and touch him, he rolled away, making an elaborate show of snoring, even when she'd been certain from the sound of his breathing that he'd been awake just seconds before. Heat swept over her at the thought of the attempts she'd made to spark his interest when they'd been away for the weekend for their wedding anniversary. Thank God no one had videoed that, because it had been mortifying to be a part of, never mind how humiliating it would have been for anyone else to see it. Daniel had nothing to be embarrassed about in comparison.

Rowan had spent a fortune on the type of lingerie that an online forum had informed her was guaranteed to 'reignite the passion'. When James had emerged from the bathroom after his shower, she'd been lying on the bed, in a position a contortionist would have been proud of, in an attempt to flaunt her best bits, and disguise the parts of her body she hated the most, which these days seemed to be the majority of it. When the person who was supposed to love you most didn't seem to find you remotely attractive, it was hard to hold on to any shred of self-esteem. James's eyes had widened in what she'd hoped was surprise, but which she had a feeling now had been far closer to horror. He'd mumbled something about having an upset stomach and had bolted straight back into the bathroom, where he'd remained for the next twenty minutes. By the time he'd re-emerged, Rowan had got dressed and downed half a bottle of champagne to drown her sorrows in the wake of James's reaction to her attempt at seducing him.

He'd been all smiles when he'd finally come back out of the bathroom, reminding Rowan that they had plans for dinner in thirty minutes.

'I thought you had a bad stomach.' Even the words had tasted bitter in her mouth and she'd taken another huge slug of champagne to try and wash them away.

'I think it was just a bit of cramp, but I feel fine now.' He'd smiled again and she'd felt like slapping the expression off his face; the mixture of humiliation and anger were a dangerous combination.

'Funny that. The sight of me without my clothes on always seems to make you feel ill just lately.'

'Rowan, please.'

'What? Not this again? Is that what you're going to say?' She took another glug of champagne. 'Don't worry, I don't want to have the same conversation we've had a hundred times before again either. It always goes the same way anyway. I ask you what's wrong and tell you how unattractive it makes me feel, and you come up with half a dozen excuses to avoid admitting that anything's wrong. Except we both know it is.'

'Having young kids and busy jobs is tough on us both. Every relationship goes through changes and dry spells. I'm sure things will shift again in the future.' He'd reached out then and put a hand on her shoulder, but she'd shaken him off and refilled her glass. She'd wanted to tell him that he was wrong, that more than eighteen months without any physical intimacy didn't represent the kind of dry spell that everyone went through, it was the goddamn Sahara Desert.

Rowan had never been confident and had often felt like she came last on the list with her parents. Her father had been a workaholic and her mother had seemed to feel hemmed in when she was at home, always finding somewhere else to go or something else to do instead. Rowan had never felt at ease with her appearance, either. At five feet nine she'd been taller than most of the boys growing up and had felt awkward and clumsy. She'd had hair that had been almost the exact same shade as Ginger Nut biscuits, which was the nickname that had stuck all the way through school. She might have eventually grown into the limbs that had once felt far too long, and started receiving compliments about how beautiful her hair was and how her height meant she could have been a model, but inside she still felt like the gawky kid with red hair. When she hit her teens she'd had a good group of friends, but she was still quite shy outside of that circle and preferred going unnoticed to attracting the kind of comments that might make her face flush red and clash with her hair. Then something had changed, maybe because she'd begun to excel at school and her confidence no longer seemed to pivot on whether or not someone called her Ginger Nut. Just when she'd begun to feel comfortable in her own skin, her parents' marriage had ended in a way that had made them the talk of Port Agnes and all she'd wanted to do was hide again.

Everything that had happened had robbed Rowan of the confidence she'd finally begun to build up and when she and her mother had started over somewhere new, she'd gone back to being the girl standing in the corner, desperately hoping to blend into the background. Except then she'd met James, and he hadn't seemed to notice how awkward she felt. They'd been friends at first, and maybe that's why she'd never been tongue-tied or embarrassed around him. Instead she'd been completely herself, the way most teenagers never truly are, and he'd liked her anyway. Over the years her confidence had grown, not just because of James, but because she was proud of what she'd achieved in her career and her personal life. Until things had started to change again, as they always seemed to do, and it hadn't taken much for that fragile confidence to unravel. James's unwillingness to touch her fed straight into the self-loathing she'd fought so hard to conquer. She was ugly, she must be, and the fact that her husband would rather fake a stomach ache than have sex with her proved it.

Rowan hadn't said any of those things to James. Instead she'd drunk more of the champagne and gone out to dinner with him as planned. They'd stuck to safe ground and talked about the children, and she'd tried not to think too much about whether there was someone else he'd rather be with; someone he wanted to touch in the way he never wanted to touch her any more. He'd never been particularly passionate, but his disinterest had grown since the birth of their second child and had tailed off altogether around the time that Izzy Hennessy, the new religious education teacher, had joined the school. Izzy worked closely with James, and Rowan had seen them together, looking far more like a touchy-feely couple than he had with his own wife. They always looked as though they were laughing at some private joke and more and more lately she wondered if she might be the butt of that joke. She didn't want to believe it of James. They'd been a couple since they were nineteen and he was the school chaplain, a man so devoted to his beliefs that he went on regular retreats to connect with his faith on a deeper level, and who volunteered with several Christian charities. His father was a retired bishop and there was no way he'd have an affair. She was sure of it. Almost.

Except now, sitting here and listening to her two friends talk about their husbands, she knew something was wrong. They were all around the same age, they all had children and marriages of a similar length. James's job was arguably the least physically demanding of any of them, yet for well over a year he'd allegedly been too exhausted to sleep with his wife. During that same period he'd started undertaking weekly 'faith walks' with Izzy. She should confront him and ask outright if there was something going on between him and Izzy, but somehow it felt far easier to bury herself in work. Although she was about to discover that she wasn't hiding her worries nearly as well as she'd thought.

'All joking aside, Row, you've been really quiet lately. Are you okay?' Pippa narrowed her eyes, seeming to answer her own question before Rowan even tried. 'You're not, are you? What's up? Is it just the job or...?'

Pippa's eyes hadn't left her face and Rowan wished her friend would look away; it would be far easier to lie to her if she did. Then she could pretend the job was the only thing bothering her, but Pippa still hadn't broken eye contact.

'Work is busy.'

'It's not just that though, is it?' The eye contact was too intense and Rowan found herself blurting out the words she'd never intended to say.

'I think James might be having an affair.' She looked from Pippa to Odette, trying to read their expressions, now that the unthinkable suggestion was out there. Membory Grange could be a hotbed of gossip and if there really was something going on between her husband and Izzy, there was a good chance one of them had heard a rumour. Although if Odette knew, she'd clearly missed her vocation as an actress, because her eyebrows had shot up in surprise and disappeared behind her fringe, her mouth forming a silent O. And Pippa had furrowed her brow.

'I can't see it. *James*?' She made it sound ridiculously far-fetched. As if Rowan had suggested that her husband was secretly working for MI5.

'Me neither.' Odette sat down next to her. 'He always seems devoted to the job and the kids, and...'

'You can't finish that sentence, can you?' Rowan looked at her friend. That should have been the moment when Odette had said 'and to you', but she hadn't been able to do it, because it was obvious even from the outside that James wasn't devoted to Rowan.

'Well, I mean, you're the headteacher and he's the chaplain, so I wouldn't expect to see you walking around the school holding hands.' Odette gave her a weak smile.

'No, but you, me and Pippa socialise together, with our husbands, and I've seen the way Seb looks at you, and how Daniel is with Pippa. It's starting to feel as if James and I are more like friends than husband and wife, and if he moved any further over to his side of the bed he'd be on the floor.'

'It can be easy to drift into complacency in a long-term relationship.' Pippa's tone was soothing. 'But I'm sure James wouldn't do anything to risk your marriage. Have there been any other signs to make you suspicious? There's supposed to be a whole list of dead giveaways if someone is having an affair.'

'Oh, there are. And wanting either more or less sex than usual is just one of them.' Odette nodded sagely and then began reeling off a list of other signs that a partner was cheating, counting each item off on her fingers as she did. 'There's taking more care of his appearance, being secretive about his phone and seeming more distant. Then there's working late or starting up new hobbies that keep him out of the house, spending money he can't account for, and criticising you more. Oh and mentionitis, where he can't stop bringing up her name, that's a big one.'

Pippa laughed. 'You sound like a divorce lawyer. How do you know all of this?'

'Because when Céline thought her husband was cheating, we did our research.' Odette wrinkled her nose. 'And he was of course. I felt so bad for my sister, but he was ticking every box. I bet James isn't.'

Odette looked at Rowan expectantly, and she wanted to be able to reassure herself and her friends that none of those things applied to James, but it wasn't true. He did seem more distant and he was out of the house more often, but he didn't fit the description in other ways and, unlike Odette's sister, Rowan couldn't tick every tell-tale sign off the list.

'I wondered if it might be Izzy. They're spending a lot of time together, but he doesn't really mention her in between, there's no unexplained spending and he never criticises me. The opposite if anything.' Rowan sighed heavily.

'Well surely that's a good thing then.' Pippa put an arm around her shoulders and Rowan desperately tried to blink back the tears burning her eyes.

'I don't know if it is. At least if there was someone else, I could pin a reason on why everything feels as if it's changing. But it's like he's slowly pulling away instead and there's a distance between us that makes me feel so lonely. If that's happening and there's no one else involved, it's almost worse, because it means he's had enough of us – of me – and I don't think there's any coming back from that.'

'Oh Row, it won't be that.' Pippa pulled her in for a hug. 'There'll be something else going on with work that he hasn't told you about. You know what he's like when he's supporting someone going through a crisis, it consumes him. He's just got this tendency to take other people's problems on as his own. That's all it will be.'

'It's true. He was like that when Graham Johnson was going through that disciplinary process, before the old head left.' Odette lowered her voice, as if even in an empty staffroom someone might overhear them. 'You would have thought it was James facing the sack, and it took him months to get over the fact that he couldn't help Graham keep his job. He'll just be navigating someone else's crisis again. Once it's over, you'll get him back, like you did last time.'

'I hope so.' Rowan sighed again, but far less heavily this time. She hadn't intended to offload any of this on her friends, but she was so glad she had because the idea of her marriage being over felt far less inevitable. She didn't want her children to go through what she'd faced in the wake of her parents' horribly messy divorce. It had resulted in Rowan's life being split between Cornwall and London, a mountain of bitterness, and her family being the subject of gossip in Port Agnes for years. Things between her and James might not be perfect and sometimes she felt lonely in her marriage, but she still loved him. He was her best friend, he had been since she'd met him when she'd first moved to London, and she couldn't bear the thought of losing him. Pippa and Odette were right, she was allowing her fear of history repeating itself to make mountains out of molehills and she needed to stop before she drove a wedge between herself and James that was entirely of her own creation.

'I know so.' Pippa nodded, emphasising her certainty. 'I also know that what we need is a night out. One where we're no one's mums, teachers or boss, and I think tonight is as good a night as any.'

'James is doing a shift at the food bank tonight, so I've got the kids and I said I'd be home by six, but you could come for a takeaway and some drinks at mine?' Rowan couldn't keep the hopeful note out of her voice; she hadn't realised how much she'd needed a night with her closest friends until Pippa had suggested it.

'No, absolutely not, we need a proper night out.' Pippa whipped her mobile phone out of her pocket. 'I'll text Daniel now and let him know that Bella and Theo will be having a sleepover at ours tonight.'

'You can't just drop that on him.' Rowan was pretty sure this wasn't how Pippa's husband had envisaged spending his Friday evening.

'I'll make it up to him tomorrow night.' Pippa grinned and Rowan tried not to let uneasy feelings about her own relationship wash over her again. Comparison was the thief of joy, she knew that, and just because she and James weren't having sex, it didn't mean their marriage was over. When she'd had girls' nights out in the past with Pippa and Odette, and one of them was approached by some sleazy chancer who wouldn't take no for an answer, it had made them appreciate their partners all the more. None of them were married to the kind of creepy guys who sat down uninvited, making leery comments about their bodies and trying to force them to accept unwanted drinks. Pippa was right, she needed a night out to get things into perspective and to appreciate how lucky she was to be married to someone as kind and caring as James. Living and working at the school was intense, and a change of scene would do her the world of good.

'If you're sure Daniel won't mind, the kids would love that. What about you, Odette? Can you make it?'

'That's the glory of having teenagers. They'll be up in their rooms and they won't know whether I'm there or not, as long as there's food in the house.' Odette rolled her eyes. 'Seb is home tonight anyway and I suspect he'll be only too glad to order pizzas in for them all. I don't really like takeaway pizza, so they'll all be thrilled to get the chance to eat junk food and watch sport all evening long.'

'It's a date then.' Pippa gave Rowan's shoulders a squeeze. 'We'll leave mine about quarter to seven. How about cocktails and tapas at Positano's for a kick off, and then we'll see where the night leads us?'

'Sounds perfect to me.' Rowan breathed out slowly. It really did sound like the perfect night, and she was more thankful than ever to have such good friends who'd never stopped treating her like she was one of the gang, despite the direction her career had taken. There was so much in her life that she had to be grateful for and she was certain that by the end of the night she'd be able to reel off a list even longer than the one Odette had shared.

* * *

'You do know that flossing stopped being a thing more than five years ago, don't you?' Odette raised her eyebrows as Pippa tried for the third time to perfect the deceptively difficult dance move that somehow left her looking like one of those inflatable tube men outside second-hand car dealerships.

'I just want my arms and hips to move in unison the way they're supposed to, but it's like rubbing your belly and patting your head at the same time.' Pippa pulled a face as she tried again, managing this time to look as stiff and awkward as the Tin Man. 'Anyway, flossing, like twerking, is timeless.'

'I don't think they are timeless and, judging by the looks we're getting, no one thinks that women approaching forty should be doing either move.' Rowan looked over at a group of young women at the far end of the bar, who seemed to be using Pippa as their main source of entertainment. When Odette had suggested they go on to a Cuban place that had a dance floor, it had sounded like a great idea, but Rowan hadn't expected the average age of the clientele to be around twenty. She'd spent the whole night furtively glancing around to make sure none of the sixth formers from school were there. That would have been mortifying.

'They just don't know a good dancer when they see one,' Pippa said loudly, gesticulating towards the younger women. She'd begun downing cocktails as soon as they'd got to Positano's, at a rate that neither Odette nor Rowan had been able to keep up with. They'd been in the Cuban for less than half an hour and she'd already downed two more mojitos. 'We should go to The Moonlight Room, it's over-thirties night on a Friday.'

'God that sounds grim.' Odette took the words out of Rowan's mouth.

'It really isn't. I promise you.' Pippa was starting to slur her words slightly. 'I went there with the rest of the English department for Henrietta Grange's leaving do and most of the other people in there were over fifty. I haven't felt that young in years.'

Pippa's laugh was getting louder too, and Rowan exchanged a look with Odette, who was shaking her head. 'That just makes it sound worse. It'll be full of divorced men, bitter about life and blaming women for their problems, but still desperate to take one home.'

'I don't care, I just wanna dance!' Pippa did an extravagant twirl, very nearly knocking a member of staff who was carrying a tray of empty glasses flying.

'Whether we go to The Moonlight Room or not, maybe it's time to get out of here?' Rowan looked at Odette again, who nodded vigorously in response, and she couldn't help smiling. Okay, so it may not have been quite the night she'd had planned, and it looked like they might end up heading home well before 10 p.m., but it had been fun. There'd been lots of laughs, a bit of putting the world to rights, and thankfully Pippa was entertaining rather than obnoxious when she got drunk. She'd said she was going to make the most of her first night out in months and she warned them that she hadn't eaten anything all day, other than half a slice of toast that one of the kids had left at breakfast. So it was probably no surprise the first couple of drinks had gone straight to Pippa's head, which had made her even keener to order more.

Odette clearly had no intention of going on to The Moonlight Room and Rowan was happy to call it a night too. It didn't matter that the evening had been cut short, it had more than served its purpose in reminding her just how many amazing things she had in her life, and just how good a night off from all her responsibilities, laughing and talking with her friends, could be. She'd probably end up getting home before James even got back from the food bank. Friday evenings were always busy, especially this close to the end of the month, when people's money had run out. They also had children to feed over the weekend, with no free school meals to bridge the gap. It was another reminder how lucky she was. Her children had never had to go without, and she'd never had to face the dilemma of having to choose heating or eating, or going hungry so that her children didn't have to. Her family lived in the grounds of an exclusive private school, in a bubble that protected them all from the hardship that so many other people had to face. She was incredibly lucky and she never wanted to forget it.

In their situation, it was no wonder James felt the need to help out with other charitable causes and give up so much of his time to support people who really needed him. It would never be enough to just be chaplain to a bunch of privileged children. Her friends were right, James was almost certainly worried and distracted because of some of the work he did. He wouldn't want to burden Rowan with it, when he knew the stresses of her own job and the expectations of parents at the school weighed so heavily on her. As soon as they were at home together, she was going to talk to him properly. Not about their sex life, but about what else it was that was worrying him and what she could do to help alleviate his burden. It wasn't just Rowan who felt the impact of him growing more distant, it affected the children too, especially Theo. She'd seen her son try to get his father's attention, but he never really did, because James was far more concerned with other people's children. She admired her husband immensely for all the work he did, but she couldn't allow that to come at such a cost to their own son. She didn't want Theo to go through the things she had as a child, when her parents had seemed incapable of ever putting her first. There had to be a balance. She loved James, he was an amazing man, and the first thing Rowan was going to do was to let him know that. She wasn't going to ask him to change who he was, but they needed to find a way forward together.

'Yes, let's get out of here before we get barred. You can dance all the way back to Membory Grange if you want to, Pippa, just please promise me you won't try to twerk in the street.' Odette linked one arm through Pippa's, and Rowan did the same on the other side.

'I can't make any promises.' Pippa shrugged. 'Anyway, I don't want to go home. You two can be party poopers if you like, but just walk with me as far as The Moonlight Room and leave me there.'

'One thing at a time, we've got to get you down the stairs first!' Rowan laughed again as they headed out, looking like they were in training for the three-legged race at sports day and needing a hell of a lot more practice to get it right.

Once they were out on the street the cool night air seemed to work a little bit of magic in sobering Pippa up.

'I think you're right about The Moonlight Room being a bad idea; it's freezing and I just want to go home and put my feet on Daniel to warm them up.' She rested her head on Rowan's shoulder for a moment. 'He's soooo lovely. He always lets me put my cold feet on him, to leech off all his body heat.'

'He's a keeper alright.' Rowan smiled into the darkness. A few hours earlier, she might have felt another stab of envy at her friend's words, but she was counting her own blessings now too and she couldn't wait to get home either.

'I'm impressed with the pace you've picked up, Pippa.' Odette still had her arm linked through Pippa's on the other side. 'I did think we might have to suggest stopping off at the food bank and getting James to help carry you home. We're virtually going past the door anyway.'

'I'm not that bad, I'm just tipsy that's all! Tipsy Pipsy, that's me.' She laughed at her own stupid joke as they rounded the corner of the road where the food bank was. It was less than half a mile back to the school grounds and Rowan was confident now that they could make it, although a big part of her was hoping they did bump into James. She liked the idea of them walking home together and maybe slipping her hand into his. It wouldn't be about making any kind of move, just reconnecting in a casual, easy kind of way, and maybe taking the first steps towards getting back on track.

They were thirty metres away from the entrance to the food bank on the opposite side of the road when James suddenly emerged with a group of other people, including Izzy. Rowan's first instinct had been to yell out his name, but something stopped her.

'Look, it's James!' Pippa's loud exclamation was too far away to be heard and Rowan tightened her grip on her friend's arm, pulling them all into the doorway of an estate agent's, where they wouldn't be seen but still had sight of James.

'I know, but Izzy is there too and I just want...' All the doubts had suddenly come flooding back. 'I just want to see them say goodbye and I don't want him to know I'm watching.'

'Right, gotcha.' Pippa gave an exaggerated nod and made an elaborate show of putting a finger to her lips and loudly shushing Odette, who hadn't said anything yet, but who then began to whisper.

'It doesn't look like anything suspicious to me. They're all just saying goodbye and everyone seems to be getting the same hug.'

'I know, but I just want to wait.' Rowan kept her voice low, but her heartbeat was pounding in her ears and she held her breath as she kept her eyes firmly fixed on her husband. She watched him hugging his fellow volunteers in turn, including Izzy, but there was nothing to mark her out from the others, who headed off into the night one by one. A few seconds later, Izzy turned away from James too, walking in Rowan's direction, holding the hand of a young man who looked to be about the same age as she was. The two of them had been the last to leave, leaving James standing outside the food bank on his own.

'I don't want her to see us standing here; we need to pretend we're looking at houses or something.' Rowan pulled her friends back out of the doorway, until all three of them were facing the window of the estate agent's and harnessing their inner Meryl Streep, pretending to peruse the best the local housing market had to offer. Rowan watched Izzy and her companion out of the corner of her eye, still hand in hand and completely oblivious to the three women, until they reached the end of the street and rounded the corner.

'See, I told you James wasn't the type; all that worrying for nothing!' Pippa shook her head, before loudly hiccupping. 'Come on, let's all go home and warm our feet up on our lovely husbands.'

'Why don't we try and catch up to James now?' Odette turned to look at Rowan and she'd been about to agree, when another figure emerged from the food bank. He and James were talking as the other man locked the door. There was nothing out of the ordinary about it, until the man suddenly turned to face James, the two of them illuminated by the light of the streetlamp, and the world seemed to move in slow motion as James reached up and put a hand on the back of the man's head, drawing it down towards him and kissing him in a way that was so unmistakably filled with passion that acid bile rose in Rowan's throat, shock and nausea presenting the very real possibility that she might throw up.

'Oh shit.' Pippa's mouth fell open as the words tumbled out, and Odette gasped in a way that made it feel like she'd sucked all the air out of the world, just for a moment. But it wasn't her friend's dramatic intake of breath that had knocked the wind out of Rowan, it was the realisation that all the feelings she'd wanted him to have for her belonged to someone else. Her greatest fears had become a reality in that instant and as she struggled to remember how to breathe, she knew nothing in her world would ever be the same again.

2

SIX MONTHS LATER

The drive from Membory Grange to Port Agnes had taken three hours so far. As Rowan glanced in the rear-view mirror, now that they were just two miles from their destination, the sight of her daughter's red-rimmed eyes made her want to start crying again too. Saying goodbye to everyone had been incredibly hard. They were leaving behind their closest friends. Rowan had given up her dream job, after less than two years, one she never thought she'd have secured at just thirty-six, and the children were being forced to change schools too. All of those things would have been enough reason for tears, but Bella had cried hardest of all saying goodbye to her father. He'd only just returned after a sabbatical to a school in Tanzania, where he'd been for almost three months and now they were leaving him behind.

'Why can't Dad come with us?' Bella had pleaded with Rowan for an answer, and she'd shot James a look that must surely have conveyed all the rage bubbling up inside her. He had begged her, literally on his knees, not to tell the children the real reason why she'd decided to quit her job and return to the village on the Cornish Atlantic coast where she'd grown up. He'd sobbed, telling her that if his father and the rest of his family found out the truth about his sexuality, they'd never speak to him again. He'd lose his job as chaplain of the exclusive private school founded on the Christian principles he espoused on a daily basis. The same principles that were forcing him to live a lie. If he'd been anyone else, her heart would have broken for him having to tear himself in two like that, trying to live up to the ideals and doctrine he'd been raised with, which were so at odds with who he really was. He was a gay man and he should have been able to be open about that and free to fall in love with anyone he wanted to. But the empathy she felt for him was clouded by anger, because he'd forced her to unwittingly live that lie too. At least James had known it was all a pretence.

Despite her anger, she still hadn't wanted to throw him to the wolves; to tell everyone what had really ended their marriage. Pippa and Odette had seen it for themselves, but they'd agreed to carry the secret too, because Rowan had asked them to. They'd probably told their own husbands, and things like this had a way of getting out eventually. There were already rumours flying around the school about why Rowan was leaving, and what had happened between her and James, but there'd been no public declaration that they were divorcing, despite the fact that she'd begun proceedings within a week of discovering his affair. The only announcement she'd made was that she'd decided to take a job back where she'd grown up, to be closer to her parents. She had no idea what James was telling people about why he'd decided not to go with her. She didn't care what anyone else thought, but she resented the fact that their children were still living a lie.

James had begged her with just as much passion not to tell Bella and Theo that he was gay, not until the time was right. It was a decision she'd wrestled with, but in the end, she'd decided that maybe he was right. There'd been so much change for them to deal with and she hadn't wanted their father's sexuality to become the talk of Membory Grange, while they were all still there. She didn't want their new start to be plagued by gossip either. She knew only too well that Port Agnes was the kind of place where everyone knew everyone else's business, but she wasn't going to feed that. They'd just have to draw their own conclusions about why she'd moved back to Cornwall without her husband. Only her mother knew the whole story and Rowan had sworn her to secrecy, making her promise not even to tell her stepfather Dean. Her father and stepparents knew James had been involved with someone else, but not the full details, because she didn't want the children to find out due to an accidental throwaway comment. She was aware it might look to some people like the marriage wasn't necessarily over for good as a result, even though that couldn't have been further from the truth.

After the initial screaming and crying on Rowan's part had finally stopped, and the pleading from James had got him the secrecy he wanted, it had all been painfully civil, until it came to the point where her children were sobbing and she couldn't be honest with them about why their father was staying behind. All Rowan cared about was how they were coping and she could have murdered James with her bare hands for standing there silently, wallowing in his own self-pity, and making her the fall guy for all that they'd lost. As Bella had pleaded for James to come with them, it had been on the tip of her tongue to scream out the truth and tell their ten-year-old daughter that the reason her father couldn't move to Cornwall was because he was in love with another man and had been for more than two years.

The fact that her husband had been sharing another man's bed at every opportunity he got for all of that time was information Rowan could probably have done without, but the one thing she'd insisted on when the over- whelming emotions had finally started to recede, had been total honesty. At least between the two of them. It was the only way they were going to be able to move forward in any meaningful kind of way and be able to co-parent. Maybe if she'd known what that total honesty would look like, she'd have asked for a watered-down version. Euan Samuels, the head of Christians in the Community, the charity that ran the food bank and other projects, was the love of her husband's life. Meeting him had forced James to confront some- thing he'd struggled to supress for years. He still loved Rowan, he'd told her, of course he did. Just not the way a husband was supposed to love his wife. He'd said he wished it wasn't true and that he'd tried so hard to ignore his feelings for Euan, but they'd been bigger than him in the end. If any of that was supposed to make Rowan feel better, it had failed.

Despite everything he'd told her, he'd seemed genuinely shocked by the decision she'd reached in the early hours of the morning, three days after she'd discovered his relationship with Euan, after they'd sat up all night talk- ing. She'd cried more tears than she'd ever have thought possible in that time, after her life had been ripped off its axis, but she already knew one thing for certain.

'I can't stay here. Sooner or later it's all going to come out and I don't want to get up every morning and go to work, knowing that everyone is talking about me and worse still, feeling sorry for me. I'm not living like that again and it's the last thing I want for Bella and Theo.' She'd shuddered at the memory of what it had been like to live in a village that had suddenly felt like a goldfish bowl, after the spectacular collapse of her own parents' marriage. Her mother had fallen in love with Dean, her father's business partner in his construction firm. He was fifteen years her junior, and they'd set up home together in the cottage Dean's mother had owned. Her father had stood outside screaming at the pair of them for hours on end and he'd seemed completely heartbroken. But within a week her mother's best friend, Marion, had left her husband of over ten years, and moved in with Rowan's father, Tony. She told him that she'd been secretly in love with him for years. It had been messy and incredibly embarrassing, especially when rumours had begun circulating that her parents had been part of a wife-swapping circle, something her mother, Katrina, had assured her wasn't true and that the only 'crime' she'd committed had been to find the love of her life when she was already married to someone else. Up until that point, Rowan's biggest worry had been her upcoming GCSEs and the burning pain of unrequited love that had finally been on the verge of changing into something with the potential to be wonderful. She'd never liked being the centre of attention and she never had been, but overnight it had happened in the most unwelcome of ways. The one thing she was certain of was that she didn't want that for her children.

'You can't leave. Where will you go?'

'Home.' The word had made it feel like she had something alien and uncomfortable in her mouth, like an oversized gobstopper. *Home.* Could she even call it that any more? She'd lived there for the first sixteen years of her life, but after her parents' divorce, she'd spent more time in London than she had in Cornwall. Her mother had moved there with Dean two months after their affair had come to light and Rowan had been forced to stay in Cornwall until she'd finished her GCSEs, but she'd transferred to a sixth form college in London for A levels. It wasn't because she'd sided with her mother rather than her father, she'd been just as angry with both of them for a long time, but London had felt like the lesser of two evils, and the chance to escape from the scrutiny of village life.

After more than two decades away, it was no wonder the word home felt so odd when she was talking about Port Agnes. It was probably why James had looked at her as if she'd suggested moving to Mars. Yet in the wake of her own marriage falling apart, she was suddenly sure that moving back to Cornwall was the only thing she could do. Her mother had returned to the village a few years ago after almost twenty years away, when Dean's mother had died and left her cottage to them. So now her parents were back to living in the same village. Her father and Marion had a son together, Charlie, who was now twenty-two and on a post-university adventure travelling through Asia. Rowan adored her little brother and she got on well with both sets of parents and stepparents, but for years it had been like a military operation keeping them apart to keep the peace. She'd always hoped they'd patch things up one day and there'd been a definite thawing of the previously very tense relationship between her parents, once her mother and Dean had moved back to Cornwall. So she knew they'd all rally around to provide a support network if she asked them to, and she needed that more than anything now that her marriage was over.

'When you say home, do you mean Cornwall?' James had continued looking at her like she had two heads.

'Yes.' She'd been more certain than ever in that moment, the doubt on his face just serving to harden her resolve.

'I could come with you.'

'What the hell for?'

'I've been thinking...' She should have cut him off then and told him he had no right to think anything, let alone make any kind of suggestion about where she and the kids might go. He'd made this mess and she was the one who needed to find a way to try and clear it up. Except for some reason she hadn't stopped him, she'd wanted to hear just how ridiculous his suggestion for the way forward was going to be, but even she hadn't anticipated what came out of his mouth next.

'There's no reason why everything has to change. At least not all at once. We could stay living as a family and raising the kids together. In fact, it would probably be easier now we all know where we stand.'

'Oh, would it?' Rowan had somehow kept her tone level, instead of screaming at him, even if sarcasm was dripping from her voice. 'And what about Euan, is he going to move in with us too?'

'Of course not.' James had tutted then, as if she was being deliberately difficult. 'But I could apply for a parish somewhere, and if Euan got a job up there he could get to know the children bit by bit, as Daddy's friend at first and then—'

'As the man who blew their parents' marriage apart?' She'd cut him off, but she was shaking her head. 'No, actually that wasn't Euan, that was you. If you think I'm being part of some weird throuple, just to make life easier for you, then you're sadly mistaken.'

'It's not about us, it's about the kids.' The pious look on his face had made her blood boil, as he tried to turn it around on her.

'Is that who you were thinking of when you were snogging his face off outside the food bank? Anyone could have seen you, but I did.' He'd tried to protest, but there were things she'd needed to get off her chest and he'd lost the right to take the moral high ground a long time ago. 'I know you think I'm supposed to understand and feel sorry for you, but no one would expect me to do that if Euan had been another woman. Either way, you don't get to have any say in where I take the kids until we can get through the fallout of what you've done, and you're ready to be honest with them. You sure as hell don't get to come with us while you work through it all. In fact, you're going to have to find somewhere else to live while I'm working my notice, because I can't spend the next few months pretending nothing's wrong.'

'If I move out everyone's going to start asking questions and what if Odette or Pippa give one of them the answer?'

'It's not going to stay a secret forever.' Rowan had sighed, because she'd been no more ready for it to come out than he had. She was still processing it herself. She might think his idea of slowly introducing Euan to the children was ridiculous, but giving them time to adjust to life in Port Agnes before they had to come to terms with everything else didn't seem like a bad idea at all. 'You've been offered the chance to take a sabbatical to Tanzania before and I think now would be the perfect time for you to go. By the time you're back my notice period will be almost over and I'll have been able to make a plan for the longer term.'

'I don't think we should rush into something so final.' James had widened his eyes. 'And Tanzania... It's not somewhere I can see myself—'

'It's up to you.' She'd cut him off, her tone as cold as ice. 'You can either face everyone now and tell them the truth, or you can give me some space and get out of my life until I have the chance to get out of yours. But I'm leaving and taking the kids with me, and there's nothing you can do about it.'

She'd been so sure back then that she was doing the right thing for Bella and Theo, and nothing that James, Pippa or Odette could say had dented that belief. She'd held on to that certainty through handing in her notice and applying for new jobs all over Cornwall. It had sustained her through the interview at the same village school she'd attended as a child, overriding her fears about taking such a huge step back in her career. She'd accepted the job and would be starting after the holidays, having rented a house in Port Agnes, still certain it was right for her children. But now, looking at her daughter's reflection in the rear-view mirror again, she was suddenly far less certain.

'Okay sweethearts, we're here.' Rowan forced a smile as she pulled up outside the place that would be their home for at least the next six months and turned to look at her children. Usually they'd have bickered about which one of them got to sit in the front seat, but they'd both been determined to sit in the back, despite the fact that on every other trip to Cornwall Bella had insisted it made her feel sick.

'I want Daddy.' Theo stuck out his bottom lip and his sister reached for his hand.

'Me too, but he said he'll come and see us as soon as he can.' Bella threw her mother a look of undisguised disgust. 'As soon as *she* lets him.'

Digging her nails into her palms to stop herself from reacting, Rowan let go of a long breath. She'd promised herself she wouldn't badmouth James to the children, no matter what. She knew better than anyone how harmful that could be to a child and she'd never forgotten her father saying that her mother couldn't possibly love her, not really, not when she'd been willing to choose Dean over her. Part of her had always believed he must be right and she didn't want Bella or Theo to ever feel that way, even if the children thought all of this was Rowan's fault.

'Let's go and have a look at your new bedrooms, shall we? Then you can FaceTime Daddy and let him see them too.' Keeping the smile firmly fixed on her face, Rowan refused to give into the tiredness that felt as if it was seeping into her bones. She had to make the best of this for the children and keep reassuring them that it was all going to be okay. She had no idea if that would turn out to be true, but the 'fake it until they made it' approach was the only option right now. All Rowan had to do was hold it together until they were both in bed tonight. Only then would she give in to the doubts that had crept in more and more the closer they got to Port Agnes, and the tears that would inevitably fall when she did.

* * *

The day after Rowan and the children arrived in Port Agnes, she woke up at 5 a.m. to a cacophony of sound. The seagulls screeching out to one another were so loud that she wouldn't have been surprised if a couple of them had been perched at the foot of her bed, their beady yellow eyes trained on her face. Thankfully the only thing at the end of the bed were suitcases. She'd done her best the night before to unpack everything they'd brought with them and to make the house feel a bit more like their home, and less like the holiday let it usually was. There'd been room in her parents' houses for her and the children to have been able to stay, and she'd received offers from both of them. But she'd have felt like she had to justify choosing one over the other and that was something she definitely didn't feel up to doing. There was also the risk if she stayed with her mother that something would be said about the ending of her marriage, which she didn't want the children to overhear. And if she stayed with her dad, he might start asking too many awkward questions that she didn't feel ready to answer either. So, despite the extra cost, renting somewhere had felt like a far better option.

The cottage was furnished, so making it feel like their home mostly relied on putting up some photographs and a few carefully selected ornaments, like the little wooden horse they'd bought on a family holiday to France. She'd included photos of James amongst the selection, knowing how important it would be to the children. Even though seeing his smiling face, as he played the devoted husband and father in the pictures, made her want to hurl the photo frames against the wall and watch them smash into a thousand tiny pieces.

The dawn chorus from the seagulls hadn't been all bad. Waking up early had given her a chance to rearrange a few things downstairs and move the furniture around in the lounge so that it had a similar layout to the house at Membory Grange. Rowan had laid claim to a few select smaller items from the family home, as well as some of the wall art, but the cottage wouldn't accommodate much and the rest had been left behind with James. He was due to drive down with a van before the end of the school holidays to see the children and bring the stuff Rowan had said she wanted but couldn't fit in the car, and she was already dreading seeing him. She was glad in a way that there wasn't much room for stuff from the old house. All of the things they'd accumulated over the years were reminders of a life she thought they'd built together, but her husband had only ever been pretending. She didn't want to look at those things every day, but she knew the children needed some reminders of the only home they'd known, at least for a while. Hopefully, before too long, they'd build up new memories and the reminders of their life at Membory Grange would become far less important. When that happened, Rowan would know they were finally healing from this. In the meantime, she was doing the one thing she always tried to do: put the children first.

They had a six-month lease on Sea Mist Cottage and she hoped that would be long enough for the children to start seeing Port Agnes as home too, so that they could put down some permanent roots. It would give James enough time to get his act together and maybe it would be a good thing if he found a parish nearby. Not in the same village, that would be the last thing she'd want, but close enough for the children to be able to see him whenever they wanted. Six months would give them all space and hopefully alleviate the doubts that wouldn't stop nagging at her brain.

The children would both be starting at the village primary school, where Rowan was the new headteacher. Bella would be going into Year 6 and she desperately hoped her daughter would make friends, and build the kind of relationships that would ease her transition into secondary school when the time came. She felt awful that Bella was missing out on her final year in the lower school at Membory Grange. There were so many things she'd been looking forward to, including the Year 6 trip to Paris, a rite of passage that Bella had witnessed older pupils of the school enjoying every year. She'd been talking about 'when I go to Paris' from the time she was in Year 3. Of course, Rowan could take her there instead, but it wouldn't be the same. None of the things that Bella had looked forward to doing in her final year of primary education would be the same as she'd anticipated. When she went to secondary school, that would be completely different from the experience she'd have had at Membory Grange too.

Worst of all was that Bella wouldn't start secondary school with a set of ready-made friends. Membory Grange hadn't just been Bella's school, it had been her home too, for almost her entire life. And it had been Theo's since before he was even born. Part of Rowan had wished that she could have held out for another year, for Bella's sake. But even the months she'd clung on for had almost killed her. She doubted there would ever have been a right time anyway. Theo would still have had to leave before he finished at the lower school, and she'd still have had to wrench the children away from their home to a new house, 130 miles away from their father. Her children hadn't wanted any of those things, but James had left her no choice. Or at least that's how it had felt. As Rowan turned at the sound of footsteps coming down the stairs and saw the look of sadness on her daughter's face, the fury she felt towards her estranged husband surged up inside her again. But she painted on a smile, so there was no chance of her own sadness making Bella feel any worse than she already did.

'You're up early, sweetheart. Did you sleep okay?'

'My room smells funny, like old ladies.' Bella wrinkled her nose as she delivered the verdict on her new bedroom and Rowan laughed, because it was preferable to crying.

'And what exactly do old ladies smell like?'

'Lavender and wee.' The line was delivered with such conviction that Rowan's next laugh was genuine for the first time in what felt like forever. She knew she shouldn't laugh at what her daughter was saying, but she hadn't been able to stop herself and she had to admit it felt good.

'What exactly are you basing that conclusion on?'

'Everyone says it.'

'I don't think they do, because it isn't true.' She gave her daughter a level look. 'And what do you mean by old anyway?'

Bella shrugged. 'Sixty.'

'Nanny Kat and Marion are both in their sixties and neither of them smell of lavender or wee, do they?' Another genuine smile crept over Rowan's face at the thought of what their reactions would have been, if they'd heard Bella describing them that way.

'S'pose not.' Her daughter pouted and pulled away from Rowan when she reached out to try and hug her. 'But my room does. It stinks of wee.'

'It probably just needs a bit of airing. We'll go down to the shops as soon as they open and get one of those plugs-ins that smell like jasmine or vanilla, and some nice bits and pieces to help it feel more like home until the rest of our stuff arrives.'

'It's never going to feel like home. Not without Dad.' Bella fired the words at her like bullets and Rowan's heart twisted in her chest. She'd known this wasn't going to be easy, but she was beginning to think she might have underestimated just how hard it was going to be. All she wanted was for her children to be happy again. She wanted it for herself too, but that wasn't her priority, because she was never going to be happy until her children were.

'I'm starving.' Theo walked into the room rubbing his eyes. They'd had takeaway pizza the night before, because they'd all been too tired to face doing a food shop once they'd unpacked, and none of the big supermarkets delivered to Port Agnes.

'Why don't we walk down to the harbour and we can go into Mehenick's for breakfast? We can get a few essentials and I'll go out and do a proper shop later, when Nanny Kat comes over to babysit.'

'I'm ten years old.' Bella gave a curl of her lip. 'I don't need a bloody babysitter.'

'Bella! We don't use language like that, do we?'

'You called Dad a lying shit.' Bella held her gaze, daring her to say otherwise and Rowan felt as if someone had punched her. She *had* said that, more than once, in the months since discovering that her husband had been lying to her for years, possibly for their entire relationship. She wished Bella hadn't overheard what she'd said and there was nothing she could do to defend herself, not without making things even worse and breaking the pact she and James had made about waiting until the children were ready. But she wasn't going to lie to Bella either, her children needed to know they could trust her if they were ever going to feel secure again.

'I did say that, but I was wrong and there's never any excuse for using bad language.' Rowan had to look away so that her daughter couldn't read her expression, because if anything gave her an excuse to swear, it was finding out that her whole life had been a lie. 'I'm sorry I said it and that you heard it, but I promise I'll never use language like that again and I want you to promise me the same thing.'

'I can't, because I don't like it here and I never bloody will, not without any of my friends and especially not without Dad.' Bella put her hands on her hips in a show of pure defiance and Rowan blinked furiously against the tears she was determined not to cry.

'I know you miss him, but you'll be seeing him in a couple of weeks. He'd hate to hear you talking like this and it's not who you are either. You're allowed to be angry and upset, of course you are, but there are other ways of letting those feelings out and I'm just asking you not to swear.' Rowan was amazed at how calm she sounded. It wasn't that using that particular word was terrible, she was sure there were plenty of ten-year-olds who used far more shocking language, but this behaviour wasn't Bella. It was the hurt on her daughter's face she couldn't bear to see, or Bella's new found belief that it didn't matter any more what she did, because her life was already ruined. Rowan couldn't allow either of her children to feel that way and she'd do whatever it took to make sure they didn't.

3

Port Agnes in August was a bustling place. Despite still being a working fishing village, it was a popular tourist destination, due to both its natural and architectural charm. The harbour and surrounding beaches were carved into a dramatic coastline that rose and fell with the cliffs on either side, with neighbouring Port Kara and Port Tremellien completing a trio of picture-perfect villages on the Cornish Atlantic coast. Narrow, winding streets led up from the harbour, lined with pretty whitewashed cottages and some more colourful ones dotted in between. At the height of summer, the sea was more often than not a vibrant turquoise, reflecting the blue skies above it, and it had a timeless beauty that Rowan hadn't been able to appreciate as a child. She'd loved life in Port Agnes back then, but for her it had mostly been about the beaches, wild swimming whenever the mood took her and rock pooling, or taking her father's metal detector down on to the sand to search for treasure when she was younger. It had been rare for him to take time off from the business, so the times they'd spent down there together had been all the more precious.

Then, when she'd hit her teens, there'd been parties and BBQs on the beach. She hadn't always had the confidence to dance with the others, but when her friends disappeared into the crowd, she would sit on the sand and watch the sunlight dancing on the water and she didn't need anything else to feel okay. When things finally started to change for her and she began to shake off the cloak of self-consciousness, she'd started to dance too. There'd even been the occasional stolen kiss in one of the caves hollowed into the rocky backdrops that flanked the sand. She hadn't wanted to escape Cornwall back then, as some of her friends had expressed a desire to do. Rowan had thought she'd live there forever, within walking distance of her parents' house, and raise her own children in the same idyllic place, but it hadn't worked out that way.

Now she was back, with Bella and Theo in tow, and they didn't look as if they'd been transported to paradise. Not one little bit. Even before her daughter opened her mouth to speak.

'God, I hate it here.'

'How can you possibly hate it? Every time we've been to visit Nanny Kat or Grandpa you've loved it.' Rowan knew that trying to cajole her daughter almost certainly wouldn't work and that the best course of action was to let Bella feel the way she was feeling and allow her emotions to play out. The trouble was, that wasn't how Rowan worked. She couldn't just let the expression on her daughter's face pass, or ignore the effect it was having on Theo, who looked close to tears.

'I didn't *love* it, I thought it was okay.' Bella had her hands on her hips again, sounding closer to thirty than ten. 'But that was when I knew I was only going to be here for a week. I don't want to *live* here. The shops only sell ice cream and tea towels, or Cornish pasties and I *hate* pasties. I can't understand why everyone's queuing for something so gross.'

Rowan had to suppress a smile at the look of pure indignation on her daughter's face as she took in the line of people outside a shop that had opened since their last visit and which proclaimed itself to be 'The home of the best pasty in Cornwall.' She remembered how envious some of her friends had been when she'd told them about her other life in London, during her visits back to Port Agnes to see her dad. She'd regaled them with tales of having every high street fashion chain within walking distance, and her friends had been agog, telling her how lucky she was and how much they wished they lived somewhere like that. Rowan had smiled and tried to convince herself they were right, and that her parents' divorce really *had* made her lucky, but she'd never truly believed it and she'd envied them for still having the life she'd been forced to say goodbye to. She wouldn't have swapped life in Port Agnes for access to any high street chain, and it saddened her to think that her daughter felt the reverse. Lowescastle, the town nearest to Membory Grange wasn't huge, but it had all the major retailers that an almost teenage girl probably considered essential. It was also where Bella had lived her whole life and where all of her friends were. Rowan could empathise all too easily with what it was like to be wrenched away from that.

'Just give it a chance. I know you miss your old friends and that it all feels really strange, but wait until you've been at your new school for a couple of weeks and I'm certain you'll feel differently.' Rowan dropped her hand to her side and crossed her fingers, hoping to God she was right but lying through her teeth about being certain.

'I don't know why we couldn't just stay with Dad.' Bella wrapped her hands tightly around her body, as if she was freezing cold, despite the fact it was twenty-eight degrees and Rowan felt hot even in a loose-fitting cotton summer dress. Everything was loose fitting these days. She'd lost more than twenty pounds since discovering James's double life, but it was no cause for celebration. She felt haggard and old, and as if the trauma of the past few months had been etched on to her face.

'You know why you couldn't stay with Dad, because he might be applying for a job in the community and, if he does, he has no idea which parish he'll be assigned to. Wherever it is, it's very unlikely to be anywhere near Lowescastle.'

'He wouldn't be leaving the school at all if it wasn't for you. He's only doing it because you didn't like it there and wanted to drag us here.' Bella's face was hard and she looked far older than she should have done. Anger and sadness rose up inside Rowan as she looked at the girl, who until a few months ago had been so innocent and childlike, and who almost overnight had become bitter and melancholy. She wanted with all her heart to turn Bella back into that girl, but she couldn't. She couldn't even tell her daughter that the choice to leave Membory Grange hadn't been a choice at all, it had been about survival. Rowan couldn't defend herself either, because she and James had agreed that they wouldn't even consider telling the children everything until he'd made a firm plan for his own future. She wanted to believe that his reticence was about protecting their children too, by waiting until the time was right, but she knew his primary concern was keeping the truth from his father for as long as possible.

'It would kill Dad if someone tells him and it would end our relationship.

Please Row, don't make me face that.' James had repeated that same plea over and over again when he'd asked Rowan to keep the truth from their colleagues and the school governors, in the days after his affair with Euan had first come to light. If they discovered what had happened, the information would definitely have found its way to her father-in-law too. She might have told James where he could shove his impassioned pleas if she hadn't known he was telling the truth about it ending his relationship with his father. She'd heard Michael spouting awful things about same-sex relationships and condemning the couples involved to eternal damnation. She'd argued with her father-in-law on numerous occasions about the subject, but she'd never once been able to make him yield any ground. It was strange, because he seemed fairly liberal about other things. He'd stood by James's sister, Helena, when she'd divorced her cheating husband, barely batting an eyelid that his daughter was very obviously pregnant by the time she remarried eighteen months later. She'd heard Michael preaching about the importance of toler-ance and forgiveness, but he'd actively campaigned against the church employing openly gay vicars and recognising same-sex marriages involving a member of the clergy. It had been one of the reasons for his retirement, jumping before he was pushed probably, and she had no doubt that her father-in-law would react every bit as badly as his son was anticipating.

It wouldn't stay a secret forever, but as much as James had hurt her, she didn't want to be the one to force him to come out to anyone, least of all his father.

'Your dad and I decided that it would be impossible for both of us to stay at Membory Grange and it's not really surprising that Dad might want a fresh start somewhere too, just like us. Then you'll have two new exciting places to get to know.'

'I don't want to get to know a new place, I want Dad to stay at Membory Grange so I can go back there to live.' Before Rowan could even respond to her daughter, Theo cut in.

'I miss my friends.' His words twisted the knife even further into Rowan's gut. He'd been so quiet since she and James had split and, unlike his sister, he'd barely complained. Instead he seemed subdued and cloaked in sadness, making his words far more impactful when they came.

'I know, sweetheart, but I promise things will get better and that you'll make loads of new friends.' Rowan crouched down to her son's level, silently praying that this wasn't another lie she'd been forced to tell him. 'Later on we'll find out if there are any clubs you can sign up to in what's left of the holidays, so that you already know some people at school before you start. But first let's go and order the biggest breakfast that Mehenick's have on the menu and start the day as we mean to go on.'

Hugging her son, Rowan tried not to think about just how much she was missing her own friends too. Pippa and Odette were only at the other end of a phone, but it wasn't the same as seeing them every day and being able to talk to them about everything she was going through. If Rowan was feeling the wrench this much, it was no wonder her children viewed a move to the village where she'd grown up as the worst thing that had ever happened to them.

4

It had been almost two years since Nathan Lark's release from prison, having served a six-month sentence for VAT fraud, but he could still sense the silence that fell over a room the moment he entered. That was the downside of coming from a village like Port Agnes. Everybody knew everybody else's business and there was a small but noticeable proportion of residents who believed he should still be locked up. He'd considered not coming back at all, and making a fresh start where not everyone knew his name and associated it with that 'nasty business' as his mother insisted on referring to it. But Port Agnes was where his family and friends were, those he'd managed to hold on to in the wake of his fall from grace. It was also where his brother, Will, and his family lived, and nothing on earth would have persuaded Nathan to live anywhere else, for that reason alone.

The Lark brothers had been inseparable from the moment Will had come kicking and screaming into the world, just eleven months after his big brother. It had earned them the nickname of 'the Irish twins', which still made their mum, Irene, blush to this day. They'd been as close as any real twins could possibly have been, sharing the same friends, the same interests and eventually starting a very successful business together, as building contractors. Life had been pretty perfect, even before they'd both fallen in love and got married eleven months apart. When Will's son, Leo, had arrived, Nathan had been certain that it was the start of the next adventure they'd share, but then the diagnosis had come that had shattered their world and changed the course of both of their lives forever.

'Hello, my love.' Ruth Mehenick stepped into the bakery from the café side of the business she ran with her husband, Jago, wrapping her arms around Nathan and giving him a tight hug. He could almost sense the disapproving looks from some of the customers around him and he definitely heard at least one loud tut. If Ruth had picked up on it, she clearly didn't give a damn. She was good friends with his mother, and she was one of the few people in Port Agnes who'd offered support to Irene during 'the nasty business'. Ruth had even driven Nathan's mother to Devon to visit him in prison and, when he'd thanked her once for giving him a second chance and seeing past what he'd done, she'd looked at him and shaken her head.

'You don't need to thank me. Everyone deserves a second chance, but as far as I'm concerned you did nothing wrong. Dickens had it right when he said that the law's an arse.' Ruth had shaken her head again then and he'd been more grateful than ever for her support. He knew a crime *had* been committed, but at the time he'd truly believed that there hadn't been a choice and that circumstances and bad timing had created a perfect storm. Ruth's opinion that he'd done nothing wrong put her in the minority, and a lot of people didn't even think he deserved a second chance. That made life very difficult when you were trying to run a business which relied on you being able to secure clients. It had been a tough couple of years, but he and Will had got through it by the skin of their teeth and things had picked up when they'd started taking jobs a bit further afield to places where the Lark surname wasn't synonymous with a criminal conviction.

'It's always good to see you, Ruth.' He hugged her back, before pulling away. 'I've come to collect Mum's order and I wondered if I could put a poster in the window, please? It's about the half marathon.'

'Of course you can. How's the training going?'

'Will and I have both managed the full distance twice.' Nathan gave her a rueful smile. 'Although that was with a couple of rest breaks, so it might be a bit more of a challenge if we don't want to stop.'

'The pair of you will manage it and Leo is going to love it, being the centre of attention at the whole event. He's such a beautiful boy.' Her face lit up but Nathan could hear the tinge of sadness in her voice. It always happened and not just with Ruth. No one could talk about his nephew without that same sadness creeping in somewhere along the line. 'We'll be helping out with catering, but don't forget to let me know how I can donate too.'

'Will's the one who's organising the financial stuff; for some reason people don't trust me.' Nathan attempted a laugh, but he didn't quite pull it off. That legacy from his prison sentence hurt the most; the thought that anyone could think he'd take money from the charity set up to raise funds for research into his nephew's condition broke his heart. Leo had been diagnosed with Duchenne muscular dystrophy just before his third birthday. It was a progressive muscle wasting disease and Will and his wife, Heather, had been told he might not make it to adulthood. Nathan shook off the thought every time it came into his head. Leo was an incredible little boy with the heart and courage of a lion, which made his name completely apt, and Nathan couldn't even bear to imagine a world without him. He wouldn't even contemplate it, because it wasn't a world he wanted to live in. Instead, he threw everything he could into helping find a cure.

'Well, that makes them idiots,' Ruth declared loudly and then looked around her at anyone who might be about to issue forth a challenge.

'You're the best.' He hugged her again before handing her the poster. 'I'm meeting Will and then we're going to price up a job in Padstow. It'll be a really good contract if we can land it, so we need to be fortified with a Mehenick's breakfast special.'

'I'll give you both some extra.' Ruth dropped a perfect wink. 'You go through and grab a table, there aren't many left, and I'll get this put up in the window straight away. You've done so well with all the fundraising this year and I know how proud your mum is of you.'

'There are some upsides that come from having long evenings to fill.' Nathan laughed so that Ruth would know he was joking, rather than feeling sorry for himself. The last thing he wanted was for her to worry about him, or report back to his mother that he sounded sad or lonely. Irene already worried about that far more than she ought to.

'I'm sure you'd have plenty of takers if you even hinted that you were looking for some company.' Ruth gave him a playful nudge. 'Eligible bachelors are in short supply around here.'

'It's a shame I'm neither eligible nor a bachelor then.' He laughed again. 'Right, I'm going through to grab a table because my brother will never forgive me if I don't deliver on my promise to buy him breakfast.'

'I suspect you two would forgive each other anything if it came to it.' Ruth gave him a final squeeze of the arm before moving off to get on with displaying the poster he'd just given her. She was right, there wasn't anything he could imagine Will doing that he wouldn't be able to forgive. They'd had to forgive one another for stuff plenty of times over the years, but they'd always had each other for support too. Having a brother like Will was something he was grateful for every single day.

To Nathan's surprise, Will was already sitting at one of the tables when he walked through from the bakery.

'Come on bro, I'm starving!' Will patted his stomach as he spoke and Nathan grinned.

'Yep, you look like you're wasting away.' Will was a bear of a man. At six feet four he was three inches taller than Nathan, and a good three and a half stone heavier. He was solid rather than overweight, but that was largely down to the running he was currently doing. Without their training for the half marathon, it might well have been a different story, given that he'd been crowned the Three Ports hotdog eating champion, ever since the annual speed eating contest had been introduced four years before.

'Heather likes to have something to grab hold of.' Will gave a little shimmy and laughed. He'd told Nathan, after his release from prison, that people were going to judge them anyway, so they might as well give them something to stare at. It was an idea Nathan had tried to embrace, but he'd never been quite as 'in your face' as his brother.

'Please don't start talking about your sex life before we eat, it's going to put me off my breakfast if I get an image of your naked behind in my head. I've already seen your hairy buttocks far more times than I ever wanted to.'

'Alright.' Will held up his hands. 'But maybe it's time you got back in the saddle. It's been over two years since you split up with Nicole. I hate the thought you might be on your own forever and you know how much it worries Mum.'

'I'm not on my own, I've got all of you.' Nathan kept his tone light. 'And it's not like there hasn't been anyone in my life since we split.'

'No one serious.' Will sighed. 'I've had loaves of bread that have lasted longer than your girlfriends and I'm a greedy bastard who eats four slices at a time.'

'Maybe I just haven't met the right person and I'm in no rush to go through all of that again anyway.' Nathan shuddered at the thought. When he'd married Nicole, it had been forever as far as he was concerned and he'd thought she'd felt the same way, until the fraud investigators had come knocking on the door.

'Well, big bro, your luck might just have changed, because guess who is sitting over there.' Will gestured none-too-subtly towards a table in the far corner of the room where a woman with auburn hair, falling in soft waves just past her shoulders, was sitting with two children. He didn't need her to turn around to know who she was; it was Rowan Adams, or Rowan Bellamy as she now was. She'd been in the year below him at school and he'd had the biggest crush of his young life on her. She'd always seemed standoffish and far too clever to be interested in someone like him. Then she'd seemed to change and they'd begun to get close, first as friends and then finally they'd kissed. He'd been certain that they were going to be together and he'd wanted that more than anything at the time. He'd planned to ask her if she'd start going out with him properly, but then her parents had split up and she'd pulled away from him again, before moving to London with her mum as soon as her GCSEs were over. Rowan had come back to visit her dad, but by then he was at college, studying construction, and his world had felt a million miles away from hers. Nathan hadn't reached out to reconnect and neither had she. He'd caught glimpses of her over the years when she'd come to spend time with her father, and heard snippets of information about her life, but she'd gone back to keeping herself to herself and they'd never spoken.

'She's married with two kids now and up here to see her parents, so I don't know why that makes me lucky.' Nathan furrowed his brow.

'Because rumour has it she's left the husband and moved back here for good. You can finally do what you should have done more than twenty years ago and take her out.'

'Are we relying on the Port Agnes rumour mill for information now?' Nathan widened his eyes, giving his brother an *are-you-mad* sort of look.

'What have you got to lose?' Will didn't break eye contact with him. 'I'd feel a lot better if you made a proper fresh start.'

'Oh, you should have said, anything to be of service to you.' He couldn't help laughing again at the hopeful look on his brother's face, but then something changed in Will's eyes.

'Please, Nath. It really would lift a burden off me if I knew you were happy with someone again.'

'I know, but I don't have to be in a couple to be happy. I promise. And I'd rather be on my own than with the wrong person.' Nathan pretended to make a show of looking at the menu, as though he hadn't known before he even left the house what he was going to order. Sometimes he just couldn't stand to see the pain on Will's face when they talked about the past and everything that the prison sentence had cost Nathan. Glancing over at Rowan's table, he realised she was looking in his direction, but she jolted as their eyes met and turned her head away fast enough to pull a muscle. He had no doubt she'd heard all the gossip Port Agnes could muster about his time in prison and what he'd done to land himself in there, but only two people in the world knew the full story and they were both sitting at Nathan's table.

'Just promise me you'll think about it. Even if you just go on one proper date with Rowan and finally tick that off your wish list. It's been on there for about twenty-five years by my reckoning.' Will clearly wasn't giving up easily.

'I promise.' Nathan nodded, but he'd already thought about it and dismissed it. Rowan Bellamy had been too good for him two decades ago and she was sure as hell too good for him now. When she'd been appointed as the youngest ever headteacher at a prestigious private school on the Hampshire/Dorset border, it had been all over the Three Ports newspaper about the *'local girl made good'*. Just because she was back in Port Agnes, it didn't mean she'd want to go out with a man who'd been splashed over the same newspaper for far less honourable reasons. It was never going to happen, no matter how much Will or Nathan might wish it would.

5
___

Rowan had been back living in Port Agnes for four days, but the first time she'd been to visit, a week after discovering James's affair, her mother had greeted her with the tea and sympathy she'd expected. Except the tea had been wine and even the sympathy had taken a different form than Rowan had expected. Of course Katrina had expressed sadness for what her daughter was going through, but she hadn't ripped James apart the way Rowan had thought she might. A tiny part of her had felt aggrieved that her mother didn't think James was the devil incarnate for cheating on his wife and children, and lying to Rowan for over twenty years about his true sexuality, but then Katrina had embarked on an affair that had ripped her own marriage apart. There might not have been two decades of lying about who she was, but she could hardly take the moral high ground on fidelity.

Rowan knew that her mother's decision to leave her father had been the best thing for all of them. Katrina had gone from being distracted and unhappy, back to the loving mother she'd been when Rowan was a little girl. Her father and Marion seemed made for each other, and now that they were all finally getting along much better it was far harder to resent her mother for what had happened. Rowan hoped her children would come to feel that way much sooner than she had done, but it was a relief to have her mum on hand for support in the meantime, especially when it came to taking care of the children.

'I'll be back by four.' Rowan had done a quick mental calculation in her head before confirming how long she'd be out. She was going into school to meet with a few of the staff who were making preparations for the start of term, and then she was going to see her dad and Marion on the way home. Although she hadn't mentioned that last bit to her mum.

'It's no problem, sweetheart, don't rush. Me and Dean are taking the kids to the beach while this weather keeps up, so you might be home before us.' Rowan's mother suddenly fixed her with a quizzical look and asked the question she'd been dreading since she'd been back living full time in Port Agnes. 'Are you seeing your dad and Marion soon?'

'I—' For a second or two, Rowan considered lying, but that was something she promised herself she wouldn't do. There'd been far too many lies over the years and it was a tradition in her family that she was determined to put an end to. 'I've spoken to them on the phone three times since we got here, but today is the first chance I've had to get over there. I'm going to pop in on the way home because Marion has got some bits she bought the kids.'

Even though her parents were now getting on far better with one another, Rowan braced herself for her mother's response. When Bella had been born, Katrina had got very huffy about what the baby might end up calling Marion. Before that, money had always been a bone of contention. Her father was a wealthy man and things had always been a bit more of a struggle for her mum and Dean, at least until they'd inherited his mother's place. Rowan had heard it all over the years, and was fully expecting Katrina to say something along the lines of: '*How nice for Marion, of course she's got the children something, it must be so lovely having money to splurge like that, because I walked away without taking anything from your father. She forgets that you know, when she acts all high and mighty like the perfect wife. I bet her ex would have something to say about that. She left him for your father so quickly that the poor sod must have whiplash.*'

It was word for word what her mother had said to her in the past, but Katrina's response this time couldn't have shocked Rowan more if she'd whipped off the floppy straw hat she was wearing to reveal a pink mohawk underneath.

'Oh brilliant. Can you give her this?' Her mother grabbed a jar from the dresser. 'It's some comfrey and mallow foot balm. She hurt her foot when we were line dancing last Wednesday, and I swear by this stuff. Nowhere in the village stocks it, but I picked up a jar when I was in Truro yesterday. Tell her she needs to get it sorted quickly, because line dancing isn't the same without her.'

There was so much to unpack from what her mother had just said that for a moment Rowan just stood there and she had to blink three times to make sure this wasn't some weird kind of dream. 'You go line dancing with Marion? I know you two can finally be in the same room these days, but I had to reorganise the seating plan at my wedding three times because of how you felt about Marion. And now you're line dancing. Together.'

Katrina sighed and shook her head. 'I know, and I wish I could go back and change all of that, it was so stupid. We all had this pent-up resentment for years. Your dad was angry at me and Dean for what happened, and I was bitter about Marion jumping into my shoes so quickly when she was my friend and I'd told her about problems between me and your father. Looking back I even found myself wondering if she'd encouraged me to leave him, because she wanted to take my place. So when it first happened, I never wanted to talk to them again and I'm sure they felt the same. Things are so much better now, I just wish I'd done it sooner, because I missed Marion, and even your dad too in some ways. Now I've got them back and we're not just civil any more, we're friends again.'

'So what changed?' Rowan sank down on to a kitchen chair hoping that her mother might be able to come up with some kind of secret formula that could help her view James as a friend again.

'It was easy when we were living in London to pretend they didn't exist and vice versa. When we got back home that got harder. I kept bumping into Marion at various things and finding myself avoiding places, or not joining groups because I knew she was a part of them. We were forced to start acknowledging each other's existence and that made it easier for us all to be around each other at things like the kids' birthday parties.'

'I was so pleased when I stopped having to have two birthday celebrations, although I think the kids were a bit disappointed.' Rowan gave her mother a wry smile. 'But that's very different from actively hanging out together.'

'I know and I really didn't think we'd get back to the point where we'd choose to, not unless we had to come together for you or the kids. But then, about six months ago, Nicky Jones started a line dancing class in the village hall. It was something I've always wanted to do, but the first night I showed up, Marion was there. She smiled and asked me if I was as nervous as she was about messing up and we started reminiscing about the aerobics sessions we used to go to together and how bad we were at following the steps. After the class, we went out for a drink, and the landlord had to throw us out in the end because we were still talking at closing time! She admitted that when we'd first come back to take over Dean's mum's cottage she'd prayed we'd sell up and go again as soon as possible. And I told her that's exactly what we'd discussed doing, but because we both loved Port Agnes so much we decided to stay, even if it meant dodging your father and Marion for the rest of our lives, unless you were there too. We laughed at how stupid that idea was and we talked about everything that had happened. Within minutes of sitting down I remembered why I'd liked Marion so much in the first place and why we'd been best friends, and now I'd say we're pretty close to being back to that.'

'Wow.' Rowan blinked a few times again, to make sure this really wasn't a dream. 'Why didn't you tell me that things had moved on so much between you?'

'I was planning to and then everything happened with James. After that it was a whirlwind of you going for interviews and getting the job at the school. Then trying to find a place for you to live. It didn't seem like a priority to tell you about me and Marion and I felt guilty for everything we'd put you through, when we could have sorted all of this out years ago. But now I think about it, in some ways the timing couldn't have been more perfect.'

'What do you mean?'

'We made some terrible mistakes and the person that cost the most was you.' Katrina moved to stand behind Rowan's chair and put an arm around her shoulder. 'Whatever James has done, and there's no denying he was in the wrong, please don't waste all the years we did on being bitter and angry, or hating him. James isn't a bad person, deep down you know that, he just did a bad thing. I suspect you're already doing a far better job of putting your feelings to one side, because of how much you love the children. But I want you to let go of the anger and resentment for yourself too, it'll only end up causing you more pain in the end if you don't.'

As her mother squeezed her shoulders again, Rowan pressed her lips together, fighting the urge to tell her mother it was easy to say from her position, when she'd been the one whose actions had broken up her marriage. Except she knew her mother was right, assigning blame wouldn't change anything and the bitterness that grew out of that would taint everything. That was the last thing she wanted for her children. She didn't want Bella or Theo to have to keep their parents separate at their own weddings, or to be afraid to tell her that they were visiting their father because of her reaction to the news. She was still furious with James for taking more than two decades of her life from her under false pretences, but she wasn't going to let her children become a casualty of that anger. She wasn't under any illusion that it was going to be easy and she wasn't sure they'd ever be able to salvage a friendship, but she was willing to try.

* * *

Port Agnes Primary School was built from granite and it was where the children of the village had been educated for well over two hundred years. At first glance, when Rowan had arrived for her interview, it barely seemed to have changed since she'd been a pupil there herself. A closer inspection had revealed that there were a couple of additional buildings in the grounds and a play area covered with a stretched awning to protect it from the weather. The playground was tarmacked, with a grassy area to one side of it that was home to a copse of trees, which had real potential to be utilised for forest school activities. She'd spoken with passion at her interview about making it into an area all of the children could use and perhaps even grow some of their own plants.

It wasn't a huge piece of land, but with careful planning they could achieve something special and one of the first emails she'd sent, after being appointed, had been to request some funding to move forward with making the space available to everyone. Having discovered that one of the pupils relied on a wheelchair, she'd been particularly keen to ensure he wasn't left out. Green space was limited in the middle of the village and larger school events were held either on the land next to St Jude's Church, or on one of the local farms. Rowan could still remember going up the hill to Home Farm, as part of a crocodile of children, marching side by side and chattering excitedly about the sports day to come.

Stopping by the gate, she looked at the school sign. There'd been a change since her last visit and the previous headteacher's name had been replaced with her own. Port Agnes Primary was her school now and she allowed the thought to sink in. None of this had been what she'd wanted or expected. Becoming head of a large, prestigious independent school while she was still in her thirties had been the stuff that dreams were made of; Rowan's dreams anyway. Heading up a village primary of fewer than two hundred pupils was a huge step backwards career-wise. Yet, in this moment, it felt as if it was where she was supposed to be, as though she'd come full circle from that little girl who'd always dreamt of being a teacher, and who'd made her friends play act at being the pupils, while she'd taken on the role of schoolmistress. She'd devoured the Enid Blyton *Mallory Towers* and *St Clare's* books as a child, so arguably Membory Grange had been the true full circle moment. Whatever the truth of that, her days of heading up an exclusive boarding school were over. She was head of a small village primary school now instead, and she was determined to feel grateful for it.

'Rowan Adams! They said it was you, but I refused to believe it until I saw you with my own eyes.' Bex White was wearing a sage green linen dress as she hurtled down the path towards her. The dress looked too tight to run in, but somehow Bex was managing it and within seconds she'd flung her arms around Rowan. 'I know it's Bellamy now, but you'll always be Rowan Adams to me. I'm still White of course, because when your husband has a surname like Handcock it would give the Year 6s a field day!'

Bex White had barely ever paused for breath back when they'd met as children at Port Agnes Primary. When Rowan had decided which characters her friends should be in her make-believe school game, something they'd spent many a breaktime playing, she'd always cast Bex as the naughtiest pupil, who couldn't stop talking. She was a natural for the part and it seemed not much had changed in that respect.

'It's so good to see you and to know I have a friendly face in my new job.' Rowan smiled as Bex finally released her. They'd been good friends at primary school and part of a group of close friends at Three Ports High School too. They'd kept in touch over the years and seen each other occasionally, but after Rowan had moved to London things had never been quite the same. Over time their lives had headed in different directions and their contact had moved mainly online. For the past ten years her closest friends had been Pippa and Odette, who were now three hours away and the test of distance on those friendships had only just begun.

'I can't believe you're going to be my boss.' Bex was grinning as she looped an arm through Rowan's. 'I just hope you're not going to shout at me as much as you used to when you were our very own Miss Trunchbull. I still think about those days when I'm walking through the playground.'

'I promise I'll do my best not to be Miss Trunchbull and I don't want you to think of me as your boss. For a headteacher, the admin manager is the single most important person in a school like this. So we're partners as far as I'm concerned.'

'Partners it is then. You and me against the rest of the world.' As Bex squeezed her arm again, Rowan just hoped it wasn't true. She didn't want her new job to be filled with conflict, she'd had enough of that to last her a lifetime.

6

The influx of second homeowners and holiday lets in some Cornish villages had priced local families out of living there, particularly in the villages closest to the coast. It meant that there were quite a few schools threatened with closure, because there just weren't enough families with school age children living in the area. Port Agnes Primary was lucky in that respect. The maximum number of pupils the school could accommodate was 196, and the addition of Bella and Theo had taken the school to its limit. Each year group had a maximum of 28, and they had been oversubscribed for the Reception class, who would be starting at the same time as Rowan, with applications coming from children living up to ten miles away. It was a good position for the school to be in and the previous head had consistently achieved good feedback from Ofsted, but there were still changes Rowan wanted to make, things she could see that could make a good school even better. Having forest and beach school activities would provide interactive learning experiences for the children, making use of the coastal and woodland environments on their doorstep. Although Rowan was aware of the need to tread carefully. The previous headteacher had been well liked and the school had an active and engaged PTA, and board of governors. Rowan needed to respect and acknowledge the good work that had been done for the school in recent years, before beginning to introduce changes, and the best way of doing that was to get to know the school and staff as well as she could.

Bex had given her the grand tour, if you could call it that in a school with only seven classrooms, an office each for her and Bex, a small staffroom and an even smaller intervention room for pupils who needed additional support. One of the outside buildings operated as the school hall, although any larger events, including those where parents were invited, were held in St Jude's Church. The hall also served as the dining room, for the children having school dinners, which were delivered by a catering service to schools that were too small to have their own kitchens. The other outbuilding was multi-purpose, and its uses included providing sensory activities and other support for children with special educational needs or disabilities. It was a lovely little school and by the time the tour was over, Rowan had a broad smile on her face. This was coming home in the best possible sense and all of a sudden it didn't feel like a setback in her career, it felt like exactly the kind of new start she'd been looking for.

There were seven class teachers, one for each year, and a part-time SENDCO, to oversee the support for children with additional needs. There was also a teaching assistant for each class, and another six academic support teaching assistants who worked with pupils on a one-to-one basis, as well as a part-time caretaker and sessional sports coach. It was a fraction of the number of staff that Rowan had managed at Membory Grange, but Bex had assured her that they were a lovely team and that working at the school felt like being part of a family. Rowan just hoped they'd all welcome her arrival, having clearly got on so well with the previous headteacher. The signs so far were good. Juliet Bartosz, who taught the Reception class, was in doing prep work, alongside Lyra Blythe, who was the Year 3 teacher, and Caden Pengelly, who taught Year 6 and was also deputy head. They were all very friendly and seemed enthusiastic about her arrival and her ideas for the forest and beach school activities in particular. Bex had told her that the caretaker, whose name was Krish, would be arriving soon to work with some of the parents from the PTA on accessibility to the grass area, for the pupil who used a wheelchair.

'Leo's such a wonderful little boy.' Bex's face had lit up when she'd described him. 'But last winter, when he started using the wheelchair full time, he stopped being able to go on the grass because it gets too wet for him. Antony had looked into getting astroturf, but your idea is far better.'

Rowan had been delighted when the PTA and governors had agreed to fund the purchase of some concrete paving grids that would provide accessibility but which grass could grow through. It meant the school wouldn't lose any of the green space, but Leo would still be able to access all the same areas as the other children. Rowan wasn't under any illusion that this was all down to her. The funds had been raised due to the hard work of the PTA and costs had been kept low by one of the volunteers offering to lay the grids free of charge.

'That sounds brilliant and it's wonderful to hear there's such a strong sense of community at the school and how involved the parents are.' Rowan had meant what she'd said. One of the downsides of Membory Grange had been the sense of entitlement that some of the parents seemed to possess, as if the fact that they were paying for their children's education meant they didn't need to make any personal investment in school life. She wouldn't miss that and she was really looking forward to working more closely with the parents of her pupils.

After Bex had introduced her to the staff who were around, the next few hours were taken up with planning for the beginning of term and the staff training day that Rowan would be leading before the children came back to school. Bex was also incredibly patient with her when she ran through the computer systems the school used, which were different from the record keeping and reporting software used by independent schools. It had been a busy morning and when Bex had produced a carrot cake, suggesting they enjoy a slice with a cup of tea outside in the sunshine, it hadn't taken much persuasion. Bex made the same offer to the other staff, before informing Rowan that she'd also extended the invitation to Krish and the volunteers who were working on putting down the paving grids. Rowan, who hadn't eaten all day, tried not to wonder whether there would be enough cake to go around. The parents working hard outside deserved it more than she did, and she'd just have to ignore the rumbling that had started in her stomach the moment Bex had mentioned cake. She should have known her old friend better than that, as Bex set a second cake out on a plate – chocolate this time – and put it down on the trestle table that had been brought out from the hall. Caden, Juliet and Lyra carried out enough chairs for everyone, and Bex switched on the tea urn belonging to the PTA.

'It feels like we're having our own little street party, we just need to decide on the occasion.' Rowan smiled wistfully, remembering the street party they'd had in Port Agnes for the Queen's golden jubilee, when she'd been sixteen, just before her parents had split up. It had been such a fun day, helping to run events for the younger children in the village, and consolidating her ambition to become a teacher one day. After that she'd gone up to the clifftop with some of her friends, at a spot where they'd be able to see the lanterns lit in Port Agnes, Port Kara and Port Tremellien to mark the jubilee, and the firework display that had been organised for afterwards. Bex had been there, along with other friends from school and the Lark brothers, who all the girls were more than a little bit in love with. Rowan had been good friends with Nathan for about a year by then, secretly hoping that one day it would be far more than that, and she'd ended up kissing him just after the lanterns were lit and those first fireworks let off. She'd been certain that the historic nature of the occasion meant their kiss must be momentous too, but before they could arrange a proper date, the end of her parents' marriage had shattered her world. It had been all she could do to get through the remainder of her exams and she couldn't focus on Nathan, no matter how much she liked him. They barely spoke again before she left for London, but that didn't mean she'd forgotten him.

'We've already got our special occasion.' Bex's voice broke into her thoughts. 'You starting as the new head and coming home to Port Agnes, where you belong is more than reason enough to celebrate.'

She raised her as yet empty mug, offering an imaginary toast and the others echoed the sentiment, but then Juliet suddenly put her hand in the air, in a hold-that-thought gesture.

'I'm not sure tea is going to cut it you know, because we appear to be having our very own Diet Coke break.' She indicated towards the grassy area where Nathan Lark, of all people, was lifting one of the paving grids off a trolly single-handedly, his white T-shirt clinging to him.

Caden let out a low whistle. 'Even as a straight man I can see what you mean, although I suddenly want to put on a coat to hide my own inadequacies.'

'Should we be objectifying him like this? It feels a bit wrong... you know, especially on school grounds and with him being a parent.' Lyra shifted uncomfortably in her seat and Rowan could have kissed her. She'd wanted to say something similar, but didn't want to seem like a complete killjoy on the first day she met her colleagues. It did feel wrong though, as did the level of disquiet she'd experienced at the news that Nathan was the father of one of her pupils. She knew his marriage had ended a couple of years ago and that they hadn't had any children, but if Lyra was right he must have become a parent with someone else and she had no idea why the thought bothered her. Whenever she'd heard snippets about Nathan moving on with his life, like when he'd first got married, it bothered her more than she could rationalise. He didn't seem to have social media, so she hadn't kept up with him in the same way as some of her other friends, but from time to time someone would mention his name and she'd realise the butterflies still hadn't completely gone away. She hadn't heard anything about him getting remarried, but there'd been one bit of news that her mother had passed on two or three years earlier, which had shocked her to the core and made her wonder if she'd ever really known him at all. But the Nathan she remembered had been funny and kind, and whatever he'd done she preferred to remember him that way. Except now their paths had crossed again and she might be forced to confront a very different person to the one she'd imagined.

'Fair point, I suppose.' Juliet pulled a face. 'Except he's not a parent, he's an uncle, which means he might not be quite so off limits and I'd definitely consider volunteering more for the PTA, and maybe even asking him out, if it wasn't for, well, you know...'

'What?' As Lyra asked the question, Rowan realised she was holding her breath. She hoped Juliet wasn't about to say what she was expecting. Whatever Nathan had done, he'd served his time, and he was now doing his bit to help out at the school. It shouldn't be the one thing people judged him by, or the first thing that came to mind when his name was mentioned. From what she'd heard he'd gone to prison for VAT fraud and if it had been a more serious crime, he'd never have got clearance to volunteer at the school. He deserved a second chance, especially when he was clearly doing his best to give something back to the community, but not everyone thought so.

'His prison sentence.' Juliet lowered her voice as she spoke. 'I mean, he might be God's gift to womanhood, but can you imagine the reaction of some of the parents if they discovered the Reception class teacher was dating a prisoner?'

'He's not a prisoner. He's served his sentence and I think he's proving by his actions that he deserves a fresh start.' Rowan kept her tone measured, despite her scalp bristling with a defensiveness she had no right to feel. The staff had clearly felt comfortable enough with the previous head to chat about anything and everything, but she didn't care any more if she sounded like a killjoy, this had gone far enough and at least one person was on her side.

'I couldn't agree more and it was VAT fraud, he's not an axe murderer.' Bex sighed. 'Okay, I know that doesn't make it right, but if I had to guess, I'd say it had something to do with his family and Leo in particular. Just before it all came out, the Larks lost their father. He'd been in a nursing home for six months and they were fundraising for Leo to get some experimental treatment in the US too. Will's wife also told me they'd been considering IVF to try for a second baby, so the embryos could be screened. That was a lot for one family to cope with and pay for. I can't help thinking that whatever money Nathan took wasn't for himself. Even if it was, he paid the price, did his sentence and had to sell his house to settle what was owed.'

'Another fair point I suppose.' Juliet pulled a face. 'I still wish he hadn't done it so I could have asked him out. As much as I might be willing to see past his criminal record, I just don't think I could cope with the snidey comments from parents who seem to think teachers should live lives that are beyond reproach. It's not fair; I haven't seen anyone I fancy in months and, when I do, he turns out to be forbidden fruit.'

'Don't worry, Jules, I'll take you speed dating with me in Port Tremellien next time I go.' Lyra made the offer and the conversation quickly moved on to the challenges of trying to date when you lived in rural Cornwall. Rowan was grateful for the change of subject, but Nathan was still on her mind.

Despite the things she'd heard about him over the years, no one had told her about the difficulties his family had gone through before he'd gone to prison and she hadn't realised he was Leo's uncle. His brother Will didn't have any social media either and the news other people had decided to pass on had focused on the more salacious aspects of his life. Rowan's trips home had always been fairly brief, so she'd only been given the information about Nathan that other people had thought was worth sharing. Now that she'd begun to discover other things about him, she found herself wanting to know more, but she couldn't justify why. She tried to tell herself it was because he was the uncle of one of her pupils, a little boy with complex needs whose family she'd need to get to know even better than the families of her other pupils. Rowan could tell herself that story as much as she liked, but when she glanced over and caught another glimpse of Nathan Lark, she knew there was more to it than she was willing to admit, even to herself.

* * *

'It looks like you're making great progress with the paving grids. Bex said you didn't want to stop for a drink, but I thought I should bring you one anyway, especially now that your brother has had to leave you to finish up.' Rowan held the bottle of water she'd taken from PTA supplies out to Nathan. She'd put a two-pound coin into the petty cash box, which Bex had said was more than they charged for water when they sold it at school events, but it had still felt like she was doing something she shouldn't. Although, that might have had more to do with who the water was intended for rather than anything else.

He put down the spade he'd been holding and smiled. He had a great smile, he always had done. She didn't know why she was so surprised to see it exactly as it had been all those years ago, but she was. Rowan didn't know what she'd expected after his short stint in prison, but clearly she'd anticipated some kind of impact; maybe missing teeth or a tear drop tattoo. Her mouth twitched at the ridiculousness of the thought. Whatever he'd been through in the last two decades, it had done nothing to dim his looks. There was just the merest touch of grey at his temples, but the rest of his hair was still dark and there wasn't any sign of it thinning in the way James's hair had started to do. Nathan's dark blue eyes had the same memorising affect they'd always had as he met her gaze.

'It's really kind of you to bring me a drink, Rowan, thank you. Can I still call you that, now you're going to be the headteacher?'

'Of course, as long as it's not in front of the children. Then I'm Mrs Bellamy.' She raised her eyebrows and smiled. 'And given my new position, I had to bring you a drink. I couldn't have the stigma of you dropping dead from dehydration, before the term has even started.'

'I'm quite good at attracting stigma. I expect you've heard.' He returned her smile, but there was a hint of something behind his eyes that she couldn't quite identify. If she'd had to guess, she'd have said it was regret, but it could have been guilt, or even embarrassment. Still, he'd been the one to bring it up, so it couldn't be a subject he was all that desperate to avoid.

'You know what village life is like.' She shrugged, wondering what Nathan had heard about her reasons for returning to Port Agnes, and the conclusions he'd drawn about her parents when she and her mother had first left. 'Unfortunately so do I, only too well, which is why I make my own mind up about people instead of listening to gossip.'

'Good to know.' They locked eyes for a moment and she had to look away, beyond where he was standing to the paving grids that had already been laid.

'I think your nephew is going to be in my son Theo's class. Please tell me that they're a friendly group. Theo is quite an anxious boy at the best of times and let's just say that the last few months haven't been the best of times.' It was more than she'd intended to say, but he'd always had that effect on her.

'I'm sorry.' Nathan briefly touched her hand and the patch of skin beneath his fingers tingled, even when he moved his hand away again. 'I can't vouch for the whole class, but most of the kids seem okay and, I know I'm biased, but Leo is great. He'd never want to see anyone sidelined, so I'm sure he'll give Theo a warm welcome.'

'That's really good to know, thank you and thanks again for getting so involved with volunteering. At my last school, the average parent would never have mucked in to help, let alone the uncles.'

'I'm not your average uncle.' He smiled again and it had been on the tip of her tongue to say he wasn't the average anything, but somehow she stopped herself from saying it out loud.

'It was good to see you again, Nathan. Hopefully I'll see a lot more of you.' Colour flooded her cheeks as he laughed. 'I meant around the school, helping out.'

'It's okay, I knew what you meant.' He was grinning in the way she'd always found irresistible, which made it worse. 'But a guy can dream, can't he?'

She didn't acknowledge his comment. 'I'll let you get back to work and don't forget to stay hydrated.'

'Yes, Mrs Bellamy.' He grinned again and doffed an imaginary cap, before picking up the spade he'd set down earlier. Walking away, she resisted the urge to turn back and see whether he was watching her, because, as ridiculous as it was, she knew how disappointed she'd be if he wasn't.

* * *

Rowan had spent far more time thinking about Nathan than she should have done. Driving over to her father's place, her mind should have been on work.

There was a lot to think about and a lot to prepare before the start of term, which was racing towards her at a scary pace. Work had stopped her thinking about James as much as she might have done otherwise, and how the fallout from their marriage ending might affect them all long term. She'd have to find a permanent home for herself and the children eventually. And she'd been so busy since arriving in Port Agnes, and so intent on getting the children settled, that the sadness was nowhere near as all-consuming as it had been back at Membory Grange.

At this precise moment she was thinking about Nathan Lark instead of work, which was absolutely ridiculous. Getting involved with anyone else was the last thing on her mind. She couldn't imagine ever wanting to do that after what James had put her through. Even if she wanted to start dating, Nathan couldn't have been more unsuitable. She hated the fact that others judged him so harshly, but Juliet had been right about one thing: the parents of her pupils would definitely have something to say if their headteacher was in a relationship with an ex-convict. She shook her head again as an unwanted image of herself and Nathan kissing popped into her mind. It was just her memory playing tricks on her, finding an outlet to ease the stress she'd have been feeling otherwise. Or maybe it was unfinished business from all those years ago. Either way she wished it wasn't happening and she just had to wait for it to pass. Once school started, she definitely wouldn't have time to worry about Nathan Lark and all of a sudden the start of term couldn't come soon enough.

'Hello, sweetheart. How are you doing?' Rowan's father folded her into his arms the moment he opened the door. Although he and her stepmother still lived in Rowan's former family home, it hadn't felt like a place she could just stroll into since she'd followed her mother to London. She still had a key and always had done, but it was her father and Marion's home, not hers, despite them reassuring her many times that wasn't the case. Whenever she'd stayed there in the holidays, she'd had to force herself not to knock on the front door before coming in. It had upset Marion when she'd done that, and her stepmother had told her it made her feel as though she'd pushed Rowan out, and that was the last thing she'd wanted to do. Marion had cried and Rowan had promised she wouldn't knock any more, but the rules no longer applied once she'd left home and she couldn't possibly have walked into the house without knocking now.

'I'm good, Dad. How are you?'

'No complaints from me, sweetheart, but are you sure you're okay? It's hard to believe you can be, after... everything. And you look thin, too thin.' Her father's concern was touching. He knew that James's actions had put an end to their marriage, but he had no idea about Euan and, for now at least, Rowan was determined to keep it that way. Her father was far more likely than her mother to let the truth slip out in front of the children before she was sure they were ready to hear it. After all, he didn't have Katrina's track record for keeping secrets.

'I'm fine Dad, honestly. I feel much better since I got home.' It was the first time Rowan had used the word and really meant it, but after today Port Agnes suddenly felt much more like home than it had done before. She was excited about starting at the school and reconnecting with Bex had made her miss Pippa and Odette a bit less too. She was starting to imagine a life here, and now that her parents were genuinely friendly it should make spending time with them far easier. This was a fresh start for them all it seemed.

'I'm so glad to hear that, sweetheart. Now come in before the neighbours start talking about the dodgy-looking woman hanging around on my doorstep.' Her father grinned.

'Is that our girl I can hear, Tony?' Marion called out from the lounge as Rowan followed her father down the hallway.

'It is and she's far too skinny. Have we got any cake?'

'We've always got cake.' Marion smiled as they walked into the lounge. 'We'd never have stayed married for this long if I didn't always have cake, and biscuits. I know the way to your heart.'

Rowan's father dropped a kiss on his wife's head. 'I knew I married you for a reason. You two have a catch up and I'll get the cake.'

'I've already had the biggest slice of carrot cake you've ever seen in your life.' Rowan knew that her protests were going to fall on deaf ears.

'Ah but this is pistachio. Your favourite.' Marion raised her eyebrows. 'And it's Charlie's too, but seeing as I can't bake anything for him for at least another six months, you need to eat his share too.'

'Oh God, moving home is going to do scary things to my insulin levels, isn't it?' Rowan grinned and turned towards her father. 'Have you heard much from Charlie lately? I've been getting most of my news from his stories on Instagram, although he does occasionally remember to send me an email.'

'You and me both, although getting an Instagram account so that I could follow him has been an eye-opener. I waste far too many hours watching other people's videos these days and Marion keeps looking at photos of Hugh Jackman.' Her father laughed. 'I'll get the cake and be right back.'

'Okay, Dad.' Rowan sat on the sofa, opposite where Marion was sitting with her leg resting on a footstool. 'How's the foot? Mum said you hurt it at your line dancing class?'

She'd done her best to keep the note of surprise out of her voice, but she hadn't succeeded and Marion raised her eyebrows again. 'Do you find it hard to believe that me and your mum go dancing together? Because I do.'

'Let's just say that you all continue to surprise me. The last couple of years have been a bit of a turnaround.' It was a hell of a lot more than that, but she wanted her stepmother to know how pleased she was that the situation had changed. 'I'm delighted, though, and it's obvious it's made Mum happy to have her old friend back.'

'Me too. I missed her a lot more than I ever missed my ex-husband, and I think your dad felt the same about Dean. Your mum and I were friends before everything happened, and so were your dad and Dean. It took us far too long to go back to that, but we're there now.' Marion had more or less echoed the same sentiments as her mother, which proved just how in tune they were.

'I'm so glad.' Rowan reached into her bag and took out the jar, handing it to her stepmother before kissing her briefly on the cheek. 'Mum sent this. She bought it for your foot.'

'She's so thoughtful.' Marion beamed.

'I think she has an ulterior motive.'

'Oh really?' For a moment her stepmother looked troubled, but then Rowan shook her head.

'Oh, it's nothing bad, she just can't wait for you to get better and go back to dancing.'

'Me neither.' Marion smiled again, her relief obvious. 'But it won't be long now that I've got this from your mum, and your dad has been looking after me really well too.'

'Wow, I can't believe how much things have changed lately.' Rowan's dad had always been a workaholic and she had a feeling it was one of the things that had come between him and her mother, to a point where they'd grown so far apart that there was no coming back together.

'He's realised that he needs to slow down and he's found a company he's happy to sub-contract to.'

'Really? I never thought he'd do that. Who is it?' Her father's inability to delegate or pass work on to sub-contractors, out of fear of losing control, had been one of the major causes of him working too much. And after what had happened with Dean, he'd never trusted anyone else.

'The Lark brothers.'

'The Lark brothers?' Rowan widened her eyes. 'Is that a good idea, given that, well...'

She couldn't finish the sentence, so Marion did it for her. 'Are you talking about Nathan's prison sentence?'

Her stepmother fixed her with a look and she couldn't have lied if she'd wanted to. She hated herself for doing the very thing she'd criticised other people for, and not allowing Nathan to move on from his past. 'I just don't want Dad to be taken advantage of, that's all.'

'Me neither, sweetheart, but he won't be.' Marion sighed. 'Whatever Nathan did, I'm sure he regrets it and knowing the family as I do, I think he must have had a good reason for it. Whatever it was, it doesn't matter, he deserves a second chance, but you know what this village can be like. There are gossips who love to keep scandal going long after it would be over otherwise and we know the damage that can do better than anyone.'

'We do, and I'm sorry. I shouldn't have said anything.'

'There's no need to be sorry, sweetheart. I know you're only looking out for your dad, but Nathan's a lovely lad, both the Lark boys are.'

'Are you talking about my new business partners?' Her father asked the question as he set a tray on the table, a slow smile spreading across his face. 'At least I know these two won't run off with my wife.'

'Dad!' Rowan couldn't help laughing. Her father had always been a bit of a joker, but this wasn't a subject he'd ever have found funny in the past. Things were definitely changing for the better.

'Oh, I wouldn't be so sure. After twenty-odd years you're still on probation.' Marion put a hand on the back of her husband's head, pulling him towards her and planting a kiss on his lips to prove she was only joking.

'Can you believe your stepmother?' Rowan's father shot her a smile, as he pulled away.

'I'd say you're a lucky man to only have had twenty years' probation.'

'I should have known you two would gang up on me.' He was still smiling. 'I messaged your brother to let him know you're here. He's going to FaceTime us in twenty minutes and he'll be on my side.'

'I can't wait to actually talk to Charlie. He's been away for too long and it'll be so nice to see him in December.'

'I was thinking we could have a big family Christmas this year.' Tony gave Rowan a hopeful look. 'And I thought that maybe your mum and Dean could join us too.'

'I'd like that.' Rowan nodded. It still seemed strange imagining her parents choosing to spend time together, let alone sharing a big family celebration out of choice rather than duty, but she was ready to embrace it. Marion was right, second chances were important and sometimes they came when you least expected it. After seeing the difference it had made to her parents, Rowan was determined to be as open to them as possible in the future, whenever they might arise.

7

'Right Leo, I think we're good to go.' Fastening the safety strap across his nephew's waist, Nathan smiled. It was impossible not to do so when Leo was beaming at him the way he was. The little boy lit up with happiness whenever they got down to Nathan's beach hut and he was transferred from his electric wheelchair, into the all-terrain one that allowed him to go down on to the sand and in to the sea. It was Leo's happy place, and spending time with his nephew was Nathan's. The only thing he'd held on to outright ownership of, after his release from prison, had been his beach hut and the boat that had been left to him by his late father, but days like this made him so much more grateful for that. The £50,000 he'd had to repay after pleading guilty to VAT fraud would have meant remortgaging his house, but the divorce had resulted in having to sell it. It had taken more than ten years of sheer hard graft, as well as renovating and selling three other properties, to be able to own his own home outright at the age of just thirty-three, but he'd done it. Now it was all gone. He'd had enough money left to buy out Nicole's share of the beach hut and boat, and to pay his mother £100,000 for the old cow shed in the grounds of his parents' home. His mother had wanted to gift him the building, but he knew she needed the money to complete the renovations to the main house, which had included creating a self-contained annex for her, leaving Will and his family the rest of the house. The brothers had done most of the work themselves, but there'd been specialised adaptations needed for Leo, which were getting more pressing, and there'd been no question in Nathan's mind about how the money should be used.

Leo's care needs had meant Will's wife, Heather, having to give up her job even before his diagnosis, and they'd been struggling to pay the mortgage on their own place ever since. Like Nathan, Will had done well on climbing the property ladder, but had remortgaged the place after Heather had left work. It wasn't just the drop in her salary, there'd been experimental treatments for Leo, and expensive rounds of IVF in their attempt to have another child. After Leo's diagnosis, they'd qualified for some NHS treatment, where the embryos would be screened for genetic abnormalities, but unfortunately the funded treatment had been unsuccessful. Heather had fast been approaching the NHS cut off and a major decline in her own fertility. So they'd thrown every-thing at funding private treatment and had finally had a successful round of IVF, but Heather had miscarried the baby two months later. It had broken everyone's hearts and taken a huge toll on Will's mental health and Nathan was terrified about what he might do. It had put incredible pressure on them all and things had got even worse when Nathan had been sent to prison.

After Nicole said she was leaving Nathan, their mother suggested they divide up the former family home so that Will and Heather could sell their place, and it had seemed the perfect solution. The agreement was that the house would be put into Will's name so that when their mum died the prop-erty would be theirs. Nathan hadn't had any objection to the proposal, even though it meant his stake in the family home would disappear. The byre, as the old cow shed was now known, and the paddock behind it, were now offi-cially in his name, so technically he owned a property outright again, but he had a long way to go before it would be anything like the home he wanted.

The best thing about the building was that it was single storey and easily accessible to Leo. One of the first things he'd done was to open up a space in the back of the byre and put in glass bifold doors which looked directly out on to the paddock. Leo loved coming down from the big house and sitting there to look out on to the field, which was currently home to three goats. He'd often stay for hours, chatting away while Nathan worked. Being with his nephew made everything he'd gone through pale into insignificance, and everything he'd lost feel like nothing. There'd been a small miracle for Will and his wife too, Heather was now almost six months pregnant with a baby girl from a final round of IVF. The pregnancy hadn't been without its challenges and Heather was having more monitoring than an expectant mother usually would. She and Will were at the hospital for another scan today, which was why he was looking after Leo. Not that he ever needed an excuse to spend time with his nephew, it was his favourite thing to do.

'Do you think the sea will be cold?' Leo looked up at him and Nathan smiled.

'It's still August, which means the temperature should be okay. But you've got a wetsuit on, kiddo, so you'll be fine either way. It's your poor old uncle who'll end up with a numb bum if it's a chilly one.' The mention of bums was met with a peel of laughter from Leo and a warm feeling washed over Nathan, that not even the iciest of waves could have taken away. These were the things to be treasured and held on to, which mattered far more than how perfect his house was, or what other people had to say about him. Hearing Leo's laughter was the best thing in the world and, whatever else happened, it meant this was already a very good day.

* * *

They'd stayed in the water for almost twenty minutes before Nathan pushed Leo's wheelchair back on to the sand. Dashing up to the beach hut, he wrapped his nephew in a dryrobe and picked up the picnic basket he'd left there, before taking Leo back down on to the beach.

'Do you want to sit on the blanket or stay in your chair?' Nathan spread the picnic blanket out on the sand as he spoke and tried not to think how much more difficult it would be to give Leo the options everyone took for granted, once he got too big for his uncle to lift him in and out of the chair. Most children with Duchenne's muscular dystrophy didn't need a wheelchair until they were about twelve or thirteen, but the previous Christmas Leo had fallen down the stairs at his maternal grandparents' home in Scotland and the accident had accelerated the deterioration of the muscles in his legs. Despite physiotherapy, he could only walk short distances with the aid of a frame and it had been his decision to use a wheelchair, which in many ways had given him his mobility back. What would happen as he got older was a problem for another day; for now Leo could choose where he wanted to sit.

'I'll stay in the chair; I don't want to get sand in my bum crack!' Leo laughed in that wonderfully infectious way he had and there was no chance of

Nathan not joining in, even though he knew he shouldn't. Leo was seven, nearly eight, but he often seemed decades older because of everything he'd had to face in life, so it was brilliant to see him being the cheeky little schoolboy he was supposed to be.

'No one wants sand in there.' Nathan pressed his lips together to stop himself from laughing again.

'I definitely don't.' Leo grinned and then suddenly gestured up the beach. 'I know that boy. He came into our classroom to see if he wants to come to our school, just before we broke up for the summer.'

Nathan turned towards where Leo was looking and saw Rowan and her mother walking down the beach with two children. One of them was a boy who looked to be about Leo's age, which must have been Theo, and the other was a girl, a couple of years older at least.

Nathan had heard about Rowan's wedding and the birth of her children on the village grapevine, and he'd felt certain that marrying a vicar would more or less guarantee her marriage lasting forever, but now she was back for good and all sorts of rumours about why would no doubt be circulating. He just hoped she was doing okay.

When he'd heard Rowan's name mentioned over the years, he'd sometimes allowed himself to wonder what might have happened between them if she hadn't moved away so suddenly. But there were a million what-ifs in life and he'd put any thoughts of Rowan to the back of his mind when he'd been married to Nicole. Except looking at her on the beach now, that night up on the cliffs came rushing back into his mind, and he had to physically shake himself to dislodge the thought. Rowan wouldn't be interested in him, even if he hadn't sworn off getting seriously involved with anyone again. His family were all that mattered and the few people who'd stuck by them after his sentencing. It was a smaller circle than he'd had before, but he loved every person in it and that counted for far more than a big group of people who had never really been there for him.

'Shall we call them over to say hello? I think it'll be really nice for him if he's got a friend when he starts at school, especially when everyone already knows each other.'

'He might not want to be friends with me.' Leo lowered his eyes and Nathan's heart constricted. He'd never been a violent person and had kept his head down in prison, avoiding any kind of confrontation if he possibly could, because physical altercations weren't his style. But the thought of anyone rejecting Leo or making him feel like he wasn't worthy made Nathan's blood rush through his veins. Not long after Leo had started using the wheelchair, a group of lads in their twenties had slowed down their car as they'd passed, rolling down the window and shouting a word that Nathan couldn't even bear to say out loud. He'd broken into a run, chasing the car down the road and only coming to his senses when he realised that he'd left Leo on his own. Nathan had always hated bullying of any kind and, when it came to defending his nephew, he knew he could be capable of almost anything and sadly he understood why Leo was afraid of rejection.

Rowan's son wouldn't be a bully, though. Somehow Nathan knew it with absolute certainty. Most people were good and kind, and they lived in a community that had rallied around Will and Heather for the most part, donating to fundraising causes, like the half marathon Nathan had organised. People looked out for Leo, and the parish council had voted unanimously to assign funds to purchasing accessible equipment for the play park. Volunteers from the PTA were helping out at the school and most of the other pupils seemed to love Leo for the wonderful kid he was. It was what had made Nathan fall in love with Port Agnes again and feel able to continue to call it his home, despite the way some people had reacted after his release from prison. As long as they treated Leo the way he deserved, Nathan didn't care what they thought about him.

'Of course Theo will want to be your friend and I bet he'll be thrilled you want to be his.' Nathan put a hand on his nephew's shoulder.

'How do you know that's his name and that he'll want to be friends with me?' There was still a slight wobble in Leo's voice and Nathan wished he could make his nephew believe that anyone would be lucky to have him as a friend.

'Theo's mum told me his name. Me and your dad used to be friends with her when we were at school. She's lovely, and I bet her kids are too. It must be hard for them, moving here and starting somewhere new. They haven't lived near the beach before.' A grin tugged at the corners of Nathan's mouth as he looked at his nephew again. 'And Theo will need someone to warn him about the importance of keeping sand out of his bum crack.'

Leo giggled. 'Okay then, I better tell him.'

'Rowan!' Nathan called out her name before Leo could change his mind and she looked up and smiled. Her long auburn hair hung around her shoulders in loose waves and from this distance it was almost as if she hadn't aged a day since she'd moved out of Port Agnes. As she got closer, he could the differences, but time had been kind rather than cruel. Her cheek bones were more prominent and there was just the hint of laughter lines around her hazel eyes, indicating a side he hadn't seen to Rowan since her return. She'd been friendly enough when they'd chatted at the school, but there'd been a definite air of melancholy about her too. Looks wise, she might be instantly recognisable as the girl he used to know, but her spirit was nowhere near as vibrant and the thought of that made him sad. Still, he seemed to remember that she'd been quite quiet when she'd first started at secondary school. So maybe this version of her was closer to the real Rowan than the far more sparky and confident girl who'd kissed him on the night of the golden jubilee. In a way he hoped it was, because he hated the thought that life might have robbed that spark from her instead. He knew what it was like for life events to change everything, and he was only just starting to feel a bit more like his old self, two years down the line.

'Hi Nathan, good to see you again.' Rowan was still smiling when she reached them. 'And you must be Leo? I've heard a lot about you.'

'Uncle Nathan said you went to school with him and Dad, a really, really long time ago.' Leo gave her an earnest look and Rowan burst out laughing.

'I didn't say anything about it being a really, really long time ago.' Nathan held up his hands in protest.

'But we can both admit it *was* an awfully long time ago.' She exchanged a look with him, her eyes twinkling, and he could see that old spirit of hers was still in there somewhere after all. 'This is my son, Theo, who is going to be in your class and my daughter, Bella, who'll be in Year 6.'

'Hi.' Leo's shyness seemed to have crept back in and he dipped his head as he spoke.

'Hi Leo. Your wheelchair is really cool; does it go in the sea?' Theo had the sort of brilliant directness, with absolutely no ill intention, that only children really seemed to possess.

'Yes, it can go anywhere and I never have to worry about stepping on a jellyfish.' Leo grinned.

'I hate jellyfish.' Bella gave a shudder.

'But you both love the idea of hanging out at the beach a lot more often, don't you?' The children nodded in response to Rowan's question and started asking Leo more about what kind of sea creatures he'd seen. As they chatted, moving slightly away from the adults to look at some of the shells that were mixed up with the sand, Rowan turned towards Nathan. 'You already know my mum, don't you?'

'Of course, good to see you, Katrina. How's the line dancing going?'

'I'm not a patch on your mum yet, but I'll get there. I've just got to take every chance I can to practise.' Katrina gave a brief demonstration of the grapevine step as if to prove her point, before turning to look at her daughter. 'Nathan's mum, Irene, goes to the same class as me and Marion. Irene and Ruth, you know, the one who runs Mehenick's Bakery with her husband, are Nicky's star pupils. I've got a lot of catching up to do.'

'It sounds like you all have a great time and that's the main thing,' Rowan said.

'You two should join us.' Katrina looked from Rowan to Nathan and back again. 'I know your dad or Dean would be happy to have the kids.'

'Thanks, Mum, but I'm not sure it's my thing and I can almost guarantee it's not Nathan's.'

'I might be tempted if I'm allowed to wear a Stetson and some cowboy boots.'

'You'd be the most popular man there.' Katrina laughed. 'Although you'd also be the only man there.'

'Oh God, is that really the time?' Rowan said suddenly, double checking her watch as if she was finding it impossible to believe. 'James is FaceTiming the kids in half an hour, so we'd better get back. It was good to see you again, Nathan, and Theo and Leo seem to be getting on like a house on fire.'

'Their names rhyme, so maybe it was meant to be.' Nathan found himself silently praying that it was. Leo had friends, but he'd never found a best friend. Nathan had always had a built-in best friend, because of the closeness of his relationship with Will, but it would make his year if his nephew could find one too.

'I think it might well be and maybe we could arrange another get-together? Theo will kill me if I call it a play date, but maybe we could meet up for a bit longer next time, before they start back at school?'

'Leo would love that. I'd give you a card with my number but...' He grinned, pretending to reach into an imaginary pocket, suddenly aware that he'd been standing chatting to her this whole time wearing only his swimming trunks.

'I'll get it off Dad; he said you've been working together.' Her tone was level, not giving away how she felt about the situation.

'Sounds like a plan.' He watched as she spoke to the children, telling them that their father would be calling soon and that they'd make arrangements to come back to the beach with Leo and Nathan again soon. He was glad she'd confirmed it in front of them, because he knew that meant she'd definitely call him. He just couldn't be certain whether it would be him or Leo who would look forward to it more.

* * *

Rowan had worried about how the children might react to seeing their father on FaceTime and whether they'd get upset, especially after he'd pulled out of the plan to hire a van to drop the rest of their things off and spend time with Bella and Theo. Apparently there was 'too much going on' at Membory Grange, something she very much doubted given that it was still the school holidays. Nonetheless, James had somehow persuaded Pippa and Daniel to drive up with the stuff instead. It had been great to see them, but Rowan had been left to mop up the children's disappointment at not seeing their father and it was why she was worried about how they might react to the video call. She needn't have been concerned, they'd both chatted away happily about life in Port Agnes, which was already feeling far more settled than Rowan had dreamt possible. She was under no illusion that there wouldn't be some ups and downs ahead, but for now everyone seemed so much happier than they had even a week ago.

Bella had got to know the twins next door, Kit and Merryn, who were due to start in Reception, but she seemed to enjoy mothering them. She'd told Rowan that Merryn was a bit nervous about going to 'big' school, and Bella had reassured the little girl that she'd be there to talk to at break times. The idea of looking out for Merryn seemed to have alleviated all of Bella's own nerves and her resistance to starting at Port Agnes Primary. Bella had also got chatting to a girl called Tiffany who lived three doors down from Rowan's mother, and who was in her class. They'd arranged to meet up in the last week of the school holidays when Tiffany got back from visiting family in Ireland.

Now that Theo had been introduced to Leo, it felt as if he had a ready-made friend to start school with too, and it gladdened Rowan's heart to see her children looking so much happier.

Both of them had always loved the beach and seemed to be relishing having it on their doorstep, as well as being able to spend time with both sets of their Cornish grandparents. And there was no doubt about it: all four grandparents were clearly thrilled to have the kids so close to home. James's parents had never been warm and, since his mother's death five years earlier, Rowan could probably count on the fingers of one hand how often Michael had asked if he could see the children. They never asked about him either, but as the former bishop should know, the quote about reaping what you sow was so often spot on.

'Daddy wants to talk to you now.' Theo thrust Rowan's iPhone back into her hand, barely pausing as he ran past her. 'I'm going to sort out my Lego. Leo said he'd do some with me next time we see him.'

Bella had already gone too, no doubt out to the back garden to hang over the fence so she could talk to the twins.

'Theo said you needed to talk to me.' Rowan's tone was tight. She had no idea what James wanted, but it was far too soon to feel ready to talk about anything that wasn't to do with the children. The house they'd bought together in Exeter to ensure they kept a foot on the property ladder while they were living in housing provided by the school was already on the market, and they'd agreed a simple fifty-fifty split in equity and their joint savings. Other than that, they'd both be retaining any individual savings and their pensions. While the children were living with her full time, James would be sending 300 pounds a month in maintenance, which would be reviewed if and when he was in a position to have them spend nights with him. But he'd already said he wasn't ready to do that at Membory Grange, and that he was worried it might be disruptive for the children and delay them settling in to Port Agnes. Secretly she'd been glad, but now she was bracing herself for James to announce that he'd suddenly had a change of heart, having seen the children's faces and realised that he couldn't bear not to spend time with them.

'I miss you so much, all three of you.' James started to cry before the words were even out of his mouth and she stared at him for a moment, trying to work out how she felt about the man she'd spent over two decades loving, but hadn't really known at all. He looked thin and exhausted and there was a part of her that hurt for him, but a much bigger part that was still incredibly angry for what he'd put her and the children through.

'It's been a big change for us all and I know the kids miss you too.' Rowan wasn't going to say she missed him, not even in an attempt to make him feel better. Of course she did, you couldn't share your life with someone for more than twenty years and not miss them when they suddenly disappeared out of it, almost overnight. But she'd grieved painfully during the months when she'd still lived at Membory Grange, and she'd had to harden her heart to him in order to survive, telling herself that the James she missed had never really existed. She had to get to know this new version of him as her children's father. But the new James would never be her husband. The most she could hope for was that they would one day be friends, for the children's sake if nothing else. She'd seen for herself the difference it made when parents were able to get along, and she wanted them to, Euan included, if he stayed on the scene. It just felt far too early to think of James as any kind of friend yet.

'I need to see you all, face to face; not being able to hug any of you is like a physical pain.' There were still tears running down James's face. 'Can I come and stay with you?'

Rowan couldn't help wondering why he was suddenly so desperate to spend time with the children, when he'd ended up cancelling his last visit. But she knew that being separated from them would have felt like physical pain to her too, and she wasn't going to give him the third degree about his change of heart. All that really mattered was that the children were happy.

'I want you to see Theo and Bella whenever you like.' It was the one thing she'd vowed she'd never stand in the way of, and that she'd never badmouth James in front of the children. In all the late-night drinking sessions with Pippa and Odette, after discovering James's secret, when the three of them had called him every name under the sun, it had been the vow she'd repeated. No matter how she felt about James or what he'd done, she'd never say a bad word about him in front Theo and Bella, and she'd never stop him from seeing them. But he couldn't have it all his own way. 'They'll be really happy to see you, but you can't stay here, I don't think it would be good for any of us. You'll have to rent an Airbnb or stay in a hotel.'

'I understand.' James bit his lip, but it did nothing to stem his tears. 'I'm so sorry, Row, if I could undo everything I've done I would. I wish to God it hadn't happened.'

She scanned around her and lowered her voice to make sure there was no chance of the children overhearing. 'The affair or the part where you got caught?'

'Row, please, I feel terrible enough as it is.'

'That makes two of us then.' A frisson of guilt knotted in her stomach, because she didn't feel as awful as she'd expected to this soon after moving back to Port Agnes. Now that she'd been to the school and reconnected with Bex she was genuinely looking forward to starting her new job; things between her parents were better than they'd ever been and then there was Nathan. She tried to push the thought of him out of her head; he shouldn't even feature in the equation of all the things she felt she had to look forward to as she built a new life for herself and the children. That new life could never include Nathan Lark, they were just too... different.

'I'm sorry, I really am.' James was repeating himself now and it wouldn't change anything, no matter how many times he said it. Maybe one day she'd be ready to accept his apology, but today wasn't that day.

'Just let me know when you've sorted out a weekend to come. It might be a good idea to give us at least a week's notice. They're both starting to make friends and I don't want them to have to cancel any plans because you've left telling us to the last minute.'

'It sounds like everyone is moving on, except me.' James sounded so sorry for himself and something inside Rowan snapped. She might be doing okay now and the children were starting to settle, but she'd gone through months of barely being able to sleep, worrying about the future, and trying to comfort her children when they begged to stay at Membory Grange, without being able to tell them why that was impossible.

'Funny how it works out when you gave yourself such a head start on the moving on front. Just text me when you've decided about a visit.' Ending the call before he could say anything else, Rowan let go of a long breath. They were all moving on, bit by bit, and she was incredibly proud of the children for the way they had turned things around in such a short time and for embracing their fresh start. The road ahead didn't seem anywhere near as bleak any more, but no matter what the future held she knew they'd make it through, because they had each other and that was all Rowan really needed.

8

The beautiful weather that had blessed Port Agnes for most of the summer seemed determined to hang around until the start of term, and the temperatures showed no signs of falling as August drifted into September.

It meant they had the perfect day for the boat trip that Rowan had arranged with Bex and her three sons. They'd been accompanied by Rowan's neighbour Anna and the twins, and another old friend Toni, with her two children. It had been even more fun than she'd hoped, when it turned out that Toni and Anna were also good friends, who worked together at the Port Agnes midwifery unit. Bella's new friend, Tiffany, was back from her holiday, so they'd arranged to take her on the trip too.

There were hourly boat trips from the harbour between 10 a.m. and 4 p.m. in the school holidays, and they'd booked the last slot of the day, but it was still so warm that all ten of the children had to be slathered in sun cream, much to their disgust.

'Mum, I can do it myself. You're so embarrassing.' Bella rolled her eyes so hard she was in danger of doing herself an injury.

'I just want to make sure it's on the back of your neck and your ears, they're the worst places for getting burned.' Rowan ignored her daughter's heavy sigh and turned to Bella's friend. 'You'll need some too, Tiffany. I promised your mum I'd make sure you were very well looked after. She trusted me to take you on a boat trip and keep you safe, so I don't want to let her down.'

'Thank you, Mrs Bellamy.' Tiffany gave her a wide grin. 'And I don't mind how much sun cream I have to have put on. I don't want to get skin cancer. My grandad had it and now the top of his ear is missing because the doctors had to cut it off. Gross!'

Bella widened her eyes and took the bottle of sun cream from her mother. 'Okay, okay. I can put it on Tiff and she can put it on me. We're not babies.'

'No, you're not.' Rowan breathed out. Her daughter sounded more like a woman than a girl far too often just lately, and there was no denying that she was growing up. She'd seen the way Bella looked at Henry, Bex's eldest son, who was twelve and just about to start in Year 8 at secondary school. Bella and Tiffany kept glancing none too subtly in his direction, before giggling and laughing. It probably wouldn't be long before boys would be on her daughter's radar in a far more significant way, and the thought terrified Rowan. It wasn't just the idea of her daughter having a boyfriend eventually, it was the prospect that one day her little girl's heart might get broken, just like hers had been, and she couldn't bear the thought of that. Sometimes she worried about what she might be capable of if anyone hurt either of her children in that way.

'Oh.' Bella widened her eyes again, clearly shocked that her mother had acknowledged the fact she was growing up. 'So does that mean we can sit over there, by ourselves?'

She gestured towards a bench on one side of the boat, only big enough to seat Bella and Tiffany. Everyone was wearing a life jacket, and they'd only be about ten feet away from where Rowan and the rest of their group were sitting, so they'd be perfectly safe. Even so, there had to be some ground rules. 'Okay, but you need to stay sitting down. Don't lean over the edge, or start doing anything silly like playfighting.'

'We're not at school today, so you don't have to act like our teacher.' Bella rolled her eyes again, but Rowan decided not to come down too hard on her in front of her new friend. It was a tough balance when she would be Tiffany's headteacher in a few days' time, not just her friend's mum, but there'd been so much for Bella to adjust to recently and just this once she'd cut her a bit of slack.

'Okay deal, I won't act like a headteacher if you don't act like school-children.'

'We're just going to sit down and take selfies. Tiff's got a really cool phone.' Bella gave Rowan a pointed look. She knew mobile phones were off the cards until she started at Three Ports High School in a year's time and had to get the bus there. Until then she had no need of a mobile, and the thought of the world that would open up for Bella terrified Rowan even more. Tiffany's parents had made a different decision, but that wouldn't change Rowan's mind, no matter how much Bella might complain about how unfair it was.

'As long as none of the pictures of you are posted online.' Rowan knew she'd failed in her attempt not to embarrass her daughter, even before Bella's cheeks coloured, but some things had to be said.

'Don't worry, Mrs Bellamy. I'm not allowed to have any social media accounts yet; you know what mums are like.' Tiffany shrugged and Rowan had to suppress the urge to laugh. It wasn't just her daughter who was ten going on thirty.

'I do indeed. Just have fun and stay safe, that's the only thing your mum and your headteacher wants.' She dropped a wink and turned back towards where the rest of the group were sitting along two benches at the back of the boat. Anna and Toni's children were younger than the others and still revelled in sitting close to their mothers, causing Rowan a mixture of envy and regret when she looked at them. Those early years with the kids had felt challenging in lots of ways, but they'd gone by so fast and she missed them now more than she'd ever have believed possible.

Bex's three boys had arrived in the space of four years and she seemed to spend most of her time refereeing a never-ending wrestling match between the younger two, who were eight and nine. She'd already admitted to Rowan that she came into work for a rest. Her older son, Henry, was glued to something on his phone, occasionally glancing up and giving one of his brothers a sharp elbow in the ribs when their playfighting encroached on his personal space. Theo was only a year younger than Bex's third son, but it might as well have been a decade, given the differences in their personalities. Theo was quiet and thoughtful, even more so since the break-up of his parents' marriage, and it hurt Rowan's heart to look at him now, sitting on his own away from the others. She would have liked to cuddle Theo, snuggling him into her side the way that Toni and Anna were doing with their children, but he wouldn't appreciate that.

Theo desperately wanted to fit in, she could see it when she caught him watching other children. He was doing it now, taking in the rough play between Ollie and Tom. But he'd never take the initiative to get involved, or ask if he could join in with their 'game'. He was too frightened of rejection and it made her want to wrap him up in cotton wool all the more, or step in on his behalf and ask if he could play, which would have made things ten times worse. Your mum being the headteacher was bad enough, she couldn't become one of those mothers who interfered in other children's games and insisted that her son be included. She had to step back and trust that Theo would find his place before too long, and try not to let her heart ache for him in the meantime. At least he'd have Leo when he started school next week. It would be lovely if they became good friends and easier because she already knew Nathan. Even as the thought entered her head she wondered if that really would make things easier, because she had a funny feeling Nathan had the potential to complicate everything.

'Okay, sweetheart?' Rowan sat down next to her son and he nodded slowly, as the boat chugged out of the confines of the harbour and past the rows of cottages and shops that flanked it on both sides. There wasn't even a wisp of cloud to break up the endless blue of the sky, and the colour of the sea changed from turquoise to teal as the boat moved into deeper water.

'Do you think we might really see some seals?' Theo turned to look at her, his eyes shining with excitement.

'The captain said there was a good chance, so we'll just have to keep our fingers crossed.'

'Dad really likes sea animals; he'd love to see a seal.' Theo's eyes were still shining, but his mouth had turned at the corners, as if excitement had given way to sadness, and she wanted to hug him all the more.

'He would, darling.' She squeezed his hand, not caring if her son thought it was deeply uncool, but he didn't snatch it away. 'How about I give you my phone if we see any seals, then you can take lots of photos and send them to Dad later on?'

'Okay.' Theo gave her a watery smile and slowly withdrew his hand, shooting a sideways glance towards Ollie and Tom, who were too busy jostling one another to notice. Bex had just sent them to a bench further up the boat, on the opposite side of the wheelhouse from where Bella and Tiffany were sitting. They were close enough for her to be able to see them, as Ollie desperately tried to get Tom in a headlock, but there was no longer any risk of them catching one of the younger children in the crossfire. Henry was now wearing ear pods, still engrossed in his phone and oblivious to the whole world around him.

'Tom and Ollie are exhausting. I barely get a word out of Henry these days, but I'm almost looking forward to when they're more interested in their phones than anything else.' Bex looked as if she was ready to have a lie down in a dark room. 'I shouldn't have had them so close together. I was talking to Irene Lark about it and she reckons it's harder work than having real twins, because they're at slightly different stages and need different things.'

'Anna might have something to say on that subject.' Toni grinned. Her own children were close in age too, but Anna was the only one to have experienced the challenge of raising twins.

'It's not a competition.' Anna smiled. 'But I think Irene might be right. Kit and Merryn have always entertained one another, in their own little way. Still, if the Lark boys are anything to go by, Ollie and Tom will be really close when they grow up.'

'As long as one of them doesn't turn to crime.' Bex laughed, but then she shook her head, suddenly looking contrite. 'God, that was horrible of me. Nathan's lovely and I can't believe he'd have done it for his own benefit. It might even have been a mistake, you hear about it all the time, don't you? People who've made a genuine error being made an example of by the courts, while the real criminals go free. It probably wasn't even investigated properly.'

'Hark at Miss Marple over there!' It was Toni's turn to laugh. 'Although you're right that Nathan doesn't seem the type to do something like that. Whatever the truth, he paid his debt, in both senses of the word.'

'He did.' Bex glanced at Henry to make sure he was still engrossed in his phone. 'Irene told me that after he sold his house and paid off the fine, he insisted that the money that was left over be used to convert the house so that she had a self-contained annex, and the rest was accessible for Leo. Meanwhile, he's trying to convert an old barn on a shoestring budget. Those don't sound like the actions of a man who committed fraud for his own gain. I'd have loved to have a sibling who was as selfless as that, instead of one who puts herself first, last and everywhere.'

'I thought we'd agreed never to mention Briony's name.' Toni raised her eyebrows, but Rowan couldn't let the comment pass. When she'd asked Bex how her sister was, she'd got an evasive answer and, now she thought about it, she couldn't remember the last time she'd seen any mention of Bex's younger sister on any of her social media accounts.

'Why aren't we mentioning Briony's name?'

'Let's just say that life is far more peaceful if Briony's name doesn't come up.' Bex gave a dramatic sigh, clearly realising she was going to have to give some kind of explanation. 'Because of her, our parents lost thousands of pounds and it pushed their retirement back by years. Whatever Nathan did, at least he faced up to it and tried his best to make it right, instead of running off like Briony. I don't care what anyone says, I still think he's a good man.'

'It sounds like it.' Anna had clearly made the decision to move the conversation away from any more talk of Bex's sister, and she turned towards Rowan. 'I hear you know Nathan quite well from back in the day?'

'I—' Rowan stopped and pulled a face, hoping it would be enough to indicate to the others that she didn't want to discuss this in front of Theo, but suddenly Bella was standing in front of her.

'Tiff thinks she can see some seals, but they're quite far away. It's a lot easier to see them from the side of the boat and I thought Theo might want to come and sit with us. Is that okay?' She gave her mother a questioning look and a wave of warmth flooded over Rowan. Whatever boundaries Bella might be pushing lately and however determined she was to start asserting her independence, deep down she was the same sweet, loving girl she'd always been.

'Please, Mum, can I?' Theo tugged on her sleeve.

'Of course you can, just be careful and don't lean over the edge to take photos, or my phone could end up in the sea, and so could you.' She handed him her mobile, knowing there was still a risk it could get lost, but not caring as long as Theo enjoyed himself. It was so good to see both children happy and excited. Reaching out for her daughter's hand, Rowan brushed hers against it. The gesture was just enough to demonstrate her love and gratitude, but not enough to embarrass Bella. 'Thank you, darling, you're a good big sister.'

'I know.' Bella grinned and Rowan had a feeling her daughter might be reminding her of that next time she wanted something. It would be worth it, though, and the only downside to her children getting along so well and disappearing off together, was that now she had no excuse not to answer Anna's question. And when Toni decided to offer a recap, she realised she'd been well and truly backed into a corner.

'I think Anna was asking you about Nathan?'

'There's nothing to tell.' Rowan gave a deliberately over-the-top shrug. 'We kissed once, when we were about sixteen. Then I moved away and that was it.'

'Until you moved back and your eyes met across the empty playground. Oh yeah and you also forgot to mention all the years you pined after Nathan at school, before you finally wore him down!' Bex laughed and ducked out of the way as Rowan pretended to make a grab for her. 'You'll have to be quicker than that, I'm used to dodging blows from Tom and Ollie. And don't try to pretend with me, I've known you since you had a crush on him first time around and I saw the same look on your face when you went over to talk to him in the playground.'

'No, you didn't. I just think it's lovely how much he looks out for his nephew and how involved he is with things around the school. I'd be the same with anyone.'

'You keep telling yourself that if it makes you feel better.' Bex shook her head. 'Although I don't know why you're pretending you don't still find him attractive. You are allowed to admit it, especially now you're single.'

'Single.' Rowan hadn't realised that she'd repeated the word out loud until the others looked at her. She was single, wasn't she? After more than twenty years with the same man, the *only* man she'd ever slept with, she was single. Not only that but it turned out her husband had slept with at least as many men as she had, probably more if she allowed herself to face the truth of just how long he'd been playing make believe.

'Sorry, I shouldn't have said anything. Me and my big mouth, nothing's changed since we were at school on that front either. It's probably why you and Toni stopped hanging out with me for so long, you both wanted to shake me off.' Bex put an arm around Rowan, but she shook her head. She didn't want her friend to feel bad; their lives had just moved in different directions over the years. It was really lovely to have her old friends back, and to be making new friends like Anna too. There was no way she was going to allow James to ruin that for her.

'Don't be daft, it's true, I am single, it's just taking me a while to get used to the fact that I'm not part of James and Rowan any more, that's all.'

'It will take a while.' Toni's voice was low. 'And no one expects you to rush into another relationship, or to throw yourself at Nathan Lark and tell him you want to pick up where you left off. You don't have to start another relationship at all if you don't want to. Just don't shut yourself off from the possibility. I did that for more than ten years after my fiancé Aaron died, because I thought I'd had my one shot at finding someone. Then I met Bobby, and for a long time I still told myself I couldn't have all the things that I thought I was going to have with Aaron, but I got all of them and more.'

'You certainly did.' Rowan smiled. Toni's heart had been shattered by her fiancé's death from a brain aneurysm, but now she had a husband and two gorgeous kids, and she seemed happier than Rowan had ever known her. Maybe Rowan could open her heart up to the prospect of a new relationship eventually too, but it could never be with Nathan Lark. Whatever the reasons for the crime he'd committed and however much she might sympathise with them, living in a village like Port Agnes meant your indiscretions were never forgotten. Rowan had been the focus of village gossip before and that was one aspect of her past she never wanted to relive.

* * *

Rowan clicked on the icon to save the file she'd been working on, even though she still wasn't 100 per cent happy with it. She'd been preparing her first staff training session, which she'd be delivering the day before the children came back to school. She needed to get this right, her new team would form a first impression of her off the back of the staff development day. She wanted them to view her as friendly and approachable, and a team player who still understood what it was like to be in the classroom, rather than shut away in the headteacher's office. She needed to balance that with setting out her intention to make some changes within the school, and articulating a vision for the future that the staff could believe in. She also wanted her new team to feel that the training was worthwhile and that they'd actually learned something, rather than just being there to tick a box. Port Agnes Primary School was a very different place from Membory Grange, so she had to approach the training differently too. This was her third attempt at finalising the materials and she suddenly felt an almost overwhelming urge to get away from the computer and give herself a chance to think.

The clouds still seemed to be hiding somewhere far from Port Agnes, and there was another endless blue sky above the school buildings when Rowan wandered into the playground. Bex was in the office, updating the children's files, and a couple of other staff had popped in to continue preparations for the start of term, but other than that the place was deserted. It was always a slightly weird sensation, being in a school without any children, and Rowan closed her eyes for a moment, trying to envisage not just the pupils she'd be responsible for, but her own children running around in this playground, making friends and taking another step towards Port Agnes becoming their permanent home. Bella and Theo were with her mother, who was going to drop them into the school on their way back from the beach, so that they could have one last look round before the start of term. Rowan just hoped it would seem as perfect to her children as it did to her. With the sun warming her face, and birdsong the only sound filling the air, a sense of contentment she hadn't felt in a very long time swept over her.

'Huh-hum.' Someone behind her was clearing their throat. Rowan's eyes shot open in response and she spun around, coming face to face with Nathan, his nephew, Leo, and Krish, the school caretaker.

'Sorry, Mrs Bellamy.' Krish looked distinctly uncomfortable. 'We were trying not to make you jump and I didn't think there'd be anyone but Mrs White here. Otherwise I wouldn't have arranged for Leo to come and try out the new paving grids. We just wanted to make sure everything's as it should be for the start of term.'

'It's not a problem at all, it's really nice to see you again, Leo, and your T-shirt is great. Theo loves dolphins too. He's desperate to see one, ever since my mum told him she sometimes sees them in the bay when she's walking her dog in the mornings. We haven't been lucky enough yet, but he's keeping everything crossed it won't be long.'

'Dolphins are the best and I get to see them all the time, when I go out on Uncle Nathan's boat.' Leo beamed. 'Maybe Theo could come with us next time?'

He turned towards his uncle, who smiled in response. 'He'd be welcome anytime and you could come too if it makes you feel more comfortable being there to keep an eye on him, and Bella of course.'

Nathan's gaze met hers and the air suddenly felt as though it had thickened, making it harder to catch her breath, but she managed to nod slowly. 'We'd all love to see a dolphin and anything that helps convince Bella that moving to Port Agnes was a good idea has to be worth doing.'

She hadn't meant to be quite so open, but there was something about the way Nathan looked at her that made it hard to keep her guard up. The young girl who'd fallen under his spell was clearly still in there somewhere. It was probably no surprise that nostalgia was such a powerful force, when the recent past had been so tricky, but it didn't mean anything.

'We'll have to arrange a date to go out.' He was still holding her gaze and her mouth opened and shut a couple of times, like a fish out of water. Nathan gave her a quizzical look and, when she still didn't respond, he laughed. 'Don't panic, I just meant let's choose a date when we can go out on the boat, while the weather is still so good.'

'Oh, yes of course.' Rowan looked down and picked an imaginary piece of fluff off the sleeve of her summer dress so that there was no chance of Nathan, or anyone else, reading the expression on her face. She couldn't even attempt to hide how she was feeling, because she wasn't sure herself. It would be lovely for Theo to have a good friend and the idea of taking them out on the boat together definitely appealed, but she'd have been lying to herself if she tried to pretend she hadn't experienced a frisson of excitement at the idea of going on a date with Nathan. There'd been a mixture of fear and horror at the idea too; that would really give people something to talk about. Even if the idea of that hadn't been enough to put her off, her life was in far too much of a mess to get involved with anyone else. Thankfully Krish saved her from further embarrassment.

'Shall we go and check out the paving grids, then?'

Rowan didn't hesitate. 'Great and maybe we can talk through some other potential plans. I was thinking of asking the PTA if we can raise funds to build raised beds, so that everyone has the chance to grow some plants, and Leo can give me some advice on what to ask for.'

Leo nodded enthusiastically. 'My nan's really good at gardening and she's taught me the name of the plants, so I know lots about them.'

'I knew I'd picked the right person to be in charge.' Rowan winked at him and the four of them headed towards the grassy area. But when Leo got there, he stopped his wheelchair.

'Are you sure I won't get stuck?' He stared up at his uncle, his eyes looking twice as big as they had before, and Nathan sank down on to his haunches.

'I promise you, buddy, there's absolutely no chance of that happening.' He put a hand over his nephew's. 'Have I ever let you down?'

The little boy shook his head. 'And I can go all the way to the woods?'

It might have been a grand name for the small copse of trees at the edge of the grassy area, but Rowan could see from Leo's expression just how much it meant to him to have the freedom to go wherever he wanted. She had so many ideas about how to make the most of the area and she'd already decided to have a forest school champion in each class from Year 3 upwards, whose role it would be to collect suggestions from their classmates about how to transform the area and the types of activities they wanted to do. Leo would be perfect for the role, if he wanted to do it.

'Yes, you can.' Nathan smiled. 'We've put a pathway of paving grids all the way down to the trees and the grass is already growing through them, so it'll look exactly how it used to soon. If you follow Mr Chodri, he'll show you the way.'

'Yay!' Leo didn't need telling twice and he manoeuvred his wheelchair on to the grass, heading down towards the wooded area with Krish almost having to run to avoid getting mown down.

'I think the project is a hit.' Rowan turned to Nathan and smiled.

'He loves being outside and even before he started using the wheelchair, it was difficult for him to go on the grass when it was wet, because he was so scared of slipping. He's a great kid and he so rarely complains about anything, but he hates being different. He just wants to be like everyone else and not feel as if everyone's looking at him or judging him.'

'I can understand that.'

'Me too.' It was Nathan who looked away first this time and she wanted to let him know that whatever had happened in the past, she wasn't going to hold it against him. People made mistakes, she'd made enough of them to know that. She might not have committed a crime, but she hadn't listened to her gut and, against her better judgement, she was still being part of James's deception. She could understand all too easily why people sometimes did the wrong thing for the right reasons, especially when it came to family.

'Mum!' Theo's voice carried across the playground, as he came running towards her, with Bella, Bex and Katrina trailing in his wake.

'Hello, sweetheart.' She wrapped her arms around her son, glad that she didn't have to stand on ceremony today. She'd have to remind the children before the start of term that when they were at school, she was Mrs Bellamy, but for today it was nice to be just their mum on school grounds and hopefully that would help alleviate some of Theo's anxiety about joining a new class. Although as Leo called out to her son, she suspected he could be of far more help on that front.

'Theo, come over here. There's a squirrel collecting acorns.' Leo's face was a picture of pure joy as Rowan and the others turned to look at him as Theo broke into a run again, hurtling down the new path towards the other boy.

'Leo hasn't stopped talking about Theo since we saw you at the beach.' Nathan was still looking in the boys' direction. 'I really hope they'll be friends.'

'Me too.' Rowan was still trying to convince herself that the reason she liked the idea of Theo being friends with Leo so much had nothing to do with his uncle Nathan. She desperately wanted Theo to settle in and be happy, and Leo was a lovely boy, that was all. But that didn't explain why when she pictured arranging a play date, Nathan was there too.

'I've got a really good idea to help them bond even more before they start school.' Rowan's mother put a hand on Nathan's arm. 'Me and Dean are having a barbecue for family and friends on Saturday afternoon. Why don't you and Leo come, and bring the rest of the family. I've already invited your mum.'

'That's lovely, but I'm sure you don't want all of us there.'

'Of course I do.' Her hand was still on Nathan's arm and Rowan knew her mother wouldn't take no for an answer. 'The more the merrier. Bex and her boys are coming too, aren't you?'

'Yes, we'll go anywhere for free food.' Bex grinned, before turning to Rowan and shooting her a look that no one else would have seen. Her friend knew what Katrina was up to as well as she did. Rowan just hoped Nathan hadn't picked up on it too.

'If you're sure, that sounds great, and I know Leo will love hanging out with Theo, which means Will and Heather will definitely be up for it too. I'll go and tell Leo now, and you'll probably hear the whooping from here.'

'I'm going to go down and see the boys too.' Bella said, running on ahead of Nathan, but Rowan waited until they were both far enough away before taking a step towards her mother and lowering her voice just enough to make sure she couldn't be overheard.

'I know what you're up to, Mum, but you're wasting your time.'

'I've got no idea what you're talking about.' Katrina widened her eyes, trying to look innocent. She was nowhere close to pulling it off, even before Bex started laughing.

'She's got your measure, Kat, but for what it's worth I think you're doing the right thing. Nathan is lovely and Rowan deserves a bit of fun after what she's been through.'

'I didn't realise you knew—'

'Of course she knows you're trying to fix me up.' Rowan cut her mother off before she could say any more. She was as certain as she could be that her mother had been about to spill the beans about the real reason she and James had split up, despite her promise to keep it to herself. Bex was an old friend, but they'd only just reconnected and she wasn't ready for anyone else to know the truth, especially when her children still had no idea. She didn't want Bex chatting about it to her husband, and her kids overhearing it and then passing it on to Bella or Theo. So she was determined to keep the conversation on safe ground.

'Right, enough of all of this, let's go down and see how the kids are getting on.' Rowan turned towards the pathway, still trying to make sense of how she was feeling. Part of her wanted to be angry with her mother for railroading her and Nathan into spending more time together, but the truth was she wasn't. She liked him and Theo wasn't the only one who could benefit from building up friendships to feel more settled in Port Agnes. As long as no one got any ideas about it being more than that, it couldn't possibly do any harm.

9

Nathan looked at his watch; he'd have to stop work soon. He had forty minutes before they were due to leave for Katrina and Dean's barbecue and he needed a shower first, having spent all morning laying solid oak flooring in one of the bedrooms of the byre. He'd worked hard to restore the original cobblestone flooring in the open-plan living area, but he wanted something different in the bedrooms, a surface that felt warmer, but that would still accommodate Leo's wheelchair if his nephew wanted to have a sleepover. One of the first things he'd done when he'd considered keeping the cobblestones was to make sure that Leo's wheelchair could handle the surface. Prioritising his nephew's needs was barely even a conscious thing any more; it had become automatic.

'How's it going?' Will suddenly appeared in the door of the bedroom, his dark hair wet and sticking to his head.

'I've made pretty good progress and I've only taken the skin off about five of my knuckles.' Nathan held up a hand as proof.

'Sounds like a productive day. I'm sorry I didn't get over in time to help. Heather had promised Leo a swim, but she had a rough night and she barely got any sleep. Her indigestion is so bad she's considering a Gaviscon-only diet.' Will grinned. 'She wouldn't have made it to the barbecue if she didn't have a nap today, so I was on pool duty.'

'It's no problem at all; I'm really glad he's liking the pool so much and it looks like you've only just managed to drag him out.'

'He'd still be in there if it was up to him. The only way I persuaded him out in the end was by telling him that we're meeting up with Theo.' Will ran a hand through his damp hair. 'But I still feel guilty that I left you here slogging away, when the only reason you haven't spent any money getting help with this place is because you keep spending it on Leo.'

'I told you before that the pool was going for such a ridiculously low price that it would have been a waste of money not to buy it, and we can all use it, including Mum. It hasn't held up any of the work on this place, I promise.' Nathan looked down at the floor so that his brother wouldn't be able to tell that he was lying. The resistance pool was perfect for Leo; it enabled him to exercise in a way that would hopefully slow the muscle loss resulting from his condition. It might not have been the incredible bargain Nathan made it out to be, but it was heavily discounted and he was happy to take on all the extra work he could get, and live with a makeshift kitchen for another six months, if it helped Leo. He'd made far bigger sacrifices for the people he loved in the past and he'd never once resented the choices he'd made, but this one really had been an easy decision. The look on Leo's face the first time he'd tried the pool had been enough to convince Nathan that it had been the right one, too, and that was all the thanks he'd ever need.

'You do know you're the best big brother I could ever have asked for, don't you?' Will's words caught in his throat and his eyes were glassy when Nathan looked up at him.

'You didn't used to think that when I was giving you wedgies, or telling everyone at school about the time you used Mum's foundation to cover your spots.'

'True, but a hell of a lot has changed since then and I could never repay everything you've done for me.'

'We're brothers, so there's nothing to repay. I did it for myself as much as you anyway. I couldn't have lived with the alternative and what's six months in the big scheme of things?'

'It's not the time, it's the impact it's had on you... I hate how it affects the way other people think about you. I still think that maybe we—'

'No!' Nathan's response was forceful, cutting Will off before he could finish. 'It's water under the bridge now and, I promise you, I don't even think about it these days. If other people have a problem with it, that's on them.'

'I just hate the idea that it might stop you meeting someone. If it hadn't happened, you'd be married with kids of your own by now.'

'Yeah, I might not have been divorced by now, but let's face it, that did me a big favour. Nicole turned out not to be the person I thought she was and I'm glad we didn't have children together. If I meet the right person, the fact that I spent six months in prison won't be a problem for them, so stop worrying. It's a complete non-issue.' Nathan looked down at the floor again, as he told another lie. He knew there was a chance that his chequered past was a barrier to him forming a lasting relationship with the kind of person he wanted to build a life with. He tried to blink away the image of Rowan that had popped, uninvited, into his mind. She definitely wouldn't be interested in someone who'd spent time in prison.

'It just doesn't seem fair, when it would be so different if people knew the whole story.'

'It would cause far more problems than it would solve, so let's just leave it in the past where it belongs. I need to get in the shower now anyway, otherwise the guests at the barbecue will have more to talk about than my criminal record. Being known as a bad boy is one thing, but being remembered for smelling like I've forgotten how to shower is quite another.'

'I suppose there are plenty of women who can see the appeal of a bad boy.' Will laughed, the idea clearly amusing him. 'You just better not let any of them find out what a teddy bear you secretly are.'

'You're never too old for a wedgie you know.' Nathan took off one of his work gloves and flung it in Will's direction, still trying to erase the picture of Rowan from his mind and the absolute certainty that she wasn't the kind of woman who'd ever be attracted to a bad boy. She shouldn't even have entered his head, but it was happening more and more lately, and there didn't seem to be anything he could do to stop it.

* * *

There were more than forty people at the barbecue and the recent dry weather meant that Katrina and Dean's garden was fully accessible to Leo.

Nathan couldn't help smiling as his nephew got a guided tour of the garden from Theo, who had scooped up his grandparents' French Bulldog, Bluey, and had placed him on Leo's lap. It was a moment that had clearly been love at first sight and the little dog looked in his element, as Leo whizzed around the garden behind his new friend.

'I think you're going to have to get a dog.' Nathan turned towards his brother and sister-in-law, as the three of them sat around one of the bistro tables that had been set out on the lawn. His mother Irene was on the other side of the garden chatting to some friends from her dance class, with a plate of food in her hand after they'd all been encouraged by Katrina to pile their plates high. Heather had already given up on her Gaviscon-only diet and was taking her life in her hands by tucking into a jumbo sausage in a bun.

'I've been saying that for ages.' Will took the opportunity of his wife having her mouth full of food to present his case. 'But I reckon this puts the seal on the deal.'

'I told you.' Heather held up a hand until she'd swallowed the rest of her mouthful. 'Once this little one is here we can think about it, and I mean *think*. I don't want to come home from hospital to find out we've got a dog.'

'Fair enough.' Will squeezed her leg. 'Although Nath could always get the uncle of the year award again in the meantime and get himself another dog.'

'I could, I have been thinking about it, but...' Nathan couldn't finish the sentence and he didn't have to, the look on his brother's face told him that he understood. Chester, Nathan's Jack Russell, had been his shadow for years, even going with him to building jobs wherever possible. Chester had been twelve when Nathan had started his prison sentence, and he'd died six weeks later. It had been kidney failure and it would have happened eventually regardless of whether Nathan had been at home, but the little dog had seemed to be doing okay. Then Nathan had gone and, according to Irene, Chester had just seemed to give up. The guilt of not being there had eaten away at Nathan and he hadn't been able to face getting another dog. He couldn't say that, though, or even hint at it, because he knew how much the truth would upset Will, and not just because he and Heather had been caring for Chester when he'd died. So he had to give his brother another reason.

'It's hard when you've loved a dog like I loved Chester. I'm not sure anyone could live up to him, or fit into my lifestyle the way he did. But maybe if you guys take the plunge, I will too, and we can leave the dogs together when I'm out at work. I'll feel less guilty that way.'

'And there I was thinking that Leo was the master of persuasion!' Heather shook her head, but she was smiling. 'A dog would be lovely and maybe by this time next year we'll both have one. What sort do you think you'll get?'

'Not another Jack Russell, it's got to be something really different to Chester.' Glancing across to Leo, Nathan could see his nephew still chatting animatedly with Theo, but Rowan had joined the boys too and he rose to his feet. 'In fact, I might take this opportunity to discover what it is about Bluey that Leo likes so much. Who knows, maybe there'll be a French Bulldog in my future.'

'I can't see you with a dog like that.' Heather furrowed her brow, and Will nudged her gently.

'Don't spoil it for him, he's just trying to come up with an excuse to go and chat to our new headteacher. He's had the hots for her since we were teenagers.'

'Oh in that case, ignore what I've just said.' Heather mimed zipping her lips shut and pretending to throw the key over her shoulder.

'You two are like a pair of kids and Rowan is not the reason I'm going over there.' Nathan shook his head, turning away before either of them spotted the lie that he was almost certain would be written on his face. He was having to do a hell of a lot of that lately.

'Just ask her out already!' He pretended not to hear Will's parting words as he headed across the garden, smiling instead at the look of joy on Leo's face as he approached.

'Uncle Nathan! Look how much Bluey likes sitting on my lap; he's fallen asleep and he keeps snoring.'

'He's beautiful, isn't he?' Nathan stroked the dog's head. 'I was just saying to your mum and dad that maybe it's about time I got myself another dog.'

'Really?' Leo widened his eyes. 'Did you hear that, Theo? We might be getting a dog.'

'Brilliant.' Theo mirrored his friend's grin. 'I really want a dog too, but Mum says we need to wait until we've got a new house. Nanny Kat says I can share Bluey until then. She's got some chickens too, do you want to see them?'

'Course!' Leo didn't hesitate and the boys headed off towards the furthest end of the garden without a backward glance.

'It looks like we've been dumped.' Nathan smiled and Rowan shrugged in response.

'It's not the first time it's happened to me.' A cloud seemed to pass over her face for a moment, but then she shook it off. 'That's kids for you, though.'

'Yes, but it's lovely to see them getting on so well. Leo hasn't always found it easy to make friends. There are things he can't do and not all kids seem to understand that. You've clearly done a great job with Theo.'

'He's a good kid, so is Bella, but things haven't been easy for them lately.' Suddenly that clouded look was back, and he wanted to say something to help, but he had no idea what. He didn't want to push her to talk about anything she wasn't comfortable with either. He knew exactly how that felt and he was very careful who he opened up to about his own past. There were plenty of people who enjoyed revelling in the drama of it all, when the only thing Nathan wanted was to put it behind him. So the last thing he'd ever do was to put Rowan in a situation where she felt she had to tell him more than she wanted to.

'I don't suppose it was easy for any of you, but they'll be fine, because they've got you and both sets of your parents. Whatever went on with their dad, and I'm not asking for the details, you've got some great examples of how to move forward.' Nathan looked over towards where Rowan's dad and his wife were happily chatting to Dean and Katrina, their glasses chinking together as they raised a toast.

'It wasn't always that way and you probably remember all the drama of when Mum and Dad split up, it was all anyone seemed to be talking about back then.' Rowan paused and tucked a strand of hair behind her ear. 'But you're right. They're really good role models these days and I hope that James and I can reach that stage much more quickly than they did. I just need to put a bit more of the hurt behind me first.'

'I'm sorry you've had to go through such a tough time.' The desire to reach out to her was almost overpowering, but the last thing he wanted to do was to come across as sleazy.

'We all have tough times, don't we?' She hesitated again for a moment, seeming to weigh up what it was she wanted to say next, and then she took a deep breath. 'It must have been hard for you too when everything... with all you've been through.'

It was obvious she was skirting around the issue of his time in prison, and it felt like the elephant in the room every time they spoke, so they might as well get it out of the way.

'I've had some tough times. I wouldn't recommend a six-month stay in one of His Majesty's less appealing properties, but it was nothing compared to when Leo got his diagnosis and they outlined the likely progression of his disease.' Nathan swallowed hard, but still didn't quite manage to dislodge the lump in his throat. That day had felt like it might kill him. He'd held his brother in his arms as Will had sobbed, the man who usually seemed the epitome of strength reduced to a helpless child again for all the power he had to change the situation. Nathan had been devastated too and filled with rage. How could it be possible that a sweet boy like Leo could be facing such a prognosis? It had shattered the hearts of everyone who loved him, but Leo had saved them all when they'd felt like giving up. He just seemed to deal with every setback; even when he'd had the accident that had piled more worry and pain on top of the original diagnosis, he'd just got on with it and looked for the positives. From time to time it hit him, like when he couldn't join in with the things that his friends did, but he never allowed the disappointment to linger for long. He was like sunshine in human form and he was the best person Nathan had ever known. 'He's shown me every day since then what it is to be resilient and whenever things get tough, I just think about him and the fact he has no choice but to face up to the challenges life throws at him every single day.'

'He's an amazing little boy and he clearly adores you.' Rowan's eyes met his for a moment and he felt it again, that undeniable attraction fizzing between them. A huge part of him wanted to take a leap of faith and act on his brother's advice. After all, what harm could there be in asking her out? The worst she could do was say no. But then he thought about the boys and how well their friendship was developing, and he didn't want to do anything that might derail that. He took on almost as much responsibility for picking Leo up from school as Will and Heather, especially at the moment, which would make things so awkward if Rowan turned him down. And she would turn him down, she had to. She was the headteacher of the village primary school and he was someone almost everyone in Port Agnes knew had been to prison. She'd probably have turned him down even if that hadn't been the case. She had two children and a well-respected career and he was a builder, who lived in an unfinished conversion of a former cow shed, in the garden of the house he'd grown up in. Apart from his stint in prison, he'd lived in Port Agnes his whole life. So he'd never have been enough for a woman like Rowan. He needed to stop wishing for something that was never going to happen and focus on Leo instead, the way he always had done.

'I feel so lucky to be his uncle and I can't wait to have a niece too. They change everything kids, don't they? I might not be his dad, but I'd do anything for Leo, and it's obvious you feel the same about Bella and Theo.'

'Definitely and I owe them so much. They've saved me these last few months.' There was a wistful tone to her voice, and for a moment she didn't even seem to be there, as if her words had taken her away to another place and time.

'You're a team, that's what a family is supposed to be, isn't it?' Nathan waited for her to respond, and she seemed to shake off whatever feeling it was that had washed over her.

'Definitely, but let's just say that one of our family turned out not to be a team player. We came back to Cornwall because...' Rowan hesitated again and then she shook her head. 'We came back because we all needed a new start. I just hope I did the right thing bringing the children to Port Agnes.'

'I'm sure you did, but if you're ever worried and want someone to—' Nathan had been about to tell her that if she ever wanted someone to talk to, he'd be more than happy to listen, but his words were cut off by Katrina calling her name.

'Rowan! Can you come and help me bring the desserts out please, sweetheart?'

'I better go and give Mum a hand, but I'll see you later and we'll have to set a date for going out on the boat, if the offer's still open? I know Theo would love it.'

'Of course the offer's still open, just let me know when.'

'Will do, see you later.' Rowan gave a brief raise of her hand before heading towards the house.

It was just as well Nathan hadn't had the chance to tell her that she was welcome to offload her problems on him. Why on earth would Rowan want to confide in him about the end of her marriage and the worries she was having about the new life she was making for them all? He enjoyed her company, but he was just going to have to do what he did so often in life, and make the best of things. If they could spend time together supporting the growing friendship between the two boys that would be enough. It had to be, because whatever he might say to Will about his past being behind him, the things that had happened meant there'd never be another chance for someone like him to be a part of Rowan's life.

10

For the rest of the barbecue, Rowan made sure she wasn't on her own with Nathan again. She'd come so close to telling him the truth about why she and the children were back in Cornwall and she didn't want to let her guard down like that again. No one outside the family needed to know the full story, especially when her own children still had no idea that their father had fallen in love with someone else.

Fallen in love. That kind of sentiment was so often used as an excuse for bad behaviour. 'I didn't want to do it, but I fell in love', or 'we didn't mean to fall in love, it just happened.' Even 'I couldn't help myself, I fell in love.' When she'd caught him kissing Euan, Rowan hadn't expected James to use any of those lines on her. She'd expected him to tell her that it was a one off and that it didn't mean anything. A moment of madness when he'd just wanted to know what it felt like to kiss another man. She'd never thought he'd break down in tears and admit that he loved Euan and had done almost from the moment they'd met. There'd never been any chance of her taking James back, even before he'd admitted the strength of his feelings for the man he loved, but once he had, Rowan hadn't felt as if she could salvage anything from their relationship.

James had never loved her, not the way he loved Euan, and it had left her questioning whether she was capable of inspiring those kinds of feelings in anyone else. Not that she wanted to, at least that's what she told herself, but it was harder to pretend when she was around other couples who seemed as though they were made for each other, like Bex and her husband, Matt, and Heather and Will. She wasn't nearly naïve enough not to realise that everyone had their ups and downs. But for some reason it was even harder to convince herself that she didn't want to experience a relationship where she was truly loved when she was around Nathan Lark of all people. She tried to pretend the only reason she felt a connection to him was because he always seemed so willing to listen, but never pumped her for information about what had happened between her and James. If she needed to talk to someone, she could call Pippa or Odette to offload on them. They'd both been in touch regularly to check how she was doing and had texted on the first day of term to say that life at Membory Grange wasn't the same without her. So it wasn't that she had no one else to talk to; the truth was she liked Nathan far more than she was comfortable admitting. She didn't want to think what it might be like to kiss him again, but she couldn't seem to help doing that either. What made it even trickier was that she could tell he was attracted to her too, and she never usually picked up on those sorts of signs. If she made a move, she was almost certain Nathan would respond positively and that could be very dangerous. It was far less risky to stay out of his way altogether and it had been a relief when she hadn't bumped into him at school in the first few days of term.

Rowan had been in the playground to greet all of the parents and children on the first day, and it had been Heather who'd bought Leo in and explained that, unfortunately he'd be missing the next two days of school as they were going to London to see a specialist. She'd apologised for the timing, but they'd been offered an appointment they couldn't turn down. Rowan had reassured Heather that she didn't need to worry about anything. She hadn't envisaged Leo missing two days of school having that much impact on him or anyone else, but she hadn't factored in how it would affect her son. With the help of Tiffany, Bella had settled into school like a dream and she already seemed to be right at the heart of things, but it wasn't going nearly so well for Theo. Day one had been fine, when Leo was there, but without him things went downhill fast.

'I'm sorry to bother you Rowan,' Bex said after knocking on her door. 'But Lyra is on playground duty and she found Theo standing down near the trees crying, and he won't tell anyone why. He's refusing to come in too.'

'Oh God.' Rowan got to her feet straight away, wanting to get to her little boy and comfort him, but then she started to second guess herself. 'Do you think it might make it worse me going out there and the other children seeing and teasing him about needing his mum?'

'Possibly, but if it was one of mine, I'd have to go out there anyway.' Bex furrowed her brow and Rowan nodded, knowing her friend was right. She didn't have a choice.

'Me too.' Heading out into the playground, Rowan quickened her pace to get to the wooded area, after giving some instructions to the other staff. The area was fenced off from the playground and the five-bar gate at the end of the new path was padlocked, so the children could only access it when staff were with them, but Theo must have climbed the gate.

'What are you doing, Theo? You need to come back into the playground.' Usually she would have called him 'sweetheart' or some other term of endearment, but that could definitely make things worse if the other children overheard. She'd thought about asking for everyone else to be sent inside, but it was lunchtime and if there was a sure-fire way of Theo being permanently singled out, making the others miss out on playtime would be it. Instead she'd asked the staff to keep the rest of the children back, while Bex went to get the key to the gate, but that didn't mean no one would be able to hear what she and Theo were saying.

'I'm not coming back over there.' Her son was clinging to the trunk of one of the trees like an eco-warrior determined to do whatever it took to stop a new road being built through his beloved woodland.

'Well, I'll have to get the gate unlocked and come and get you then.'

'No! I want to go home.' Theo sniffed, his voice coming out in that shuddering half-talking, half-crying kind of way it did when he was really upset.

'There are only two hours left after lunch and then Nanny Kat will come and pick you and Bella up and take you back to the cottage until I get home.'

'No, I mean to our old house with Dad.' This time the sob that punctuated Theo's words was unmistakeable.

'Oh, sweetheart.' Rowan hadn't been able to stop the word from slipping out, despite her best intentions. 'I know it's hard and that you miss some of your old friends, but I promise you'll make new ones. You just have to give it a bit more time.'

'No, I won't. They call me Cry Baby Bellamy because I got a bit sad when

Leo wasn't here. They all hate me because you're the headteacher and when
Leo's not here any more I won't ever have any friends again.'

Rowan's throat burned with the effort of trying not to cry. She wanted to
fold her little boy into her arms and take away his pain, but she couldn't do
either of those things. She had to try and comfort him in some other way. 'Leo
will be back tomorrow and then you can hang out together again. You really
like him, don't you?'

'Yes, but—' Another sob punctuated his words. 'Dylan said Leo will be
gone forever soon, because his legs don't work and soon nothing will and then
he'll... then he'll die.'

The last word came out in a strangled sob and as the tears ran down
Theo's face, she had to blink hard against her own. She couldn't even promise
him that his friend wasn't going to die. This was a lesson she didn't want him
to have to learn yet, but she'd vowed to herself, after all of James's lies, that
she'd try to be as honest as possible with her children. It was bad enough that
she was still being complicit in James's deception, she wasn't going to lie about
anything else if she could help it. Theo and Bella needed to grow up knowing
they had at least one parent they could rely on. But she had no idea how
much Leo had been told about his muscular dystrophy and the last thing she
wanted to do was cause him any distress or fear, by telling Theo something
about Leo's condition that even he didn't know.

'Leo has a disease that affects the way his muscles work and that's why he
uses a wheelchair. There are lots of muscles in the body and they're all important. The reason Leo isn't at school is so that the doctors can help keep his
muscles as healthy as possible for a very, very long time. He'll be back
tomorrow and I bet he'll be as happy to see you as you are to see him, but you
won't be able to come out here and play together if I can't trust you to stay
where it's safe. So when Bex... *Mrs White* gets here and unlocks the gate, I
want you to come back into the playground and promise me, that whatever
the other children say, you won't ever do anything like this again, because you
could really hurt yourself and I can't let that happen, you're far too precious.'

'You promise Leo is coming back tomorrow?' Her son held her gaze and
she nodded, silently praying that nothing would happen to make her break
that promise. For all she knew, Leo and his parents could be delayed in
London, but she had a feeling that if she didn't make the promise, Theo would
double down on his refusal to come back into the playground.

'Okay.' Just at the moment he finally agreed, Bex came sprinting across from the playground, panting hard.

'Sorry it took so long, someone had put the key back in the wrong place and it took me ages to find it.'

'Thank you.' Rowan took the key and unlocked the gate, resisting the urge once again to scoop her son into her arms, waiting instead for him to walk through the gate. 'Come on Theo, it's time to come back.'

Reluctantly her son walked slowly towards her and she handed the key to Bex to secure the padlock again. With a hand on Theo's shoulder, she'd waited until they were halfway across the playground and in earshot of some of the other children she recognised from his class before putting on her best head-teacher's voice.

'Right Theo, because of what you did you're not allowed outside for the rest of lunchtime, or afternoon break.'

Her son had looked up at her, his eyes wide and she'd given an almost imperceptible nod of the head to let him know she understood that this was what he needed: a make-believe punishment that would keep him away from the children who'd been giving him such a hard time. It wasn't a solution they could use long term, but if it worked as a stop gap, it would just have to do for now.

* * *

On Friday morning, Rowan had been almost as relieved as Theo to see Leo being dropped off in the playground. She'd tried to talk to Theo the night before about how he was feeling, but he'd shut her down, saying he didn't want to talk about it. She hadn't been able to check on the situation at lunchtime because she'd had a meeting scheduled with one of the teaching agencies that would be providing cover when the Year 4 teacher went on maternity leave after Christmas. Thankfully Caden, who was sharing playground duty with a couple of the teaching assistants, had popped his head around the door as soon as her meeting was over and told her that Theo and Leo had spent lunchtime together, and that Theo seemed 'back to his old self'. She'd been really grateful to her new colleague for looking out for her son, but Caden had no idea what Theo's 'old self' was like, because that little boy had all but disappeared when she and James had split up. So when her phone

pinged with a text message from her soon-to-be ex-husband, just before the
end of the school day, she couldn't imagine it saying anything she wanted to
hear.

> I was going to call you, but I knew you'd be working.
> I'm really struggling and I don't know if I can carry on
> like this. I know you're angry and that I've got no
> right to ask, but I need your help. Dad's been on my
> case wanting an explanation for everything and I
> can't keep a lid on this for much longer. I've made
> such a mess of things and I can't see a way out. Can
> you call me when you get this? PLEASE.

Rage bubbled up inside her. He was struggling? The gall of it was stagger-
ing. Their little boy was broken hearted and James expected her to feel sorry
for him. He hadn't even confirmed arrangements yet to come and see the children, despite claiming to be desperate to weeks ago. She wanted to call him
right then and there and tell him exactly what he'd done to their son and that
she was terrified he might always be the frightened little boy he'd become
these last few months. Theo had always been gentle and sensitive, but this was
far more than that. She didn't call James to tell him any of that, though. She
needed to take her time to work out what to say. No matter how angry she was
about James's inability to see the impact of his actions on anyone but himself,
she knew Theo and Bella would want to see their father. He could wait for a
response though; let him stew. She certainly wasn't going to make it her priority, because today she wanted to be the one to pick her own children up from
school and take them home, instead of someone else doing it.

Rowan had worked late every afternoon on the first week of term, relying
on her parents and stepparents to pick the children up and take care of them
until she eventually got home, but tonight was going to be different. Tonight
they were heading home together and they'd be having takeaway pizza, and
then popcorn and a movie. So all talk of their father and anything else could
wait; tonight was just for the three of them.

Shutting down her computer, she headed outside. Caden and Krish would
be locking up and Bex had headed off early to take one of her children to the
dentist. So Rowan planned to wait in the playground with the rest of the
parents, until the children were let out of class.

One of the first people she spotted was Nathan and even though common sense told her to steer clear, if she was speaking to him she'd be less likely to be collared by one of the other parents for the kind of conversation that would ruin her chances of getting away on time.

'Hey.' She'd gone for a simple greeting, but she sounded like someone desperately trying to sound cool and failing miserably.

'Hi.' Nathan smiled and she tried not to let it affect her, but she liked the fact that just seeing her made him smile. 'How has your first week in charge been?'

'Good.' She didn't want to say any more than that, not with so many people already craning their necks to try and hear the conversation.

'I'm glad. I think the whole village realises we're lucky to have you, so it's good to know you're not about to go running for the hills.'

'Definitely not.' She returned his smile, trying not to acknowledge how much his compliment meant to her. 'How about you? How has your week been? How did Leo's appointment go?'

'It's been a busy one. Will and I are trying to get through as much work as we can before the new baby comes. And Leo's appointment went as well as these things ever can.' Nathan tried for a casual shrug but didn't quite pull it off. Before she could respond, Bella was suddenly tugging on her sleeve.

'Mum, Mum, can I go shopping in Truro tomorrow with Tiff? Her mum said she'll pick me up at eleven and I can have a sleepover. Then she'll drop me home on Sunday afternoon.'

'I don't see why not. That sounds lovely and it's very kind of Tiffany's mum.' Rowan didn't allow her smile to slip off her face, despite feeling a bit bereft that her daughter would be elsewhere for most of the weekend, because she was thrilled that Bella already seemed to have found such a good friend. Rowan's mother knew Tiffany's parents well, and they were both doctors at the local GP practice, so she felt confident about agreeing to the sleepover, even if it meant giving up her precious time off with her daughter.

'Woo hoo, thanks Mum. I'm going to go and tell Tiff that you said it's okay.' Bella shot off again, just as Theo and Leo emerged from the classroom, chatting away. Her son looked like a completely different boy from the one who'd tried to hide amongst the trees the day before. The two of them appeared to be in no hurry whatsoever to reach Rowan and Nathan, and they'd stopped altogether now for Theo to show his friend something in the book he was holding. Rowan turned to look at Nathan.

'Do you think Heather and Will would agree to Leo coming over to ours for a few hours tomorrow? I know Theo would love it and he won't feel so much like he's missing out when Bella goes off with Tiffany.'

'I'm on uncle duty for the weekend, while they spend a night at a hotel down in Looe. Mum's got longstanding plans with her friends and it's their last hurrah before the baby arrives.' Nathan smiled. 'Although I think they both just want to flake out and sleep while they've got the chance.'

'That's lovely and no worries, maybe some other time.' She was already trying to think of things she and Theo could do that would make up for the fact that his sister was off having fun with a friend, while he was stuck at home with his boring old mum.

'I could still drop Leo over if you like, but he might get a bit shy about things if he needs the toilet or anything. He can be a bit like that until he really trusts someone.' She knew Nathan wasn't just making an excuse to tag along, because she'd reviewed Leo's EHCP, the plan to manage his care while he was at school.

'If you don't mind coming with him, you'd be more than welcome.' She was throwing all caution to the wind now, still telling herself it was just for Theo, even if the thought of sharing the day with Nathan held more appeal for her than she wanted to admit.

'I'd love to, or we could always have that planned trip out on the boat. The weather looks great.' He cast a look over his shoulder, clearly every bit as aware as she was that they were being watched. 'That's if you don't mind the risk of being seen out with me in public, on our own.'

'Of course I don't, and we won't be on our own anyway.' She'd added the last part as much to remind herself of the fact as anything else, but a look passed across his face that was impossible to read.

'Great. If Bella is being picked up at eleven, how about we meet outside Mehenick's at half past? My boat is moored in the harbour and I can pick up a few bits from there for lunch and we can have a bit of a picnic.'

'That sounds lovely. What can we bring?'

'Just yourselves.' The look that had clouded Nathan's face lifted as the children finally reached them. 'How do you two fancy a day out on my boat together tomorrow?'

'Yay!' Leo beamed at his uncle.

'Really?' Theo turned towards his mother. 'Can I *really* go?'

'Of course you can, but I'm afraid I'm going to be coming with you.' Rowan's tone was teasing, but for a moment she couldn't work out whether her son was genuinely disappointed. Then his face broke into a smile too.

'That's okay, as long as we get to go on the boat.' His face transformed again, but this time into an anxious frown and she knew what was coming next even before he spoke. 'What about Bella? We can't leave her at home by herself.'

'Of course we wouldn't leave Bella on her own, but she's having a sleepover at Tiffany's. So it'll just be the four of us.'

'I can't wait.' The grin on Theo's face was the sort she hadn't seen in months and she could have kissed Nathan for being the one to bring it back. Even as the thought entered her head, she pushed it down again, but she wanted him to know how grateful she was.

'Me neither.' Turning towards Nathan, her fingers itched to touch his arm, but she forced herself to resist. 'Thanks so much for inviting us.'

'It'll be fun, see you tomorrow.' The expression she hadn't been able to read was back and she hated the thought that she might have somehow upset him, when he'd been nothing but kind since her return. All she could do was try to prove that she wasn't judging him for what had happened in the past, even if her job meant she had to keep a firm boundary between them. Everyone should have the chance to leave their past behind if they wanted to, and she was determined to move on from hers.

11

Rowan was doing her best not to overthink things, but nervousness had been washing over her in waves ever since she'd agreed to spend the day on Nathan's boat. She'd tried to tell herself that it was apprehension about taking two young boys out on the water. Since having Bella and Theo and realising she was responsible for keeping them safe, she'd become far more risk averse than she had been when she only had herself to look out for. Although the truth was, even back then, she hadn't been a huge risk taker. If she was completely honest with herself, it explained why she'd ended up marrying James. He'd become her safe space after leaving Port Agnes. He was her first friend when she'd moved to London and, looking back, she suspected it should probably have stayed that way, but they'd become boyfriend and girl-friend instead; at least, that was the title they'd given themselves. There'd never been any grand passion, not even in the early days. She had nothing to compare it to, but she was pretty certain that a couple of nineteen-year-olds in a relationship, away from home together at university, should be having to fight pretty hard for that not to become sexual.

James had always cited his religious beliefs for wanting to wait until they were married and she'd respected that, but he'd never seemed to find the waiting a challenge. Maybe it hadn't seemed as odd because neither had Rowan, not really. They'd kissed, but it hadn't been anything like what was described in the books or the movies, or anything like it had been when she'd kissed Nathan. She hadn't wanted to rip James's clothes off. She didn't think about what it felt like to kiss him even when he wasn't around, or replay the moment in her mind for months – years – afterwards, the way she had with Nathan. It had felt nice and safe and comforting in a world where that was all she'd craved since the breakdown of her parents' marriage, and she'd decided she was more than happy to settle for that. Her parents' own grand passions with their new partners were what had killed their marriage as far as she was concerned, and that kind of thing looked dangerous to Rowan. She wanted any children she might have to grow up in a calm and steady household, and it had felt as though James was the perfect person to provide that.

After they got married, sex was suddenly on the table. They hadn't consummated the marriage on the night of their wedding, agreeing that they were too tired and that they wanted their first time to be special. They'd been three days into the honeymoon, and half a bottle of Tequila down, before it had finally happened. Rowan wasn't completely naïve; she'd had enough conversations with friends over the years to know that first times tended to be pretty rubbish, especially for women, and even more so if you were both virgins. She hadn't expected fireworks and it had been okay. The trouble was it had never got beyond okay and there had *never* been any fireworks. They'd quickly moved into a routine of having sex on a Saturday evening, almost as though it needed to be diarised for it to happen. The only time they'd really increased the regularity had been when they were trying for Bella and Theo.

After conceiving the children, sex had slipped down the priority list and moved to one Saturday a month, before tailing off altogether. Rowan hadn't missed it, because there really hadn't been much to miss, but it had bothered her that there was no intimacy between them and James didn't seem to find her attractive. Sex itself was overrated in her opinion and she'd stopped feeling butterflies at the thought of kissing someone, and the prospect of taking that further, when she'd finally stopped thinking about that kiss with Nathan. Except now he was back in her life and she could lie to herself as much as she wanted to about the reason for the nerves bubbling up inside her, but she knew it wasn't all about keeping the boys safe on the boat. Nathan Lark made her feel things she'd only ever felt with him and even the idea of giving into a grand passion of her own terrified her. That was a road to trouble she didn't want to travel down, but when he was standing in front of her, as he was now, and it was just the two of them on their own, it was almost impossible not to think about it.

'Irene's still in the bakery with the boys. I think she's buying enough food for us in case we get shipwrecked.' Rowan smiled, feeling guilty now for the way her heart had sunk at the sight of Nathan's mother when she and Theo had arrived outside Mehenick's Bakery. Irene had quickly explained that she was only there to drop Leo off, as Nathan had gone down early to do some preparations on the boat.

'That's Mum for you. I think she feels guilty because she's off out for a day with her friends to the Japanese gardens in St Mawgan and then for dinner.' Nathan straightened up as he spoke. He was already onboard, but she was still standing on the concrete slope that led down from the harbourside, which made it possible to access the smaller boats, uncertain whether or not she should join him. 'I think Mum feels guilty that I've got Leo for the whole weekend, but she should know better than that. I can't think of any other way I'd rather spend it.'

'I'm the same. I used to dread weekends a bit before I had the kids. I don't know, maybe it's just because I've always loved my job, but the days felt weirdly empty without work. James and I couldn't seem to get into any kind of a rhythm with filling our time in a way that we both enjoyed.' She caught Nathan's eye then and heat rose up her neck as he raised his eyebrows.

'I don't know your ex but he's clearly a man with very little imagination and no concept of how lucky he was.' Nathan was looking at her so intently that she wanted to drop her gaze, but somehow she couldn't. She had a feeling he was flirting with her, except it felt far deeper than that. Although it had been so long since anyone had flirted with her that she couldn't be entirely sure. Either way the navy blue of his T-shirt almost exactly matched the colour of his eyes, which were still holding her gaze. If she'd thought he'd done it on purpose, it would have been enough to put her off, but she would have bet her car that he hadn't. The fact that he didn't seem to have any idea how good looking he was just made him all the more attractive; he'd always been that way, even when they were back in school. Nowadays his physique was broader and she found herself wondering what it would be like to be held by him again. The way he was looking at her meant the butterflies were threatening to get completely out of control and travel to places they had no right to visit. Places that would only lead to trouble.

'Right, we've got enough food to feed an army!' Irene's voice broke the spell and all the tension Rowan hadn't even realised she'd been holding in her body seemed to relax. Being on her own with Nathan was something she needed to avoid, she knew that now. Not because she didn't trust him, but because he still had the same effect on her after all these years. It was a feeling she'd begun to think she'd imagined, something that had played into a fantasy of what chemistry between two people should feel like. Except it felt alarmingly real when they were alone together. Now, with the boys excitedly chattering about the day ahead, and Irene listing all the things she'd bought for the picnic, Rowan could finally think straight and put her feelings back into the box labelled 'the past' and get on with life as a single mother of two.

'Come on, Mum!' Theo called out to her as he followed his friend down the wide metal gang plank that led from the concrete slope to the boat, enabling Leo to access it in his wheelchair. 'You're going to get left behind and miss all the fun otherwise.'

'Yes, go on, don't risk missing the fun.' Suddenly Irene was handing her the bag with the picnic inside and pushing Rowan gently in the small of her back. 'You really deserve some fun and so does Nathan, so it would be a crying shame if either of you missed out on the chance of it.'

Before Rowan could even answer, Irene had turned and walked back up the slope, and all she could do was follow her son's urging to hurry up and join the others. She and Nathan were only spending time together to give the boys a lovely day out, that was all. There was no need for her to over-analyse how she felt towards him. He was just the uncle of her son's new best friend. That was where her relationship with Nathan Lark begun and ended.

* * *

If Irene's wish had been for them to have fun, then it had certainly been granted. Leo and Theo had been having the best time, and Rowan and Nathan had reminisced about the old days at school. She wasn't sure whether it had been an attempt on his part to avoid talking about their more recent histories, neither of which had been the stuff of dreams, but it had been so much fun to share memories with someone who remembered all the same people she did, including a biology teacher called Mr Dandridge, who'd had about six strands of hair that he'd somehow knitted into what looked like a shredded wheat perched on top of his head. He'd also seemed comically adept at putting a condom on a banana, when he'd doubled up as the sex education teacher in Rowan's GCSE year, even though at that age not a single one of his pupils could imagine anyone on the planet wanting to have sex with Mr Dandridge. Rowan couldn't remember laughing as much as she had when they were reminiscing for years, but they'd both been thrilled when Nathan had googled Mr Dandridge and discovered he was not only a well-respected author of text-books about genetic engineering, but had also shaven off his shredded wheat hair and swapped it for a bald but very distinguished look. Best of all he'd recently got married to a very attractive middle-aged American woman called Marcy. Mr Dandridge had found a happy ever after and somehow that had made the day even better.

All Rowan's worries about safety on board the boat had been assuaged too. Nathan had made adaptations in order to ensure the boat was fully wheel-chair accessible. The old cabin had been replaced so that it was a canopy with an open front and back, and Nathan had supervised both boys to have a turn at 'driving' the boat. It also meant that Leo was able to move his wheelchair through to the bow, which had high rails all the way around to ensure neither he nor Theo were in any danger of going overboard. They were still up at the front and, right now, the two of them were doing what looked remarkably like a recreation of the scene from *Titanic*, but with far more giggling.

'Are they doing what I think they're doing?' Rowan turned towards Nathan with a smile on her face, which he quickly mirrored. The two of them were standing close to one another, as he guided the boat back towards Port Agnes.

'Yes, they are. Leo knew from an early age that Heather had named him after her favourite actor and he always wants to watch Leonardo DiCaprio films when he gets the chance. We just have to fast forward certain bits.'

'Like the *"paint me like one of your French girls"* scene?' Rowan widened her eyes as Nathan nodded. She'd been just eleven when she and her friends had secretly watched *Titanic* for the first time and they'd all fallen a little bit in love with the leading man. Leonardo DiCaprio had been her crush, until Nathan had edged him out, because not even a Hollywood actor could hold a candle to him. Although she'd rather have flung herself into the sea than admit that.

'That's definitely one of the scenes he's not allowed to watch, but Leo loves the one where Jack and Rose are at the bow of the boat. Whenever we go out on the water, he can't resist putting his arms out like they do in the film, because he says it makes him feel like he's flying too, even though he can't walk.'

'Oh, Nathan.' Rowan couldn't stop herself from putting a hand over her heart. She'd sworn she wouldn't show how sad she felt for Leo or his family, because it was patronising and the little boy was an incredible force of nature who refused to let muscular dystrophy define him. But her heart was breaking at Nathan's words and she couldn't stop her eyes from filling with tears, despite how much she wanted to blame the sea breeze that was whipping around them.

'I know. Most of the time I manage to put the fact that we're eventually going to lose him out of my mind, but then he goes and says something like that and it hits you.' Nathan closed his eyes for just a moment, before turning to look at her. 'The only way to get through it is to think about what he said. Really think about it. He's finding a way to grab the joy in life and fly even when he can't walk. So I can't allow myself to wallow in self-pity and think about what his condition means for me. I have to follow Leo's lead and be the uncle he needs me to be. He's never going to be more well, or more physically able than he is right now, so we have to get the most out of every stage before life moves on. That's why days like this mean so much to me.'

'From what I've seen you're a fantastic uncle and Leo's an incredible child.' It was on the tip of her tongue to ask him whether he wanted to have children of his own one day, but she didn't want to make it sound like she was diminishing his bond with his nephew in any way. It was obvious he couldn't have loved Leo any more than he did, even if he had been Nathan's child. 'I take it the boat's name is in his honour?'

'It is, but Leo's just Leo. Will didn't want him to be Leonardo. I renamed the boat after his diagnosis and it has the long version of his name because it means courage of a lion and that's something Leo has definitely shown he's got.'

'He has and I think we could all do with being a bit more like Leo.' Rowan let go of a long breath and stared out at the sea for a moment. When she looked back at Nathan, he was still watching her. 'Don't look at me like that. I know my hair probably looks like Medusa was dragged through a hedge backwards.'

'I was looking at you because I've just realised you have no idea how incredible you are or how brave you've had to be. Okay, so you might not have had to face what Leo does, but you came back to Port Agnes to give your children the best possible life, even though I know it's hard for you to be here. You're like a breath of fresh air at the school and Leo absolutely adores you, he said all the kids do. And I'm sure they're not the only ones.' Nathan was doing that thing again – looking at her in a way that made it feel as if she was the only person in the world he wanted to look at. He'd always had that knack, even as a teenager. 'It's obvious you've had to get yourself and the kids out of a really tough situation. Like I said before, I don't need to know the details of what happened with their dad, but you just have to look at how well they're doing to know you've made all the right decisions for them. The fact that they're thriving is all down to you.'

'Thank you, but I don't think I've been brave at all, sometimes we just have to do what's necessary to survive, don't we?' She watched his face and there was an almost imperceptible nod; he understood exactly what she meant. Prison must have been incredibly tough on Nathan and it was still almost impossible to believe he'd done something to deserve a sentence. Either way, he'd got through it and it hadn't changed who he was, at least not in any negative way. He was still the same Nathan she'd been drawn to all those years ago, but there was a new strength within him too and she knew he was someone his friends and family could rely on. After all, she'd witnessed it with her own eyes. Whatever he'd done in the past, she wouldn't have hesitated to trust him. No one was a good enough actor to pretend to be the kind of person Nathan had shown himself to be with his nephew, and she wasn't going to hold his past against him. A big part of her wanted to ask him about his time in prison, but if that was something he wanted to share with her, it needed to come from him.

'Yes, sometimes we do, but I promised myself I'd do more than survive. That's something else I owe Leo, to not give up on getting the things I really want out of life. If he can find a way to fly, then none of the rest of us have got any excuse.'

'And what is it that you really want?' Her words were almost a whisper and she wondered for a moment if they'd been lost on the wind, when he didn't answer. His eyes were still fixed on the sea ahead of him when he finally spoke.

'I want what Will and Heather have got: loving someone who loves you too and building a family together, that's definitely the dream.'

'It really is.' She hadn't meant to sound so wistful and she was grateful that the wind really had stolen her words this time. They must have done, because Nathan didn't react to her reply. She didn't want him to feel sorry for her, or to see the tears that had filled her eyes again at the realisation she'd never had that, despite having two children with James, and it was something she wanted one day, every bit as much as Nathan did.

12

'Oh look Leo, Uncle Nath has obviously spent half an hour getting his hair right this morning for your *play date*.' Will put air quotes around the last two words and laughed. 'You must be worn out, Leo. I don't think you've ever done as many activities as you have in the past few weeks. Of course it's got nothing to do with the way your uncle Nath looks at a certain someone.'

'Who?' Leo furrowed his brow, clearly trying to work out the identity of this mystery person and Nathan decided to intervene before he made the connection. That was absolutely the last thing he wanted, his nephew telling Theo how much Nathan liked his mum. He could take any kind of ribbing his brother wanted to send his way, except this, because it was far too close to the truth. After the first time they'd taken the boys out on the boat together, he and Rowan had arranged a series of other get-togethers and Will wasn't exaggerating when he said that Leo had never been so busy.

'Your dad's just talking about that really good surfer who's down at the beach a lot. You know the one with the curly hair and the bright blue surfboard. I think his name's Billy. Your dad knows I like watching his technique, so I can try and get as good at surfing as he is.'

'No chance.' Leo grinned. A seven-year-old's directness could be brutal, but Nathan had to laugh. That was one of the many things he loved about his nephew, he never pulled any punches.

'Why not?'

'Because you're too old and too...' Leo thought for a moment, clearly searching for the right word. 'Wobbly.'

'I suppose I did ask and I'm not going to push my luck any further by asking what kind of wobbly you mean. I'm going to choose to assume that you mean when I'm standing on the surfboard.' Nathan laughed again and so did Will.

'Yeah, of course.' Leo shrugged. 'You're okay at surfing and I like it when you teach me, but once I get better than you I'll have to have lessons from someone who's really good.'

'You will, kid, you will.' Nathan ruffled his nephew's hair. They'd been doing adaptive surfing together since Leo was two years old and Nathan had been volunteering with a local organisation that supported children and adults with additional needs to experience surfing. There'd been a sticky patch after his time in prison when he hadn't been sure if he'd be able to continue, because he no longer had a clear DBS check. Thankfully, in the end, *Waves 4 Everyone* had allowed him to continue volunteering because the crime he'd been convicted of presented no risk to children or vulnerable adults. He'd hated the fact that the friends he'd made in the organisation had been forced to have those kinds of discussions about him and, even though none of them had ever said anything negative to his face, it still felt like they viewed him differently. Everyone else seemed to.

'Do you think Theo will be good at surfing? He gets a bit worried about doing things sometimes and I don't want him to get upset.' Leo furrowed his brow again and Nathan suddenly felt as if his heart had doubled in size. This boy was incredible. He had so much to contend with, but he was worrying about his friend instead of himself and it struck Nathan for about the millionth time, that if more people were a bit like Leo the world would be a much better place.

'We're only going to take it easy today and let Theo see if he likes it or not, while the weather is still okay. This might be our last opportunity to go surfing this year.' It was the first week of October and the Indian summer was still clinging on with the temperatures much warmer than usual for the time of year. Even so they'd be reliant on wetsuits to be able to get into the water. 'If he does like it, next summer we can all go to Port Tremellien instead, the waves are much better there.'

'All of you? Next summer?' Will inclined his head and gave Nathan a knowing look. 'Quite the long-term plan you're making there, bro.'

'Anything for my nephew and his best friend.' Nathan attempted a neutral look but knew he hadn't managed it. He would do anything for Leo, that much was true, but he had to admit it was more than that. He'd taken Leo out with Rowan and Theo at least twice a week for the past month, shouldering even more responsibility for his nephew than he normally would. Heather's blood pressure had been raised at her last antenatal check and there was a worry about the baby not growing quite as much as expected. Will had tried to play it down, telling Nathan that the midwives didn't think there was any major cause for concern, but he had seen the fear on his brother's face. The two of them were working harder than ever to get contracts completed before the baby arrived and their mother had taken on more of the school drop-offs and pickups so that Heather could rest. But Nathan had been determined to do what he could too, picking Leo up twice a week and taking him out every Saturday, to give Will and Heather a break.

It was how that first invitation for Rowan and Theo to join them on the boat had snowballed into more of a regular thing. Despite how busy Rowan was in her new role, it was obvious her children's happiness was her number one priority and she seemed delighted that the boys wanted to spend so much time together, even if it did mean her having to give up her Saturdays too, and at least one afternoon a week straight from school. It had crossed Nathan's mind to say she didn't need to come with them every time, but he knew she almost certainly wouldn't allow her son to go out unsupervised with someone who had a criminal record. It would just have made things awkward to bring it up, and it seemed stupid to risk the arrangement when he liked having Rowan around as much as he did.

The first time they'd gone out on the boat together had been a huge success. Theo had been a bit anxious at first, and Leo had been the one to put him at ease. His nephew was happiest whenever he was on or near water and, if Nathan had believed in that kind of thing, he'd have sworn that Leo had been a seal or a dolphin in a former life, or maybe even an old sea captain. It made sense that he loved swimming, because it was something that was far less restricted by his muscular dystrophy than many other activities. But he was completely at home on a surfboard too, or out on the boat with the wind whipping around his face, sometimes making it almost impossible to talk. It was all about the freedom, Nathan supposed, and he completely understood that. The nights he'd spent locked up in a prison cell, longing to go outside just to look at the stars, were when he'd truly appreciated – for the first time – just how lucky he'd been to grow up in a place like Port Agnes, where all that freedom had been his for the taking. Now he wanted to give that same freedom to his nephew whenever he could and, even though Will was right about him wanting to spend time with Rowan, it was Leo who mattered the most. Leo had always mattered the most. That was why, even though he knew Rowan liked him too, there could never be anything between them. Even if she could have looked past all the downsides that would have accompanied getting involved with him, he couldn't risk ruining the friendship the four of them had built up. It was far too important to Leo.

'Are you going to go and say goodbye to Mum?' Will looked at his son. 'She's on the sofa in the lounge and you know what it's like when she sits down these days, she needs at least two people to help her up again!'

'She looks like a giant football.' Leo giggled at the mental image he'd created for himself.

'She does, but just promise not to tell her that, okay.' Will winked, waiting until Leo had manoeuvred his wheelchair through the kitchen door and had headed down the hallway, before turning towards his brother. 'So come on then, when *are* you going to ask Rowan out, just the two of you, without the kids as an excuse to get together?'

'Never. It's not like that.' Nathan kept his tone light, but Will knew him far too well.

'Yes it is, and it always has been. You liked her for ages when we were at school and by all accounts she felt the same way. Now she's back and you're both single and you clearly still like each other – anyone can see that – so what's the problem?'

'She's been badly hurt by whatever happened in her marriage. I don't know the details and I'm not going to push her to find out, but whatever the reason I get the distinct feeling she doesn't want to start dating.' It was the truth, but there was more to it and Will knew that too.

'You think she'll turn you down because you went to prison, don't you?' Will's jaw was rigid and this was exactly the conversation Nathan had wanted to avoid. There was no point going over this again, it wouldn't change anything. He'd made his choice years before and he had to live with the consequences of that. Nathan had always known there'd be a price to pay and he'd never once doubted it was worth it. Although just lately the price had felt a lot higher, because Will was right, Rowan would never date him. The best he could hope for now was to be her friend, which would force him to watch from the sidelines when she did start to date again. Maybe it was for the best, that was what he was trying to tell himself; there was just too much to lose if it all went wrong. They got on so well when the four of them were doing things together, sometimes they'd be joined by Bella and her friend Tiffany too. The insights Rowan had into things and her way of looking at the world gave him a new perspective. They'd spoken about everything from their favourite music to their childhoods. The deepest conversations had come in quiet moments, like when they'd been heading back to Port Agnes on the boat, or while they sat watching the children playing, the day the boys were trying to launch a kite on the beach. They'd insisted they didn't want any help, Leo was the brains and Theo was the muscle and it seemed to be a winning combination.

'It must have been so nice to have a brother to do things with, especially with you and Will being so close in age. I'd have loved that.' The wistful tone to Rowan's voice would have given her away, even if her words hadn't. 'I hated being an only child. I love Charlie to bits, but he didn't come along until my childhood was all but over and, even now, he feels more like a nephew than a brother. It's different when you don't grow up together.'

'Yes, we were lucky, we got a built-in playmate and best buddy. There's nothing I wouldn't do for him and I know he feels the same.' Nathan had paused for a moment, a memory he'd kept locked away trying to resurface, but he pushed it back down again. That wasn't a story he could share, but there were plenty he could. 'Despite how well we got on most of the time, we had some pretty epic fights too and some of the jokes went a bit too far, like when I superglued the side of his head to the car window.'

'Should I even ask?' Rowan was even more beautiful when she smiled and that's when she looked most like the carefree girl he'd known all those years ago, before life had layered on the kind of worries that it inevitably did. He'd found himself hoping that being in Cornwall would help bring her old smile back bit by bit, and he was determined to do whatever he could to help that process along.

'Will always fell asleep on long car journeys. He'd lean his head against the window and it didn't matter how bumpy the road was or how many twists and turns there were, nothing woke him up. It used to drive me mad, because I'd be bored stiff, wanting to talk or play some stupid game, and he'd just be sleeping. So I squeezed the best part of a tube of superglue on the inside of the window, just before we set off and as soon as Will leant his head against the window, he realised something wasn't right.'

'Oh my God, what happened?'

'A bald patch the size of a two-pound coin for Will, a month's grounding for me and a punch in the guts when he eventually got free. But that's brotherly love for you.' They'd both laughed and then Nathan had turned to look at her. 'Maybe it's just as well I haven't had any kids of my own; God knows what kind of monsters I'd have created.'

'From what I've seen with Leo, you'd have made a great dad and you've still got time to meet someone you want to start a family with.' She'd held his gaze for a moment and then she'd broken into another one of those disarming smiles. 'Just make sure the strongest glue you have in the house is a Pritt Stick!'

All he'd intended to do was share a funny anecdote, but Rowan had still managed to challenge his thinking about what the future might hold. He'd almost come to terms with the fact that he wouldn't be a father, but he'd never really asked himself why he'd drawn such a line under the possibility when he'd gone to prison. Nathan had allowed it to become the full stop to so many aspects of his life. He'd sold the home he'd worked so hard to create when he'd split with Nicole, all the plans they'd had for starting a family walking out of the door with her. When they'd got married, he couldn't ever have imagined this would be his future, or that he'd be happier now, in the building site he called home, than he'd ever been with her. When Nicole had decided to leave while he was still waiting to be sentenced, Nathan hadn't been sure how he could possibly be happy again, but then he realised he didn't miss her the way he should and he knew she'd made the right decision for both of them.

What was that saying? That life happens when you're busy making plans. It certainly had to Nathan, and just because there was no longer a plan set out for having children, it didn't mean that it couldn't still happen one day. It was just one of the things his conversations with Rowan had helped him to realise and he'd come to value her friendship in the last few weeks more than he'd ever have imagined possible. They might have been thrown together by her desire to help her son settle into a new life in Port Agnes, and the amount of responsibility he had taken on for Leo with Heather so close to having the baby, but whatever the reasons a friendship of their own had undeniably grown out of it.

'Did you hear what I said, or are you just ignoring me because you don't think I'll like the answer to my question? You think she'd never go out with you because you've been to prison, don't you?' Will had been waiting for a response and he wasn't going to let him off the hook.

Nathan shook his head. 'It's not even something I think about, because I'm never going to ask her out. I value her friendship far too much for that. So stop worrying. We said we wouldn't keep raking over this.'

'I know, but if you hadn't gone to prison, things would have been so different and it feels so wrong that no one but us knows the whole story, not even Heather or Mum.'

'We agreed that was the best solution for everyone and nothing has changed to convince me otherwise.'

'The best solution for everyone but you. You were the one who lost everything and it's not right that no one knows why.' Will swallowed hard enough for Nathan to hear it, and he reached out and squeezed his brother's shoulder.

'I'm happy, Will, I promise you that. Nicole showed me who she really was, and I love how the byre is shaping up. The house I had before was her dream home, not mine. This time it's going to be all me and my back garden is the place where we used to camp out as kids. The only downside is the neighbours.' He grinned and Will's face finally seemed to relax.

'Yeah, sorry, we're a lot to put up with and we'll be throwing a crying baby into the mix soon too.'

'I can't wait.' Nathan already knew just how much he was going to love the new addition to the family, because the bond he had with Leo was something he felt right to his core. It made the consequences of the crime that had been committed worth it a thousand times over, no matter what they continued to be.

* * *

Rowan wasn't sure she'd ever felt quite so physically tired, but it was a state of almost blissful exhaustion. When Nathan had suggested that she and the kids join him and Leo at a *Waves 4 Everyone* activity, she hadn't expected to end up trying surfing herself, much less discovering she had a bit of a talent for it. Growing up on the Cornish Coast, she *should* have tried surfing years ago, but back then Rowan had far too often missed out altogether rather than risking making a fool of herself. She was still that person in some ways, but it was funny how having children could force you to override so many of your own insecurities for their sake and that was exactly why she'd ended up finally giving surfing a go.

'Everyone is going to laugh when I fall off. I don't want to do it.' Theo had clung to her side, looking every bit as anxious and upset as he had on the day she'd found him clinging to the tree on the edge of the school playground. His friendship with Leo had done so much to help, but all those insecurities didn't just disappear overnight. The end of her relationship with James had clearly had a profound effect on their sensitive little boy and it didn't help that there were some children in his class who seemed to have an innate ability to hone in on his anxiety and do and say whatever they could to make it worse. There were some of the children from the school down on the beach with their families, making the most of the last days of unexpected sunshine and it had completely thrown Theo, who had decided he wasn't going into the water now that they were here. In that moment, Rowan had made a decision.

'No one is going to laugh at you, they'll all be far too busy laughing at me. What's funnier than seeing the headteacher fall face first into the sea?'

Within minutes she'd squeezed herself into a borrowed wetsuit and her first few attempts to stay on the surfboard had ended up exactly how she'd expected. She'd been able to hear the laughter of people on the beach, but she hadn't cared a bit, because one of the people laughing had been Theo. It was Nathan who'd eventually helped her to stay on the board and, once she'd got the hang of it, she'd found it far easier than she'd ever have thought. The most disconcerting part of the process had been when Nathan had held her a couple of times to help steady her, and her body had reacted to his touch in a way she was glad no one but her would ever realise. It had been so different to when James touched her. If he'd helped her in that situation, all she'd have felt was a steadying hand and relief that she might not be about to fall again. When Nathan had held her, it was as though he was touching every part of her, her nerve endings tingling in response, and there'd been a physical ache when he'd let go again because that brief instance of his hands on her body hadn't been enough. She had to put it down to the lack of intimacy she'd had with James for so long making her vulnerable to every little thing. Rowan couldn't accept that it was all about Nathan, because if she did she'd be travelling back down that dangerous path she was determined to avoid.

Theo had eventually taken to the water too and had ended up loving it just as much as his mum. Leo was a superstar, who'd clearly been doing this a long time, and even though he couldn't stand on the board, it was clear just how much joy it brought him to be in the water, taking part in an activity he loved. Nathan was endlessly patient with everyone, making them laugh when they were nervous or if they got things wrong. The way he treated people and made everyone feel at ease was the most attractive thing about him, which said a lot given just how good he looked in a wetsuit. He looked pretty good now too, as she crossed the garden towards where he was sitting, his face illuminated by the glow of the fire pit in front of him.

'Are the kids okay?' Nathan looked up at her and she couldn't help thinking how nice the words sounded, almost as if he was talking about their family together.

'Yes, they're all watching *Wonka* for the umpteenth time, and Bluey is stretched out on Leo's lap, of course. That dog never wants to be anywhere else when Leo is around.' They were looking after Bluey for her mum and Dean, who were away at a spa hotel in Dorset for the weekend. Tiffany had come along to have a sleepover with Bella, and Rowan had asked Nathan and Leo if they wanted to come back for a takeaway too, as a thank you for the surf lessons. The cottage they were renting had bifold doors from the garden to the open-plan living area, which made access easy for Leo's wheelchair and it was one of the reasons she'd enquired with the landlord about extending their lease.

Everyone had been ravenous after an afternoon in the water and the takeaway had been demolished in less than twenty minutes. After dinner the children had asked if they could watch a movie, with Bella taking charge of gathering together enough snacks to feed a small army.

'You're not going to watch it too, are you?' She'd wrinkled her nose at the sight of her mother and Nathan still hanging around as the film was about to start. 'You keep saying you're going to try out the fire pit.'

It was a none-too-subtle hint from her daughter, who she was now absolutely convinced was a thirty-year-old trapped in a ten-year-old's body, but

Nathan had smiled and said it sounded like a lovely idea. So now here they were, outside on their own, sitting under a blanket of stars in the flickering light of a fire pit. It couldn't have been more romantic and the idea terrified Rowan, mostly because she hadn't been able to stop thinking about what it would be like to kiss Nathan again, ever since he'd come back into her life.

'Leo loves Bluey so much. I keep thinking I should take the plunge again, but losing my last dog really broke me up.'

'I'm so sorry you lost your dog and I really understand what you mean. We had a therapy dog at Membory Grange. It was an idea I introduced shortly after I took over as head. So many of the kids who become boarders at a young age struggle and, for the really young ones, it's almost like an attachment disorder. So I thought getting Basil would help. He was a cross between a Poodle and a Jack Russell, and he loved the kids as much as they loved him. I'm sure he heard more of their problems than the school therapist, and the truth is I loved him too. I cried into his fur when my marriage was breaking down and I feel guilty for leaving him behind. I just hope he doesn't think I've abandoned him.'

'I'm sure he doesn't, but I feel like that's what I did to Chester. I took him everywhere and he was my shadow his whole life, then overnight I disappeared. I went to prison and that was hard for everyone. I thought the worry might kill Mum, and I know it really upset Leo that I wasn't around. All of that was way harder to contend with than the sentence itself, but at least they understood where I'd gone and that I'd be back eventually. Chester didn't understand that. Nobody could explain it to him, and he died while I was in prison. His kidneys had been failing, but he was doing okay until I just suddenly disappeared and then he went downhill really quickly. It was almost as if he decided life wasn't worth living any more. I did that to him. The choices I made broke my mother's heart and made Leo sad, but my biggest guilt is the fact that Chester thought I'd just walked out of his life. He'd been my constant companion for well over a decade and then one day I just wasn't there any more.'

'It wasn't your fault and I'm sure your family would have given Chester the very best care.' The stinging sensation in Rowan's eyes had nothing to do with the heat from the fire pit. Tears were prickling, but she couldn't allow them to fall. Nathan carried so much guilt, and she had no doubt now that he deserved the right to move on, but his sentence had left scars no one could see. She just wished she could find the words to make that better.

'I know they did, but I loved him so much, probably more than it's sensible for anyone to love a dog, given that the chances are they aren't going to be around for long. But it's so difficult not to let them get under your skin, when they know how to be loyal and loving in a way that not a lot of people do. So it's hard to risk putting my heart on the line like that again, you know?'

'I do.' Rowan stared into the fire pit, the words she was desperate to say almost escaping from her throat, even as she tried to weigh up whether she really should confide in Nathan, but then he knew better than anyone what it was like to be the centre of attention for all the wrong reasons, and she felt she could trust him not to repeat anything she told him. 'James is going to be coming to Port Agnes.'

'Oh.' Rowan could see the muscle going in Nathan's cheek in the flickering firelight. 'Are you two going to give things another try?'

'God no, there's no going back after what happened. He wants to see the kids, but he's told us he's coming a couple of times and then something comes up, but now he's definitely coming in the second part of half term week. I've found him an Airbnb. He wanted to stay here, but I didn't think that would work.' As she looked at Nathan again, the tension seemed to drain from his face.

'That's good, isn't it? I'm sure the kids will want to see him too, and I can understand you not wanting him to stay here. I couldn't think of anything worse than having to be under the same roof as Nicole.'

'Exactly.' She took a deep breath. 'I'm not good at being in the same room as someone who lied to me the way he did.'

'You don't have to talk about it if you don't want to.' The gentle tone of Nathan's voice was enough to convince her that she *did* want to talk about it.

'He had an affair.' It was a relief to finally say the words out loud and to know that Nathan was the last person who'd go around spreading gossip about why her marriage had ended.

'Then he's an idiot.' His eyes didn't leave her face, but she could easily have lowered her gaze or looked away like she had so many times before. Except this time she didn't. This time she did the one thing she'd been longing to do for weeks and pressed her mouth against his, gently at first, but then more urgently, vague traces of a citrusy aftershave mingling with the woody smoke in the air, and her body flushing with a heat that had nothing to do with their fire. If they'd been alone, there was no way of telling what would have happened, but she knew what she wanted to happen. Except they weren't alone, and she forced herself to pull away from him, immediately looking over her shoulder to make sure the children hadn't suddenly appeared. It was just a kiss, but no one wanted to see their mother kissing, especially someone who wasn't their father.

'Well, that was unexpected.' Nathan grinned and suddenly the woman who'd been brave enough to make the first move was back.

'But not unwelcome?'

'Definitely not. I've been waiting to do that again for well over twenty years, and I've got to say it was even better than last time.'

'That's down to you, because I certainly haven't had a lot of practice.' The words were out of Rowan's mouth before she could stop them this time. James had never been keen on kissing, which made a lot of sense now. She remembered reading an article once about how sex workers often didn't kiss their clients, reserving that for the people they loved, because it felt far more intimate than sex itself. Maybe James had felt the same way. Either way, it meant the kissing in their marriage had been a series of perfunctory exchanges – accompanied by hellos and goodbyes – and that the kiss she'd had with Nathan when she was sixteen had remained the best kiss of her life, until now. He was looking at her quizzically now and she had to offer him some kind of explanation that wouldn't immediately give away the fact her marriage had been a sham. 'James was my only *proper* boyfriend. So I never got the chance to kiss a lot of frogs, I just married the first one who asked me instead.'

'You definitely don't need any practice, although I guess we should make sure that wasn't just luck.' There was a glint in Nathan's eye and his obvious desire for her made him even more attractive. She should just laugh it off, this wasn't the right time in her life to start giving in to her feelings, and Nathan almost certainly wasn't the right person. Yet she couldn't deny she liked him, and not just because he was gorgeous and made her feel like she was too. It meant she couldn't laugh it off, because she didn't want to stop feeling this way – as if a part of her that had been left to die was suddenly being reawakened.

'I think you're probably right. We need to make sure it wasn't a fluke, but next time it needs to be when we're on our own. If the kids saw us...' She shook her head. 'I don't want them worrying and they still haven't really come to terms with the fact that James and I aren't together any more.'

'It's okay. I think if Leo saw us, he'd be thrilled because it would mean he got to spend even more time with Theo. Although I'd be worried about him getting ahead of himself and thinking we'll all end up as one big happy family.' Nathan laughed and she suspected he was right. Maybe it was wrong to use that to her advantage, but if it meant saving Nathan from the pain of the truth, she could justify it to herself.

'Theo might be the same and it probably won't just be the kids who get ideas into their heads, especially when it comes to our mums. So if we are going to go out without the children, to see if this was just one kiss or whether it might be something more, maybe we should keep it to ourselves for now. At least until we know if there's anything to tell anyone else.'

'You want to meet in secret? For the kids' sake?' His eyes were locked on hers and she was certain he could tell she was lying, and that the reason she wanted to keep this a secret wasn't just for the children, but because of the way people would talk if they knew something was going on between Rowan and Nathan. She forced herself to hold his gaze, nodding slowly, and then he shrugged. 'It's a good idea, like you say, at least until we know if there's anything to tell.'

He leant forward and brushed his lips against hers this time, a moment that was over almost before it had begun, in keeping with the spirit of the agreement they'd just reached, and it left her wanting more. She didn't want to think about whether keeping this secret would doom the chances of it working out before it even began. She was just going to do her best to enjoy it for what it was and for once in her life not worry about what the consequences might be.

13

When Rowan came back into the school offices after the Harvest Festival service, she shivered. It was like a refrigerator and every window in the outer office was open. The previous Saturday had turned out to be the last warm day. There was a definite autumnal chill in the air now and she couldn't think of any reason why Bex would have thrown all the windows open.

'Has there been a fire while I was out?' Rowan had only intended it to be a joke, but Bex sniffed the air, as if she was expecting to smell smoke.

'No, why?'

'I just wondered why you had all the windows open, when it's so cold in here.'

'Oh God, sorry.' She moved to the first window and pulled it shut. 'It's just that I had another very early start with Tom and I could barely keep my eyes open because it was so warm and cosy in here.'

'Did he have a bad night?' Rowan could still remember the torture of broken nights, even though her two had been pretty good sleepers. Bex's youngest son, Tom, was eight, but he still had lots of nights when he didn't sleep all the way through.

'Not so much a bad night as a very early morning.' Bex tried to suppress a yawn, but didn't quite manage it. 'He came into our room at 3 a.m. and said he couldn't sleep, so I ran through all the usual things with him... you know, is there anything you're worried about, do you feel sick, are you thirsty, blah, blah, blah.'

Bex looked exhausted just describing it, and Rowan gave her friend a sympathetic nod as she continued. 'Of course Tom says no to all of that, but I get him settled back into his own room, lie down, shut my eyes and start to have a very nice dream about Tom Hardy taking me horse riding.'

'You dreamt about Tom Hardy taking you horse riding?' Rowan raised her eyebrow and smiled.

'Yes, but that's not the point of this story.' Bex hesitated for a moment. 'Well, I suppose it is in a way, because there I was, in the land of make believe, having a very nice time riding along a sandy beach, when suddenly one of my eyelids was literally prised open and my Tom is staring at me, eyeball to eyeball, telling me I need to wake up because he's awake. It was 4.30 a.m. and by the time I'd played another round of why-can't-you-for-the-love-of-God-just-sleep, it was quarter past five and not worth me even trying to get back to dreamland, find that beach again, and see whether Tom Hardy was still waiting for me. Especially as Matt was already up to start work on the farm, so I couldn't even cuddle up to him as a consolation.'

'Sounds awful and I really wish I could send you home early, but with the meeting after school...' Rowan pulled a face. Given the choice she'd have sent herself home early too, but there was a meeting between the PTA and some of the governors, who were coming to outline a strategic plan to improve the school and how the PTA's fundraising efforts might support that. Rowan had already attended the governors' meeting earlier in the week and the hot topic was that the school was due for an Ofsted inspection by the end of the academic year. The chair of governors, a belligerent ex-detective chief inspector, who'd been part of the panel when Rowan was appointed, had told her that 'with your reputation and past experience we expect nothing less than an outstanding grade; it's why we employed you.'

No pressure then. It wasn't that Rowan didn't have high expectations too, but the school could get an inspection at any time and, given that she was only a few weeks into her headship there hadn't been time for any radical transformation. The school had been graded as good at the last inspection and she was determined to improve on that, as long as she had time to implement the changes and garner the support she needed from the governors, parents and staff to make them happen. It was why she'd smiled sweetly at former DCI

Keith Hounslow and assured him that being graded outstanding was her goal too. Keith's granddaughter was at the school, and he reminded Rowan of some of the parents at Membory Grange, who radiated entitlement. Some of them had even been known to remind Rowan that they 'paid her wages'.

There had been lots of upsides to working at a private school, mostly around how freely available resources were and the fact that she didn't need to manage budgets like a professional juggler to be able to replace broken equipment or recruit an additional staff member. But it hadn't been as idyllic as it looked from the outside, despite the beautifully manicured grounds of Membory Grange. The environment had been elitist in many senses and being at Port Agnes Primary had reminded her why she'd wanted to go into teaching in the first place. It felt like she could make a real difference to the children there, with the decisions she took and the way she led the school. There was a sense of the school being a hub of the community too, instead of an exclusive enclave, quite apart from the life going on in the nearest towns and villages, as Membory Grange had been. Maybe it had been a metaphor for her own life. Rowan suspected that hers and James's marriage might have looked idyllic from the outside, but that had been a façade too, such a good one that she hadn't fully realised it herself until she got out.

Bex's response to her apology brought her back to the moment, all thoughts of her old life fading into the distance. 'It's okay, Henry has maths homework on Thursday evenings and I don't want to go home until that's done. I hid in the car park behind the village hall last week working my way through an entire tube of salt and vinegar Pringles while listening to a podcast about mindful eating, until I was sure it would all be over.' Bex laughed. 'I cannot watch Matt pushing himself to the edge of a heart attack by shouting over and over again that multiplying a half by another half equals a quarter, and Henry sitting there saying "I just don't get it. It makes no sense that multi-plying something can make it a smaller amount". Matt got so close to the end of his tether that he snapped a ruler into four pieces to demonstrate, and I think if it hadn't been the ruler something in his head would have snapped instead. Neither of us are cut out for teaching, but especially maths. I stopped being of any use once they got to about three and it turns my kind, patient, level-headed husband into an unexploded bomb! Your kids are so lucky to have a teacher in the family.'

'Hmm I'm not sure they'd agree with you on that. Bella told me at the grand old age of six, when I was helping her to write some comprehension sentences, that I was the worst teacher she'd ever had.' Rowan smiled wryly at the memory. 'I think when you've spent all day dealing with other people's children the well just runs a bit dry and maths is *hard*. Henry's right: a lot of it makes no sense.'

'I feel better now, although it doesn't excuse the whole tube of Pringles.'

Rowan laughed. 'I think we might need a few tubes on standby for after the meeting and a very large glass of wine for when we get home.'

'I could always fill our coffee cups with something if Keith is going to be there.' Bex pulled a face, which suddenly softened into a smile. 'Talking of wine and Pringles, do you fancy coming to watch the half marathon on Saturday with me and Toni? I think Anna's coming too and we can have a picnic if the weather is good enough. The forecast looks dry and I don't mind wrapping up in a coat if it means I can sit in a folding chair, drinking wine, eating crisps and feeling like I'm doing my bit by sending a donation to Just-Giving from my phone. After all, we can't all be runners.'

'We can't, some of us have got to be in charge of sponsorship. And a wine and Pringles picnic? That sounds like the kind of catering I could cope with.' Rowan smiled again. At Membory Grange everything was OTT, with parents trying to outdo one another. Even something as simple as having a picnic while their children played cricket would turn into a game of one-upmanship, and it had always been impossible for Rowan to relax. This sounded like far more fun. Although she already knew she wouldn't be drinking, not when there were parents of her pupils around. The last thing she wanted to give them was anything else to talk about. She'd already overheard a discussion through her open office window about the alleged *real* reason she'd come back to the village. Everyone seemed to have their own theory and it would only be a matter of time before someone hit on the right one. But that was a worry for another day, and if anyone could take her mind off things it was Bex, who was outlining exactly how she thought the picnic should go.

'I might be able to stretch to a sandwich or two, maybe even a sausage roll, but I draw the line at anything that needs a knife and fork. I've got one hand for eating and one for holding my wine, sitting comfortably in my folding chair and cheering on Matt and Henry in the main race, and Ollie and Tom in the kids' race. Nathan has done such a great job of organising everything and there's going to be an inflatable fun course and barbecue for the kids straight after their race, run by some of the volunteers, so I won't need to be on full-time mum duty either. Are Bella and Theo doing the race?'

'Bella and Tiffany have bought matching outfits for the kids' race, and I think the boys are doing it too and then presenting medals to the runners who finish the half marathon. So I'll be entirely at a loose end for at least part of the day.'

'That should give you plenty of time to cheer on the hero of the hour, for organising the whole thing. You and Nathan seem to have been getting along very well just lately.' Bex gave her a knowing look and Rowan was tempted for a moment to confess that she and Nathan had kissed, and that she really liked him, but that would have been breaking her own rule. She'd had a video call with Odette and Pippa the night before and had confided in them, telling her friends just how different it felt to be kissed by a man who was clearly attracted to her and not just going through the motions.

'I didn't know what was missing until I found it,' was how she'd put it, before pulling herself up sharply, and desperately trying to underplay the situation, after Pippa had responded by saying that a kiss like that sounded 'potentially life changing'. She and Nathan could never be anything serious and it was the last thing she wanted anyway. The problem was it was just far easier to remember all of that when she wasn't describing what it felt like to kiss him, which was why she absolutely couldn't mention it to Bex. Instead, she arranged her face into what she hoped was a neutral expression.

'Nathan's such a nice guy and I'm glad you said hero of the hour, because I hope people in Port Agnes see the real him at the half marathon. He's obviously devoted to Leo and whatever he might have done in the past, I very much doubt he's that person any more.' Rowan didn't miss the twinkle that appeared in Bex's eyes and she needed to shut that down. 'But before you get any ideas, we're just friends. I don't think Theo would have got through the first part of this term without Leo, and Nathan has been doing as much to encourage their friendship as I have.'

'They're such lovely kids, and I'm sorry Theo is still having a bit of a hard time with some of the other boys. I know we're supposed to think all kids are great, but that Kayden in his class is a nasty piece of work and if I catch him bullying Theo again, he's going to find all his permission slips for anything fun mysteriously going missing until it's too late for him to take part.'

'Lyra has already offered to cast him as the back end of the donkey in this year's nativity play, with Hunter Welch as the front end.' Rowan couldn't help laughing again. Hunter was known for his fascination with toilet humour and, in his world, there was nothing more hysterical than passing wind. 'Of course we'd never really do that, but it does help to imagine him getting a bit of karma every now and then.'

'I want to believe in karma.' The smile had melted off Bex's face. 'But when you've got a lovely kid like Leo going through all of that, it's pretty hard to, isn't it?'

'It is and it's also impossible not to fall in love with Leo the moment you meet him.' Rowan bit her lip. It broke her heart to think that the gorgeous little boy, with the impish grin, who could make her son giggle when he was feeling sad, just by pulling a funny face, might not get to make it to adulthood. All the fears she had for Theo, and even Bella, paled into insignificance when she thought about what Leo and his family were facing. Nathan had told her they'd had to learn to push the fact they were eventually going to lose him to the backs of their minds, and focus on the now, but even that was hard when his condition was progressing in front of their eyes. As the headteacher, Rowan wasn't supposed to have favourites, but aside from her own children, Leo was hers and she knew he would have been even if he hadn't been her son's best friend. He was a lesson in making the most of every day, no matter what it might bring, and she wished there was something she could do that would really make a difference for him.

'Knock knock.' A voice behind Rowan made her turn around. It was an older woman with a blonde bob, carrying a huge cake tin. 'Sorry, Bex, I just wanted to get into the meeting room to get set up.'

'Oh my God, Gwen, have you made lemon drizzle?' Bex took the cake tin off the other woman and inhaled the air, answering her own question before Gwen got the chance. 'You have, haven't you, it smells divine.'

'I put extra lemon and sugar on the top just for you, but I might also have left a big bit of eggshell in the slice I'm going to give Keith if he turns up.' The woman dropped a perfect wink and then turned to Rowan with a smile. 'Sorry, I probably shouldn't have said that in front of the new headteacher. I'm Gwen Jones, treasurer of the PTA. Sorry I missed the last meeting but I was on a belly dancing retreat in Morocco.'

As the woman stuck out her hand and Rowan took it, she tried to work out whether or not she was joking, but Bex saved her from having to guess.

'This is the woman whose belly dancing classes have given God knows how many women their body confidence back. I know she gave me mine after I had the kids. Not only that, but she delivered them all too, before she retired as a midwife.' Bex looked over her shoulder. 'She also has the measure of Keith Hounslow and is the only one who can get him to shut up when he needs to. All of which are reasons why I want to be Gwen Jones when I grow up.'

'Me too.' Rowan smiled, already knowing that she was going to like the woman standing in front of her every bit as much as Bex did.

'Being like me can get you into quite a bit of trouble girls, but it's lots of fun and it would certainly keep you very busy. Although I'm only volunteering in the hospital shop for fifteen hours a week now.' Gwen made it sound as if she was taking it easy, but she was clearly involved in lots of different things and Rowan could imagine what an asset she was to the PTA. 'I fit in as much as I can, but dancing is probably my biggest passion. I know your mum from line dancing actually, Rowan, and she's no shrinking violet either.'

'She never has been and I used to find that embarrassing as a kid, but I'm seeing the appeal more and more these days.' As Rowan spoke she realised it was true, at least to a certain extent. After enduring so much gossip when her parents had split up, she'd actively tried to blend into the background in life, making sensible decisions and the 'right kind' of choices, instead of following her heart. Just look where that had got her. Lately a big part of her wanted to be bolder and to say what she meant, and do what she wanted like her mum and Gwen, instead of what everybody else expected her to do. But she was the headteacher of a village primary school that was always going to mean not overstepping the line of what was acceptable, and she had her own kids to think about too. Embarking on a relationship with Nathan was for the version of Rowan who knew she had the right to grab happiness and be part of something that felt real, after so many years of make believe. But keeping it secret was for the version of Rowan she had to be, the one who didn't want her children to become the topic of everyone's conversation. She might have a long way to go before she was anything like as authentic as Gwen or her mother, but Rowan Adams was finally coming out from behind Rowan Bellamy's shadow and she deserved a bit of time in the sun. Even if she and Nathan were the only people who ever knew about it.

* * *

The weather had been perfect for the half marathon. Dry and warmer than average for the time of year, but not so hot that it made the run trickier than it already was. It also meant the kids could make the most of the giant inflatable course on the green behind the row of shops and cottages that flanked the harbour on one side. Rowan and Bex had decided to source their picnic from Mehenick's Bakery, who had pledged to donate all the profits from the takings that day to Nathan's fundraiser for research into muscular dystrophy.

'I didn't expect you back so quickly. Bobby did brilliantly; was he completely worn out?' Rowan turned towards Toni, as runners continued streaming past them heading towards the finish line situated just before the mouth of the harbour. The course ran from Port Agnes, around the far edge of the neighbouring village of Port Kara and then back across farmland before dropping down into the village again. The children's course had been confined to a much shorter 2 km route around the village itself. The adults' race started an hour after the children's one and the runners in the full half marathon were just beginning to cross the finish line, one of the first of whom had been Toni's husband.

'He's thrilled that all the training has paid off, but as for being tired, it doesn't sound like it.' Toni flopped back into the chair she'd vacated only moments earlier to go and congratulate her husband on finishing in the first ten runners. 'The reason I'm back so early, is because he's already headed off to see if he can join in with the kids on the inflatables. I told him Mum and Dad have got it all under control, but I've got a feeling he's really going to check out the barbecue they're doing for the children too.'

'I think he's earned a burger after that.' Bex handed Toni another drink. 'And here's to having husbands who not only race in half marathons, but actually want to spend time with their children.'

'Cheers.' Bex tried to clunk her plastic glass against Toni's but it didn't have quite the desired effect. 'Do you think we should feel like we've let womankind down for not entering the race ourselves?'

'Nope.' Toni's response was emphatic. 'There's plenty of women running and they need someone to cheer them on. I for one intend to be sitting here doing that until the very last person crosses the line. A decision that has nothing to do with the fact that my parents and the rest of the volunteers are running what amounts to a free kids' club.'

Toni's voice was deadpan, but the twitch of her lips gave her away. She was enjoying a couple of hours of down time and, with a job like hers, no one could say it wasn't well deserved, which was why Rowan felt guilty that Anna wasn't with them. 'Do you think I should offer again to go and help out at the barbecue for a bit, to give some of the volunteers a break?'

'Absolutely not.' Toni's response was just as definite as before. 'Anna and Brae have provided all the food, and roped in Ella and Dan to help them. We've all offered our services too, but Anna told me to enjoy the break and, seeing as she's my boss, I'm not going to argue!'

Toni held her plastic glass in the air, raising another toast, and Rowan let her shoulders relax. It felt so odd doing nothing, but Toni was right, they'd been told to enjoy watching the race and that everything was under control. Rowan's parents and stepparents were part of the team of volunteers supervising the kids on the inflatable course too and there really was nothing she could do to contribute. It was strange, after playing such a central role for every event at Membory Grange, not to feel like she *should* be doing something. She'd never found relaxing easy, it gave her far too much time to think, which was something she'd tried to avoid doing too much of since her marriage had imploded. The only way she'd coped with everything that had happened was to focus on solutions, rather than feelings.

Problem: James had cheated on her and fallen in love with someone else, making living and working together unbearable.

Solution: Find a new job over a hundred miles away and make a fresh start.

Except she still hadn't really worked through how she felt about it. She'd been the same with responding to her soon-to-be ex-husband's messages about wanting to see the kids.

Problem: James was struggling and missing the children. They wanted to see him too, but it was too soon to go back to Membory Grange, especially for Theo. The children were just starting to settle in Port Agnes and she couldn't allow that to be disrupted.

Solution: Arrange an Airbnb for James to rent over half term, so that he could see the children and they could stay with him if they wanted to.

Everything was in place for his visit but she hadn't worked through how she felt about him coming to Port Agnes, somewhere that up until now she wasn't known as the chaplain's estranged wife. All she was doing was finding solutions and pushing the feelings back down inside.

'Okay, so we've been ordered to take it easy. I can live with that.' Bex plinked her plastic glass against Toni's again. 'But I am at least going to get up off this chair and watch the presentation of the winner's cup. Leo's grandma is giving a speech with one of the other fundraisers about what the funds will be used for so it should be well worth a listen.'

'I've got a feeling it might be emotional.' Rowan swallowed hard. She'd already cried watching Theo and Leo complete the kids' race together, but she had no idea that it was about to happen again, long before Irene made her speech.

'Talking of emotional, here come the Lark boys now.' Bex stood up, followed by Toni, as some of the other spectators started to cheer. Rowan got to her feet too and leant forward to see the two brothers closing in on the home straight. Will had a look of pure agony on his face and Nathan was virtually holding him up. They were both wearing T-shirts emblazoned with a picture of Leo's face and, as they got closer, she could hear Nathan calling out encouragement to his brother.

'Come on, Will, we're nearly there. You can do this, it's for Leo and he's waiting to give his dad a medal. He's going to be so proud of you, just picture his face. Only another 130 metres and we'll be there.'

Will grimaced and nodded, gritting his teeth, the pain with every step etched on his face as the two brothers moved past where Rowan and her friends were standing. They were close enough for her to see the muscles in Nathan's arm pulsating as he supported his brother's weight. His T-shirt was damp with sweat and clinging to his body, somehow making him even more attractive. He wasn't just a good man, although that much was obvious despite his past, he was beautiful too and that combination was making it almost impossible for Rowan to keep her feelings for him in check.

There were other people chanting Will's name now and telling him he could do it, but it was Nathan's name that Rowan was repeating under her breath, willing him to do whatever it took to help his brother to the finish line. Almost as if drawn magnetically, she found herself moving along the line of spectators in parallel to Nathan and Will. There were other people moving towards the finish line too and by now Nathan was almost carrying Will, whose feet were barely grazing the ground.

Theo and Leo were already in position, holding out their medals, a heavily pregnant Heather cradling her bump beside them.

'Come on, Dad, you're nearly there!' Leo echoed his uncle's words of encouragement and Heather was calling out Will's name too and telling him how much she loved him. Rowan wanted to shout out to Nathan, to let him know that she could see what he was doing and how brilliant she thought he was, but that would have brought attention to them and that was the last thing they needed. She just wanted one person in the crowd to will Nathan on and to let him know he had support too. She was sure it was there, not everyone judged him on one mistake, otherwise there wouldn't have been so many people at the event in the first place, but she still desperately wanted someone to recognise what he was doing, right here in this moment, and let him know how amazing that was. Then suddenly, there was a voice shouting Nathan's name.

'Come on, Nathan, I've got your medal! Nathan, Nathan, Nathan!' It was Theo, jumping up and down, chanting and waving the promised medal in the air. A bubble of emotion caught in Rowan's throat as she watched her son's excited response; he was so happy and it was obvious he'd made a connection to someone new, something he'd struggled to do for so long. It was crazy to feel as if she might burst into tears, but the moment had caught her completely off guard. She knew Theo had taken a shine to Leo's uncle during the time they'd spent together and that it had been Nathan's gentle encouragement that had persuaded him to keep going when he'd wanted to give up when they'd tried surfing. James would never have done that. He'd have told Theo that he obviously wasn't cut out for surfing and that they shouldn't waste any more time on it, given that Theo had never found any sport he was good at. James had been a star athlete in his own school years, excelling as a gymnast, and it had been a constant source of disappointment to him that Theo had never taken to any of the activities he'd been introduced to. Now she could see it was because he hadn't been encouraged to persevere. James's time had been too important to him to 'waste' on activities he didn't think would pay off. There'd always been other people who needed his help or charities he had to support. Although now she wasn't so sure that his motives to be out of the house so often had been all they seemed. Rowan wasn't blameless. She'd allowed herself to become wrapped up in work and not make enough time to prioritise her own children. Bella was a confident girl, to whom things came easily, but the choices Rowan and James had made had clearly affected their gentle, sensitive son far more. The job at Port Agnes Primary was challenging in its own way, but for the first time, she was able to prioritise spending time with her children and, despite some of the difficulties Theo had experienced settling in, she could see in her little boy's face that it was already paying off.

As the Lark brothers finally crossed the finish line, Will found the strength to stand on his own two feet and wrap his arms around his wife and son, as Leo tried to hang the medal around his father's neck. She'd expected Theo to place the medal around Nathan's neck in the same kind of sedate style as an official at the Olympic games, but instead he took a flying leap, flinging himself into Nathan's arms and hugging him so hard it made tears fill her eyes. This man, who'd come into their lives less than two months ago, already meant so much to Theo and she couldn't bear to think what another loss might do to him. She and Nathan hadn't even been on a date by themselves yet, but the stakes suddenly felt much higher and she had to tread very carefully. She couldn't risk anything jeopardising their friendship, when it clearly meant even more to her son than it did to her. It didn't matter how good it felt having someone in her life who was as attracted to her as she was to him. She wasn't going to do anything that would threaten Theo's fragile and new found happiness. She was never going to allow her children to slip down her list of priorities again.

14

As more of the runners continued to cross the finish line, two food trucks arrived and parked on the side of the harbour, with a sign on an A-board between them announcing that fifty percent of all profits from the sale of food would be going to the MND charity, which was just as well as Mehenick's had almost sold out. There was music playing over a sound system and the event had almost turned into a mini-festival.

The two boys had continued to hand out medals until Heather, Will and Leo were called over to talk to a journalist from a local television crew. Rowan had watched as they'd called Irene and Nathan over to be part of the interview, too. Irene had happily complied with the request, but Nathan had shaken his head and gone back to collecting empty water bottles dropped by some of the runners. She wondered if it was a conscious decision to stay out of the spotlight, or because as the organiser of the event he felt the need to muck in with the volunteers. Either way, it was clear that all that mattered to him was maximising revenue from the event.

When Rowan, Bex and Toni had gone to check how the children were getting on, Bella had been tucking into a burger, announcing happily that it was her second one. Apparently she'd earned it because she'd been round the inflatable course three times. She seemed delighted to be in the company of Tiffany and some of their other friends and Rowan had taken it as yet more evidence of how well her daughter had settled in to life in Port Agnes. But when Bex had suggested that she, Rowan and Toni have a go at completing the obstacle course, Bella had begged her mother not to be embarrassing. Not wanting to spoil her daughter's day, Rowan had left the other two to it and had headed back to see how Theo was doing. She felt a surge of pride, watching him congratulating the final few runners, still beaming every time he handed out a medal. Leo was back with him and she smiled at the sight of her little boy and his best friend, a feeling of contentment washing over her. Theo had never had a best friend, and the realisation that he'd found something as special and life-affirming gladdened her heart.

'Your son has been a little superstar.' Rowan hadn't realised that Nathan was standing behind her and she wanted to blame surprise for the quickening of her heart, but that would have been a lie.

'He loves Leo and he's a pretty big fan of yours too.'

'The feeling's mutual; he's a great kid and it's not hard to see where he gets that from.' Nathan had a way of looking at her that she wasn't sure she'd ever experienced before, almost like he was seeing her on a different level to the way the rest of the world did.

'I think you're the one who should be having praise heaped on you today. The whole event has been incredible.'

'I'm just a small part of that and we've been really lucky with the weather.' Nathan shrugged like it was nothing, but she couldn't let it go.

'Are you always this self-effacing? I don't remember you being like that when we were kids; from what I can recall you were confident, some might even say cocky.' She grinned as he pretended to look offended.

'Wow, that's an arrow to the heart. There I was hoping you'd never got over the fact that we didn't get a chance to see where that kiss might have led, and you thought I was cocky?' He shook his head slowly, but he couldn't disguise his smile and it was her turn to ask him something.

'Are you trying to tell me you never got over it?'

'I never forgot you, Rowan Adams and I was desperate to ask you out properly after that first kiss. I wanted to know if things between us might actually go somewhere, but then everything happened and almost overnight you were gone. We've both changed a lot since then, life has a way of doing that to you, but this is our second chance to see where this might go and everyone deserves one of those, don't they?'

Her eyes met his and she knew this wasn't just about them finally going out on a date, he wanted to know if she believed he deserved a second chance in a far wider sense.

'Of course they do, as long as—'

'Right, it's time to say a few big thank yous.' The voice booming across the loud speaker system and cutting Rowan off sounded vaguely familiar and, when she looked up, she realised it was Gwen Jones standing next to Nathan's mother. 'Will, Heather and Nathan, we need you up here for this too, where are you?'

As Gwen scanned the crowd, Nathan caught hold of Rowan's arm. 'What was it you were going to say about second chances? As long as what?'

His question sounded urgent, but people were gesturing at him to move to where his brother and sister-in-law were now standing, next to Irene and Gwen.

'It doesn't matter now, just go up and take some well-deserved praise, you've earned it.' He tried to protest again, but then Will walked over and grabbed him by the wrist, giving him no choice but to take his place at the front of the crowd.

Gwen was a natural at public speaking and listed off all the people they needed to thank for such a magnificent fundraiser, as well as the winners in each of the race categories. Theo had flushed with delight when his name had been called out and Rowan wasn't sure she'd ever felt more proud of him. Gwen saved the biggest thanks for the organisers of the event, including Nathan, and a cheer rose up from the crowd as each name was announced. Rowan glanced in his direction, trying to gauge Nathan's response to the obvious approval of so many people, but he just looked as if he didn't want to be there. After she'd finished the official business, Gwen handed the microphone to Irene who told the assembled crowd that being a grandmother had saved her when she lost her husband, and how 'holding her baby's baby in her arms' had changed everything, and that all she wanted was for Leo to have the chance to experience all the same milestones. Rowan had already had to blink back tears, even before the microphone was handed to Heather.

'Thank you all for coming. Will and I just want to echo everything Gwen has said about the brilliant volunteers for this event, especially my amazing brother-in-law, Nathan, whose idea this whole thing was. We're also incredibly grateful to Gwen, who has taken on the role of treasurer for the event to make sure that all the money collected gets to the charity as soon as possible.' The wobble in Heather's voice had been obvious, but as she took a deep breath her eyes filled with tears. 'Most of you know our son, Leo, and when he was born all we wanted was for our baby to be healthy. At first we thought we'd got that, but as the first couple of years went by, we realised that he wasn't like other children. He was special in so many ways, but one of those ways turned all our lives upside down. The reason this work is so important is that it helps children like him... it helps children like him to...'

She repeated the last part of the sentence and furiously wiped her eyes, but it was clear the emotion of the moment was becoming too much for her and she folded herself into Will's arms, thrusting the microphone towards Nathan as she did.

'You can see how much this means to my brother and sister-in-law. Leo is their whole world and, if you've met him you'll understand just how special he is. The best way any of us have of helping Leo and other children with muscular dystrophy to have long, active and happy futures is to support the research currently being undertaken, so that one day children like Leo will be able to run in events like this, or race down the beach into the sea and their families will be able to plan for their future just as they would with any other child. Leo is an incredible boy, capable of so much and, like Mum said, all we want is for him to grow up and have the chance to fulfil his potential. If you haven't already given by sponsoring our runners, buying tickets for the children's events, or purchasing food and drink from any of the caterers donating their profits to the cause, then please consider making a direct donation to the charity, the link to which is on our Facebook page: *Leo's Lions*. Let's have one more big cheer for Leo.' Nathan looked across to where his nephew was sitting, Theo still at his side, and Rowan felt weighed down by melancholy, her own worries suddenly ridiculously small and her heart breaking for Leo and the family who adored him. Nathan had been very careful to avoid using any terms that might scare the little boy, like the mention of death or further deterioration of his condition, but it was there in the subtext, in a way that would be easy for any moderately informed adult to pick up on. The research into muscular dystrophy was vital and Leo, and children like him, deserved all the support in the world.

Right now, the little boy was waving at the crowd who had responded to

Nathan's request for one more cheer with huge enthusiasm, and Theo was grinning again too. She wondered if either of the boys had any understanding of Leo's prognosis, or how quickly his disease might start to progress. The language used in the speeches seemed to Rowan to have been deliberately vague, but she had no idea how she'd have handled it if Leo had been her child. If he asked whether he was going to die, would his parents be honest with him? She didn't know, because there was no right answer. This shouldn't be happening at all. It wasn't right, and it was impossible to imagine herself in that scenario because it was far too painful to contemplate. What Nathan had said was so true though, Leo and his family *should* be able to look to the future and know it was going to come. It might not be promised to anyone, but most people lived with the expectation that it would. Leo's parents had to live with the very real possibility that their son wouldn't make it to adulthood and that the years before that would be filled with challenges no child should have to endure. Losing a child wasn't a prospect any parent should have to face and, as difficult as the last year had been for Rowan, it was nothing in comparison to what Leo and his family had to deal with.

'Are you okay?' Bex gave Rowan an appraising look when she went to find her a few minutes later. 'You look like you're about to burst into tears.'

'It's just Leo. It's so unfair. There ought to be a cure, or something they can do to slow things down, he's such a great kid.' A tear rolled down her face, but her throat was burning from holding back a thousand more. She wanted to sob and rage against a world where this could be allowed to happen, but she couldn't do that, not when Leo was only about thirty feet away from her, with a huge smile still plastered on his face. She had a reputation to keep too. People expected her to be calm and professional, and she'd never been the sort to show her feelings in public anyway. It gave people far too much to talk about and an insight into her emotions she didn't want anyone else to have, because it made her far too vulnerable. In the wake of her husband's affair coming to light, she'd never once shown her emotions in public, even when she'd felt like she was dying inside. Yet now here she was, with raw emotion dangerously close to the surface and she had to gulp air like a dying fish to stop herself from sobbing.

'You're right, he is a great kid and we've got to have hope.' Bex squeezed her waist, seeming to realise that a full-on hug would have pushed her over the edge. 'That's why fundraising events like this are so important and it's why Nathan set Leo's Lions up, to give them all hope.'

'Or to line his own pockets.' Rowan recognised the man who'd just interjected into their conversation without invitation. His daughter, Milly Harwood, was in Year 4. Rowan knew she shouldn't react to his comment and that she had to stay professional, but the sadness that had been welling up inside her seemed to have turned to white hot anger, and that was far harder to control.

'You should be very careful what you accuse people of, Mr Harwood.' She narrowed her eyes and there was an edge to her voice she barely recognised. Even when she was using her 'headteacher' tone, it never sounded quite as unforgiving as this.

'Why? He's got form for it, and you have to wonder why he does all of this.' Mr Harwood gestured around him. 'You can't tell me he's not pocketing some of the money.'

'Gwen Jones oversees all the finances so that would never happen.' Bex was the first to reply, but Rowan was right behind her, with an even more forceful response, one she seemed to have absolutely no control over.

'How dare you accuse Nathan of something like that, when it's obvious to anyone that he adores Leo and would do anything for him. But you'd rather ignore the evidence and judge him for one thing, wouldn't you, Mr Harwood? Well, I hope you've never made a mistake you want to move on from, but if you have, I hope no one gives you an opportunity to do that, because you clearly don't believe anyone deserves a second chance. No matter how hard they work and how obvious it is that they're a good person, most people never do anything as amazing as the things Nathan has achieved today. Still, you can just go home and polish your halo, can't you? Safe in the knowledge that you've never done a thing wrong in your entire life. The school will just have to work extra hard to teach your daughter that kind people show forgiveness to others.'

It was as if the version of Rowan she'd pushed down for years had suddenly come busting out and, even if she wanted to, she didn't think there was any way she could have stopped herself. The colour seemed to have drained from Mr Harwood's face; his mouth was moving but for a moment nothing seemed to come out, until he finally said just two words, before scuttling away and disappearing into the crowd of people still milling around the harbour.

'I'm sorry.'

Bex looked at Rowan for a moment and then started to laugh. 'That was brilliant, absolutely bloody brilliant.'

'Was it? I think I might just have lost my job.' Rowan blinked a couple of times, just to check that she was awake and that all of that had really happened.

'Okay, what are you laughing at? What have I missed?' Toni suddenly emerged from the crowd, but all Rowan could do was shake her head.

'Our amazing headteacher just tore a strip off one of the parents for accusing Nathan of setting this whole thing up to scam money out of people.'

'That is pretty amazing, and from the woman who wouldn't even have a drink in public in case someone saw her. On that basis, I might have to upgrade what you just did to legendary.' This was high praise indeed from Toni, a woman who wasn't known for using any kind of superlative.

'I hope you still think that when you're having to set up a GoFundMe after I lose my job and can't pay my bills.' Rowan still couldn't believe she'd said what she had, but despite her fears about losing her job, she was glad she'd done it. And as she looked at the expressions on her friends' faces, she couldn't stop a smile from creeping across her own.

'Oh, don't worry about Rob Harwood. He won't want anyone to know he's been told off by the headteacher, he'll be straight down the pub to get himself a pint and lick his wounds. Although he might try and prove that he was right by repeating what he said about Nathan and seeing whether he can find someone who agrees with him.'

'Sadly, someone will.' The smile slid off Rowan's face as she realised it was true, the thought turning anger to sadness again. Nathan didn't deserve this, he was a good man. She was certain of it.

'It doesn't matter what a few judgy people think, Nathan Lark has you on his side, Rowan, and you're a force to be reckoned with.' Bex raised her eyebrows. 'Although I must admit I didn't realise quite how on his side you were.'

'I'm not it's just—'

'Yes, you are.' Toni nodded. 'I've been where you are, trying to pretend that it's something else, but you really like Nathan. You might not be willing to admit it yet, but it's obvious you do. So if there's a reason you feel like you need to hide how you feel, you need to get a bit better at it.'

'Or you could just enjoy it.' Bex linked an arm through Rowan's. 'You could stop being the woman who feels as if she needs to be perfect all the time so that no one can say anything bad about you. But, do you know what? Even being perfect will give people something to talk about behind your back if they want to. So why not do what you want to do for a change?'

'It's not like I've hidden my friendship with Nathan, we've being going out with the boys all the time since they became friends.' Rowan was doing her best to make it sound like that was all there was to it, but she could see the way her friends were looking at her – as if her feelings for Nathan were written all over her face for the whole world to see. That was the last thing she wanted, so she was just going to have to try harder to have a poker face and pretend that this was completely platonic. Unfortunately, Bex didn't seem to be willing to let it go.

'You have, but that's for the kids. What about you, Rowan? What have you done that's for yourself since you came back to Port Agnes?' Bex didn't blink as she held her gaze.

'The kids are my responsibility, and I can't just go out having fun, forgetting they exist, like their father did when he found someone else he'd rather be with.' Despite her intention to keep her cards close to her chest, Rowan seemed to have unlocked a part of herself she could no longer control, because she hadn't meant to say that either, and Bex was squeezing her arm in sympathy.

'That's not what you're doing at all. I'm sorry James didn't realise how lucky he was. If you want a night out where you tell us all the gory details and we verbally rip him to shreds, you know we're there for you. But we're there for you practically too, to help out with the kids, and you've got great support from your family. Even if James doesn't step up and do his share of the parenting, don't use the kids as an excuse not to do something for yourself, because Nathan might well be just what you need. In fact, I'd be willing to put money on it.'

Rowan nodded, because she didn't trust herself to speak again; anything at all could have come out of her mouth. She might have ended up telling her friends that she was scared of opening herself up to getting hurt again, or of making a fool of herself and everyone seeing her life fall apart at the seams all over again. Part of her knew that Bex was right and that she could be bolder and more honest, because it had felt so good to tell Rob Harwood exactly what she really thought. But that kind of behaviour got you noticed and gave people even more to talk about. Rowan wasn't sure she was ready to live that way or whether she ever really would be.

15

Nathan had started reading a news article just before he'd gone to bed the night before that had come up as an alert on his phone, about the development of a new type of gene therapy. The researchers were hopeful that it might be significant in delaying the progression of some forms of muscular dystrophy. It had led him down an internet rabbit hole of reading and research, and he'd finally fallen asleep just after 2 a.m. He'd been up again at six to do some work on the byre before he was due to take Leo over to Tony and Marion's house. He'd been taking his nephew over there at least once a week for the past three years. They had a huge in-ground swimming pool with a retractable roof, which meant it could be used all year round, and Leo loved it even more than the swim spa that Nathan had installed at home. Not long after he and Will had first started working in partnership with Rowan's father, Tony and Marion had invited the whole family over for a barbecue, and as soon as Leo's eyes had landed on the pool it had been obvious he was desperate to go in.

Water had become Leo's passport to freedom as his symptoms had progressed. He'd been diagnosed earlier than usual, at just eighteen months, and his symptoms had been far more severe at a much younger age than most children with Duchenne's muscular dystrophy. He hadn't hit any of his mobility milestones and, when he wasn't even trying to crawl at almost eighteen months, he'd undergone the tests that had led to his diagnosis. Will and

Heather had discovered that they both carried a faulty gene, which gave them a 50 per cent chance of passing the condition on. They'd been trying for another child at the time of Leo's diagnosis and those plans had immediately been put on hold.

Since Leo's fall, the speed of progression terrified Nathan if he thought about it too much, and most of the time he tried to box it away and push it to the back of his mind, otherwise he wasn't sure he'd have been able to function. He had to believe that the outcome for Leo would be far better than they'd been warned it would be. The wheelchair was helping him now that his legs no longer worked the way they should, but there wasn't the same kind of solution for the most important muscle in the body – the heart. When that started to weaken, or the muscles involved in the respiratory system were no longer able to help him breathe, the options were painfully limited. Research had to find a cure before then, because the alternative didn't bear thinking about.

When Leo was in the water, it was almost as if his condition didn't exist and the joy it brought to his face made Nathan happier than anything else in the world. That same smile had been on Leo's face when Nathan and Will had first helped him into the pool at Tony and Marion's house, and again when Nathan had taken him to their place for a second time and Tony had been the one to help him into the pool. The third time they'd visited, Nathan had been lost for words when he'd realised Tony had bought a mobile pool hoist to help Leo get in and out of the water. It was that kind of thing that had restored his faith in people, something which had been severely tested in the wake of his prison sentence. There were only a very small minority of people who'd blatantly shunned him since his release, but the gossip had been far more widespread and he knew how much it had hurt his mum. Along with losing Chester, that was his biggest regret. Maybe he should have regretted the sentence more, or the crime itself. But he couldn't regret the crime because it hadn't been motivated by greed, the way a lot of people seemed to think it was. The crime had been committed because of a desperate desire to find a solution for a situation that didn't have one, and he couldn't regret that, no matter what it might have cost him.

'Nathan.' He'd known it was his mother coming even before she called out, the aroma of the bacon rolls she'd made reaching him before she spoke. He hadn't asked her to make him breakfast, but it was no surprise that she had. Irene had always been the sort of mother who lived up to that word in every sense. Her priority had been to make sure her boys were happy, well fed and had as much of what they wanted as it was possible for her to give them. His parents had loved each other and they'd had a happy marriage, but he'd never once doubted that he and Will had come first for his mother. When their father had died, they'd talked about the prospect of selling the family home, but she'd wanted to try and hold on to it. It had been a wonderful place to grow up, a solid Georgian house with almost two acres of land and the byre which at the time had been a semi-dilapidated barn-cum-dumping-ground.

By the time they made the decision to convert the main house for Will and his family, with a self-contained annex for Irene, Nathan's brother had already remortgaged his own place twice. The money had been used for trips to the US to explore experimental treatments for Leo and with the prospect of private IVF looming, there was more and more pressure on Will. They'd been pushed to their limit financially, even before they'd realised that the window for IVF was closing. The one thing they really wanted was a cure for Leo, but that was something no one could offer them and they desperately needed hope. Having another child might be the only thing that could give them that, and Nathan had been willing to do whatever it took to help his brother. He wasn't trying to excuse the VAT fraud. It had been a stupid thing to do, to think that it would be possible to get away with submitting false accounts that inflated the cost of building materials. It had meant receiving payments the business wasn't entitled to. Ignoring letters from HMRC to come clean and put the business's affairs in order to avoid prosecution was even more idiotic, but it had gone so far by then and the end goal had seemed far more important. Those VAT relief payments had helped towards the costs of the IVF treatment and had landed Nathan with a prison sentence. But he defied anyone not to be tempted in those circumstances, and now Heather was just weeks away from giving birth to a daughter. That's why he could never regret what had happened, even if it had hurt his mother far more than he'd realised it would. When she held her granddaughter, some of that pain would finally be lifted. He was sure of it.

'I'm in the kitchen.' It was a bit of an exaggeration to call it that, but the area where his kitchen would eventually be sited was finally plastered and waiting for the units to be fitted, which Nathan would be doing himself. For now he was finalising the preparation for the heating system, which had involved hours of chipping away at part of the cobblestone floor to lay the pipework.

'Okay, darling. I've brought you some breakfast to make sure you eat before you go out.' His mother appeared a moment later, carrying a tray which she set down on his workbench before he had a chance to take it from her. 'This kitchen is going to be huge when it's finished and the views are going to be amazing.'

Irene moved towards the bifold doors on one side of the room, which over-looked the paddock and the neighbouring farmland beyond it, with fields stretching as far as the eye could see. As hard as Nathan had worked to climb the property ladder by himself, it now felt as if this was where he was meant to be. He lived 200 feet away from all the people who meant the most to him, and eventually a renovated and extended version of the byre would be even more of a dream home than the house he'd renovated when he'd been married to Nicole.

'The views will be amazing and I know I'm going to be happy here.' Nathan stood up to greet his mother and she put her hands on his shoulders, holding him at a distance as though she really wanted to look at him.

'I hope so, darling, I really hope so, because no one deserves to be happy more than you.' She drew him to her then, holding him so tightly that for a moment it was hard to breathe. When she pulled back, her cornflower-blue eyes were filled with tears.

'What's wrong? I didn't say that to upset you. I really think I'll be happier here than I've ever been before, so please don't be sad.'

'I'm not.' Irene swallowed hard, shaking her head. 'It's just that you've given up so much to move here, and I'm crying out of happiness because I think you're right and that all the sacrifices you've made will be worth it.'

'Selling the house wasn't that much of a sacrifice, I had to settle things with Nicole anyway and—'

'I'm not talking about selling the house.' His mother cut him off, looking at him in a way that made him catch his breath, and in that moment he realised she knew the secret he'd been certain was his and Will's alone. They should have realised they couldn't fool their mum, she knew them far too well. Even so, he couldn't say the words out loud, because once they were out there they couldn't be taken back. He had to keep denying it, otherwise there was no way of knowing what the consequences might be.

'I'm afraid I don't know what you're talking about then.'

'Yes, you do.' She squeezed his hand. 'But we don't have to discuss it, because I understand why you don't want to. I just needed you to know that I know the truth and I'm prouder of you than you'll ever begin to understand.'

'Despite the fact that I'm Port Agnes's most famous ex-con?' He grinned and she put one hand on the side of his face.

'No, because of that.' His mother planted a kiss on his cheek, pulling away and gesturing towards the plate she'd left on his workbench. 'Just make sure you eat something before you head out. And remember, if this girl is the right one, what's happened in the past won't matter to her. And I think Rowan might be the right one, I really do.'

His mother headed out of the door before he could answer, but when he replied to the empty room it was no less heartfelt.

'Me too, Mum. Me too.'

* * *

If anyone had told Rowan when she was sixteen that her father would one day allow himself to be pelted with water bombs by his grandson and his best friend, who would be laughing uproariously in the process, she'd never have believed them. Even more unbelievable would have been the idea that her father's former best friend and business partner would go from being his arch enemy back to being his friend again. Much less that they'd be standing side by side in the pool, ready to be pelted with water bombs by the boys. Her mother and Marion were far more sensible, sitting together on the side of the pool, laughing. Their excuse for not getting wet was that they were going out together soon, taking Bella and her best friend Tiffany to get their nails painted for the very first time at a beauty salon in Port Tremellien. Rowan hadn't been sure about the idea at first, Bella wasn't even eleven yet, but the salon had a special package for children, with pretty nail art, but easily removable polish. It wasn't something that would damage the girls' nails or need another visit to the salon to remove it, and Tiffany's mother had already been planning to take her there for her next birthday anyway.

Tonight the girls would be having a sleepover together at Katrina and Dean's house, and the boys would be staying with Tony and Marion, mostly so that Leo could maximise his swimming time. Tomorrow her parents and stepparents would be taking all four children out to lunch and then to the cinema in Truro. None of these were things Rowan could ever have imagined, and it gave her hope for a future where she and James might be able to have a similar kind of co-parenting relationship and, who knows, maybe they could even be friends. His stay in the Airbnb was fast approaching, but he'd been conspicuous by his silence for over a week, missing his regular FaceTime with the children and sending just a four-word text in explanation.

Sorry, something came up

Rowan had a feeling that something was Euan Samuels. As hard as it might have been for James to supress who he really was for so long, none of that excused sidelining the children. James had already broken several promises to them since they'd left Membory Grange and Rowan had every intention of telling him in no uncertain terms that all of that had to stop now.

'Here we go, boys, bombs away.' Nathan was on the other side of the pool to her, loading up water bombs for Theo and Leo to drop on her father and Dean. He was laughing conspiratorially and, if anyone had looked in on the scene, they would have sworn all of them were family and that Nathan was the kind of father who knew exactly how to have fun with his children. He would be a great dad and it made Rowan's chest ache that a stupid mistake might have robbed him of that chance. *Maybe it wasn't too late, but at her age...* Rowan shook the thought from her head. It was ridiculous to think like that. In just a few minutes, she and Nathan would be going out on their first real date. For all she knew it might also be their last, so all the stupid thoughts that were racing through her mind needed to stop right now. It was just sixteen-year-old Rowan making an appearance, that was all. The same girl who'd practised pairing her name with his: Rowan and Nathan, even Rowan Lark. But that girl had to stay firmly in the past, where she belonged. Rowan wasn't a carefree sixteen-year-old any more and life wasn't make believe. She knew that better than anyone.

'Right, we need to make a move, girls, if we're going to get to our appointment.' Katrina stood up, and Marion and the two girls quickly followed suit. All of them bidding farewell in a flurry of excited goodbyes.

'If you boys have had enough of water bombs, we can get you in for a swim.' Tony's suggestion was greeted with an enthusiastic response from both boys, and he turned towards Rowan. 'You and Nathan can get off now; Dean and I can get the boys sorted.'

'Are you sure?' She glanced over to where her stepfather was already setting up the mobile hoist, wondering if he or any of the others realised that she and Nathan weren't just heading off at the same time, they were going on a date. They'd done their best to be discreet, acting like the friends that until very recently she'd been determined they should remain. If the others did know, they were clearly deciding to be discreet too; Rowan's father smiling as he responded to her question.

'Absolutely, we're old hands at this. Nathan knows we can handle it, don't you?' Her father looked towards him and he nodded, before turning in Rowan's direction.

'Your dad has been great letting Leo come here and swim whenever he wants.'

'It's been an absolute pleasure.' The sentiment in her father's voice was so sincere she caught her breath, but it wasn't just because of what he'd said. It was what it signified, and how much her father had changed from the bitter, hate-filled person he'd been when her parents had first split up. If she'd ever doubted that people were capable of change if they were given a second chance, she had to believe it now.

'Are you ready to go?' She smiled at Nathan, and the same butterflies she'd felt at sixteen seemed to be out in full force when he smiled back, and she knew that no matter how much she wanted to pretend, this wasn't just a casual first date.

'I am if you are?' He smiled, giving her one final chance to step back and protect herself in the only way that could be guaranteed, by not getting involved. Instead she found herself nodding and followed his lead, stepping straight into the unknown.

16

There'd been a handful of occasions during their marriage when Rowan had expressed concern to James about their lack of intimacy. It was usually after a conversation with friends, like the one she'd had with Pippa and Odette just before she'd discovered his affair, when she'd question whether there was something fundamentally wrong with their relationship. James would pull out all the stops to convince her that there wasn't anything wrong, by planning some kind of romantic grand gesture. Over the years there'd been a trip to Paris on the Eurostar to have dinner on the Champs-Élysées, a diamond ring, a couple of huge bouquets and a dozen heart-shaped cupcakes delivered to her office. People would tell her how lucky she was to have such a romantic husband, who clearly adored her, and she'd push her concerns about their lack of intimacy back down. But the truth was she hadn't wanted any of those grand gestures. She'd wanted a connection between the two of them that they didn't have with anyone else, something that placed their relationship into a different category to the ones she had with her closest friends or family. She'd wanted fun and laughter and, yes, a physical connection to the man she'd chosen to spend her life with, but it hadn't been there and the things James had tried to substitute it with hadn't made up for it.

Rowan hadn't realised quite how sad and hollow that had left her feeling until she'd got out of the situation. She'd buried herself in work and motherhood, but since coming home to Port Agnes she'd finally allowed herself to acknowledge that she wanted more than that, and it was Nathan who'd been the catalyst for admitting those feelings to herself. She had no idea where things between them were going to go, but reconnecting with him had proved that the feelings she'd had decades earlier hadn't just been teenage infatuation, they were real. A powerful physical connection with the potential for fireworks wasn't just the stuff of novels and rom coms. She'd felt it when she was with Nathan and, even if he wasn't meant to be a part of her life in the long term, she'd always be grateful to him for opening her eyes to the truth. She'd allowed James to manipulate her into believing their marriage was normal, but the truth was he wasn't entirely to blame. She'd played her own part in manipulating herself. She'd wanted to believe their marriage was okay, so she'd ignored all the signs to the contrary. Now there didn't seem to be any going back to the pretence that a platonic relationship was enough for her and she didn't want to. When she'd agreed to go out with Nathan, he'd called and asked her if there was anywhere in particular she wanted to go. Her response had been immediate.

'I just want to do something fun. Nothing fancy. Why don't you take me where you planned to take me all those years ago, when you were first going to ask me out?' She'd tried to keep the playful tone out of her voice, but she hadn't quite pulled it off, because there'd been a part of her that had suspected his mind might have been on one track at that age. He might well have planned to take her somewhere they could find some privacy, to spend the entire time kissing her and trying to take their relationship to another level. The thought of him wanting to recreate a date like that – one that had never happened – sent tingles up her spine. But she was terrified too, because she couldn't help wondering if there might be something wrong with her, something that made her fundamentally undesirable when things reached that stage. She didn't feel that way when she was with Nathan, but anticipation could be very different to reality and the idea of being a huge disappointment to him almost made her want to pull out of the date altogether. She was overthinking it though; Nathan wouldn't rush her into anything she wasn't ready for, Rowan was certain of that.

'Okay, you asked for it.' He'd laughed in response to her instruction. 'Just make sure you're wearing socks.'

'Why do I need to be wearing socks?'

'You'll find out.' She'd been able to hear the grin in his voice and picture his dark blue eyes crinkling in the corners and suddenly, whatever the date might involve, it couldn't come soon enough.

'Are you enjoying yourself?' Nathan was looking at her now, and she couldn't believe her answer wasn't obvious. They'd been laughing almost non-stop since arriving at the bowling alley just outside Port Tremellien, mainly because of how truly terrible Rowan was at bowling, even with the guardrails that were meant for children up to stop her ball rolling into the gutter. After several disastrous attempts, she'd got it into her head that using the heaviest ball would mean she couldn't bowl it hard enough for it to go off at an angle and that it would go straight down the middle instead. In reality, before the ball had finally rolled slowly along the guardrail and knocked over two pitiful pins, Rowan had travelled part way down the lane too, dragged by the weight of the ball, Nathan had clearly been trying his best to keep a straight face, while he checked that she hadn't hurt herself, but then he'd started to laugh.

'I mean you could just go a bit further down and kick the pins over, or we could ask the kids two lanes up if we can borrow the launcher they're using. I think you need it more than they do.' He'd gestured towards the blue plastic ramp in the shape of a dragon and she'd laughed too. Nathan's teasing was all in good fun, and she'd started it, ribbing him about the way he walked up to the line to ready himself before he bowled, doing an exaggerated impression of it like a graduate from the Ministry of Silly Walks. When she'd told him after her next turn that she thought the teenage boys in the next lane were laughing at how awful she was at bowling, she'd felt the first frisson of embarrassment, wondering just for a moment if she was making a fool of herself in front of him. But the next time Nathan had walked up to the line, he'd done a pirouette spin before releasing the ball with a grunt a tennis player would have been proud of, making sure that if the teenagers were ridiculing anyone, it wouldn't be Rowan.

Nathan wasn't afraid of laughing at himself and when she'd asked him to help her bowl her next shot, he'd moved behind her and checked if he could put his hand over hers to show her how he would throw the ball. It had felt as if electricity was thrumming through her body and she'd been left almost bereft when he'd stepped away again. About five minutes before he'd asked Rowan whether she was having a good time, she'd realised she was on the best date of her life. She couldn't tell him that, though, it would have sounded ridiculous. So she had to play it down.

'It's been really good fun and I'm so glad you decided to take me on the same date you would have done the first time around.'

'I hope you still feel that way when I take you for dinner. A portion of chips from Penrose Plaice to share, straight out of the bag, and we can split a can of Coke too. That was top of the range for my budget back then.'

'I think you should let me pay for dinner; it's only fair as you paid for the bowling and that way we could have a can of Coke each.' Rowan laughed again, but as soon as the words were out of her mouth she wished she hadn't said them. She liked the idea of sharing a can of drink with Nathan. It spoke of the kind of casual intimacy she'd never had with James, the sort of thing a normal couple might do.

'My mother would never forgive me if she found out I let you pay for your own chips, but I'm sure I can persuade Brae to give us two straws, if he's working today.'

'I don't mind sharing, if you don't.' Rowan felt suddenly shy and Nathan nodded.

'I can't think of anyone I'd rather share a can of Coke with.' He smiled again and she felt another huge jolt of attraction towards him, one that went right down to her toes. The date couldn't have been any more simple or any more perfect, and Rowan's only regret was that it would eventually have to end.

* * *

Rowan wasn't sure if her parents knew that she and Nathan were dating, but she suspected they did. It was hard to believe they wouldn't be able to pick up on the energy that seemed to fizz between them whenever she was close to Nathan. They'd been on three dates in the last two weeks and spent time together with the children in between, and she was certain her whole family would have been delighted at the prospect of her and Nathan getting together, but it was far too soon to even consider making it public. It didn't really matter whether her parents had already worked it out, because none of them would discuss it in front of the children. When her mother had asked how she felt about James potentially introducing them to a new partner, she'd said he'd have to be certain it was serious and long-term first. The children needed stability, and Theo in particular was vulnerable about things changing, so they all needed to act with caution. Her parents understood that. The children saw Nathan as a friend and she wanted to keep it that way, although it was getting harder and harder for her to think of him in those terms.

'Thank you for dinner, it was amazing.' Rowan turned towards him as they pulled up outside her cottage. They'd driven to Port Tremellien and had drinks at a new bar overlooking the beach, watching the sunset turn into nightfall, before eventually heading to dinner at a Thai restaurant which had a fabulous reputation, but that Rowan had never tried. There was always a chance of someone seeing them together, but all three of their dates had happened outside of Port Agnes, apart from when they went to Penrose Plaice for a portion of chips, and no one watching them together could have claimed to know for certain that they were a couple. They'd kissed again at the end of the first two dates, but despite the opportunity there had been to go further, and despite how much Rowan had wanted to, she'd put the brakes on both times. James was the only man she'd ever slept with. Part of her was still scared that their lack of intimacy and the fact that he'd fallen in love with another man was due to some kind of failing in her. Added to that, she was also nearly forty and had been through two pregnancies, which made the prospect of someone seeing her naked terrifying. But it wasn't just someone, it was Nathan. In a way that made it better, but in another way the stakes were far higher than they would have been if this had just been a rebound fling. As much as she might try to tell herself that dating Nathan was just a way of moving on from a bad marriage, she knew it wasn't true. He meant far more to her than that, he always had done, but up until now it had all been on her terms. Just as she'd suspected, Nathan hadn't given even the slightest hint of wanting to push her into something she wasn't ready for, but the truth was she was more than ready. She was just terrified of getting it wrong.

She couldn't even use going home to the children as an excuse for not being as brave as her body was begging her to be. Bella was staying at Tiffany's, and Theo and Leo were at a cub camp in the village hall. The newest cubs were doing their first 'camp out' in the warm and dry, rather than under canvas, partly because of the time of year and partly because, as the cub leader had told the parents, there was a high rate of wanting to go home at their age. Irene was one of the volunteers and she'd assured Rowan that she'd take the boys home with her if the need arose. There was unlikely to be a lot of sleeping going on for the boys and, as Rowan looked at Nathan she realised that getting a good night's sleep was the last thing on her mind, too.

'I'm really glad you liked it.' His voice was warm, but somehow it still elicited a shiver of anticipation. 'And I love going out with you.'

'Me too.' Rowan twisted her hands in her lap. There'd been so many times during the evening when she'd wanted to reach out and touch him, but instead she'd knotted her fingers together and she was doing the same thing now. They had to take this slow, not just because of her insecurities, but because of the risks to their friendship if they got it wrong. The trouble was, the more time she spent with Nathan, the more her feelings deepened into something more than friendship. Her attraction to him was even stronger than it had been all those years before, and even though she knew she should thank him again, lean over and give him a kiss, before disappearing inside, something else entirely came out of her mouth.

'Do you want to come in?'

'Do you want me to? I don't want you to feel like there's any pressure to invite me in.'

'You know I want you to, and I've wanted you to at the end of every single date, it's just that I'm scared I might have forgotten how to do this.' Her voice was low and she couldn't meet his gaze. She had to get this out now, or she might never be able to tell him, and she needed him to know before they went any further. 'My marriage to James was so lonely for years. There were always a thousand things he needed or wanted to do rather than spend time with me. In the end we were more like friends, maybe not even that.'

'Then he's an even bigger idiot than I thought.' Nathan took her hand. 'If I come in, I want you to know there's still no pressure. I would give anything to spend time with you, except if I thought it wasn't what you wanted.' She looked at him then and she could see in his eyes that he was every bit as attracted to her as she was to him, and that there was no putting the brakes on this time, because she didn't want to.

'Let's go inside.' Getting out of the car, she moved with an urgency she suspected wasn't entirely decent. Within seconds they were inside the house and as she pushed the door shut behind them and turned to face him again, he closed the gap between them, pausing for a moment.

Rowan reached up and put her hands on the back of his head, pulling his mouth towards hers and kissing him, making all the lies she'd told herself in over two decades with James painfully obvious. *Maybe everyone's love life died off when they'd been together a while. Passion didn't matter in a relationship. She didn't need to feel desired to be happy.* When Nathan kissed her, she knew what she'd been missing and suddenly her fingers were fumbling with the buttons on his shirt, her body arching towards his.

'Are you sure?' He whispered the words into her hair, but she didn't have to ask him if he felt the same. His feelings for her were obvious as their bodies pressed together.

'Oh, I'm sure.' Rowan helped him pull his shirt over his head, before slithering out of her dress. She was too much in the moment to feel self-conscious any more, or even remember that no one but James had ever seen her like this, or touched her the way Nathan was touching her. Except the truth was it wasn't remotely the same. When Nathan touched her it was as if electricity was pulsing through her body and when she kissed him again, she wouldn't have been surprised if fireworks really had been going off somewhere above her head. But she wouldn't have noticed even if they had been, because all she could see was Nathan and all she wanted was him, in a way she couldn't imagine ever wanting anyone else.

17

Nathan kept catching himself smiling for no apparent reason at all, except for the fact that he felt happier than he had in a very long time. He could have tried to convince himself that the look on his face was down to the fact that the bare bones of the kitchen construction had now been completed, or because he and Will had just signed on the dotted line to work with Rowan's father on another very lucrative contract for the conversion of five farm buildings on the outskirts of Port Tremellien into executive homes, which would start in the spring. But those things would have been a lie. The reason he was smiling was Rowan.

Nathan would never have believed they'd get this second chance after so many years, or that it would turn out that his feelings for her would never really have gone away, just been buried in an attempt not to compare every other woman he met to the girl he'd been in love with but had never had the chance to tell. It scared him a bit, because he knew there was a possibility of history repeating itself and getting over her might be impossible this time around. It had been hard enough the first time and even after she'd left Port Agnes with Katrina and Dean he'd held on to the hope that they might be able to pick up where they left off, but she'd ghosted him long before it was even a thing. Their kiss hadn't been his first, but it had meant more to him than any of the others and he hadn't been lying when he'd told her that he'd thought about it for a long time afterwards.

By the time she'd come back to Port Agnes to stay with her dad he'd moved on, telling himself that the only reason he still thought about her from time to time was because of how abruptly it had ended. If it hadn't been for Leo and Theo's friendship they might never have got to know each other again in any meaningful way, but watching Rowan with her children was like getting to know her on a deeper level. She loved them fiercely and she would do whatever it took to make sure they had fun, even if it meant making a fool of herself by falling off a surfboard over and over again until Theo was laughing so much that he stopped being afraid to try it.

At first, he was more than happy just to have her friendship. There was no denying that Theo's presence brought joy to his nephew's life, but spending time with Rowan had brought it to his too. After Nicole had left him, he hadn't been interested in anything serious. Women either seemed to want him to live up to some kind of bad boy fantasy that just wasn't him, or they suddenly viewed him as fundamentally untrustworthy when they discovered his past. He supposed it made sense in a way, but their assumption that he'd cheat on them because he'd been convicted of a crime was wrong. He'd never been unfaithful and, even in more casual relationships, he'd never dated two women at the same time.

Maybe his certainty that Rowan would never date him was what had allowed them to get to know each other properly. He'd just enjoyed hanging out with her and, even when they'd kissed again, he hadn't been sure it would go anywhere. He'd half expected her to pull out of agreeing to go on a date, but then it had happened and things seemed to take on a momentum all of their own. Spending the night together could have been a huge disappointment, but that couldn't have been further from the truth and he was as certain as he could be that she'd felt the same way. If it had been just a way of getting her husband out of her system, she wouldn't have asked him to stay the night, or been the one to reach out for him again the next morning. She made Nathan feel wanted in a way he would have found it hard to describe. Afterwards Rowan had made them breakfast, like they were a proper couple, and he hadn't been able to stop himself from saying what was on his mind.

'This has been incredible and I know there are all sorts of rules we're supposed to live by in the dating world, but I'm horribly out of touch with them. So I'm just going to have to come out and ask if you've thought about what happens next?'

'A fourth date?' She'd grinned then, standing in her kitchen wearing an oversized T-shirt, her tousled hair looking so different from when she put it up for work, and he'd had to force himself not to reach out for her again, because they needed to have this conversation. Suddenly she looked shy. 'Does this make me easy, spending the night with you so soon?'

'If you're easy then so am I, but we've waited more than twenty years and if you count all the times we've been out together since you got back, it's at least fifteen.'

'That sounds far more respectable.' She laughed, but he hadn't been able to join in.

'Does being respectable matter to you?'

'It has to in my job.' Shrugging, she reached for his hand. 'But I want to do this again, because it really has been amazing.'

He couldn't ask her for any more than that, and he'd understood when she'd suggested continuing to keep it just between them, '*at least for now, so we don't confuse the children*.'

It was early days and he respected that Rowan's children came first. There'd been a couple more dates and some get-togethers with the children, none of which had done anything to diminish how strongly he felt about her. Quite the opposite in fact. Now it was the end of October and half term week, and they had a series of things planned to do together in the first few days, before James arrived to see Bella and Theo, after which they were hoping to grab the chance for more time on their own.

It might be way too soon to tell anyone that he and Rowan were more than friends, but if he couldn't keep this stupid smile from spreading across his face every five minutes, it was going to give him away long before he had the chance to tell anyone anything. Shutting the door to the byre, he set off to the main house to pick up Leo. They were going to the cinema again with Rowan and her children and all he had to do was stop his face from revealing just how much he was looking forward to seeing her.

'Is there something you're not telling me?' Will gave him an appraising stare the moment he walked into the kitchen.

'What about?' Nathan did his best to attempt wide-eyed innocence.

'Whatever it is that's making you grin like a half-wit every time I look at you.' Will peered at him again. 'It's the same expression you used to get when you'd set me up for something and you couldn't wait for the pay off. Like the time you sprayed Deep Heat into my swimming trunks. When I got to the beach and put them on I couldn't get out of the sea for about half an hour, until my balls had stopped burning.'

'That was a classic, you've got to admit.' Nathan couldn't help laughing. The two of them had spent most of their teenage years thinking up pranks to play on one another. It must have driven their parents mad, but it had bonded the two of them even closer together.

'Stop trying to sideline the conversation, I need to know what you keep smirking at, because if you're thinking of trying the Deep Heat trick again, just be warned that I'm fully prepared to wax your new handmade kitchen units with fish oil in retaliation.' Despite his threat, Will was laughing too and part of Nathan was desperate to tell his brother the truth.

'I promise I'm not up to anything. Life is just good at the moment and who wouldn't be smiling knowing they get to spend the day with Leo?' Nathan winked at his nephew as he came into the room.

'Is the film really going to be in 3D?' The little boy's excitement was written all over his face. 'The dragons are going to look so cool in 3D.'

'They really are and I got you and Theo one of these each, so you can look the part.' Nathan handed Leo a sweatshirt depicting a scene from the movie they were going to see.

'Thanks, Uncle Nathan!' His nephew's smile was broader than ever as he turned towards Will. 'Look, Dad, it's got my favourite dragon on it. Theo's going to have one the same so everyone knows we're best friends.'

'That's brilliant, darling. I'll help you get it on, but I'm just wondering why your Uncle Nathan hasn't got one for him and his best friend?' Will raised his eyebrows, his lips twitching in the corners, even before Leo responded.

'Do you mean Theo's mum? Because she's definitely Uncle Nathan's best friend, he wants to sit next to her *all* the time.'

'Oh, does he now?' Will looked at his brother and laughed. 'I suppose that solves one mystery; now let's get you into this sweatshirt, Leo, so that you can both get off to meet your best buddies.'

Nathan didn't even try to protest. It wasn't a conversation he wanted to have in front of Leo and his face would probably just have given him away anyway. Instead he started to gather his nephew's things together and he'd just picked up the little boy's jacket when his phone pinged with the arrival of a text from Rowan.

I'm so sorry, but we're not going to make it to the cinema today. James has turned up at the cottage in a terrible state and I can't leave him. I don't know how it's going to affect our plans for the rest of the week, but I'll let you know when I do. Please tell Leo I'm sorry and that I'll make it up to him xx

Nathan stared at the message for a moment, trying to process all the implications and read between the lines. He'd known that James was coming for a few days, but it was Saturday and he hadn't been due to arrive until Tuesday. But Rowan's husband had shown up early and he was clearly upset. She had to make that her priority, the rational part of him understood that, but he still wished it wasn't true and the words 'I can't leave him' felt like they were written ten times larger than the rest. When he glanced across at Leo and saw the excitement on his nephew's face, he didn't want to tell him about the change of plans because he knew that look would disappear. Even though he had every intention of taking Leo to the cinema and giving him the best day possible, it wouldn't be the same without Theo and Rowan. Nathan didn't even want to think about how her text had left him feeling, because he'd sworn to himself, after Nicole, that he'd never allow his happiness to depend on another person. Yet in barely three months of having Rowan back in his life, Nathan had allowed it to happen. It was funny how little he'd learned from the lessons that life had tried so hard to teach him, but one thing was certain, the smile he'd been so desperately trying to hide had disappeared all by itself.

* * *

Rowan wanted to cry at how upset Leo must have been after her text. It had been bad enough seeing the disappointment on her own children's faces, when she'd told Theo they were staying at home, and Bella that she'd had to call Tiffany's mum to come and collect her. But the two of them had seen their father sobbing on the doorstep, so at least they understood why. Part of her wanted to kill James for turning up like that and not being able to hold it together in front of them. She'd never wanted them to witness anything that might tip a horrible situation into something truly traumatic. There'd been times after discovering his affair, when trying to hold in her pain in front of the kids had felt like it was going to kill her, but she'd done it. Now she'd been forced to let her children down, and hurt Leo and Nathan in the process, all because the man standing in front of her couldn't deal with the consequences of his own actions.

'I'm sorry, Row. I just had to leave and the Airbnb is booked out to someone else until Tuesday, so I had nowhere else to go.' There were tears in James's eyes, but she felt almost nothing as she looked at him. He'd cried when she'd confronted him about the affair, but all the tears had been for himself; at how hard he'd fought against his feelings for other men, until Euan had come along and he just couldn't do it any more. Despite her own pain, she'd felt his too and had understood how his upbringing had shaped the choices he'd made. But he'd never cried because of what he'd done to *her*, or the choices he'd taken away from Rowan with his lies. Far worse than that was the fact he'd never cried when he'd talked about not living with their children any more. The realisation had made it far easier to leave and take them with her. A part of her heart had hardened towards him and it was why she didn't feel as sorry for James as he did for himself. The situation was a mess and there were no winners, but what her children needed would outrank her sympathy for him every time. James had claimed to be desperate to see them on several occasions, but in the end he'd been able to wait a whole three months. Rowan could never have done that. Three days without her children would have felt like a lifetime, but three months would have been unbearable. She already knew desperation to see the children wasn't the reason he'd turned up early, she just needed to know what was.

'What do you mean you had nowhere else to go? Why couldn't you just stay at Membory Grange for three more days like you planned?'

'Everyone knows.' James gave a shuddering sigh and wiped his eyes with the back of his hand. 'I've been up all night, and this morning I just got in my car and left. Euan doesn't even know I've gone.'

'I see.' Rowan thought about her old friends and colleagues, and the parents at the school, some of whom would revel in any kind of scandal. She doubted that Odette and Pippa would have deliberately spread gossip, but they would have told their husbands, both of whom worked at the school. There had been rumours flying about as soon as Rowan had handed in her notice and James was never going to be able to shut them down forever.

They'd both known that this day would come. It was time the children knew the truth.

They were good kids, and they'd want their dad to be happy, something he was very far from being right now. The secret was clearly eating away at him and he'd found out the hard way that these things had a habit of coming out no matter how much you tried to keep them hidden.

'I had a parent come up to me on the last day of term and tell me how disgusting it was that I had the audacity to stand up in chapel and lead a service when I was living a life of such appalling sin. He said he was intending to talk to the new head and that he was going to ask the church to have me removed, not just from my job but as an ordained priest.' James let his head drop back for a moment, swallowing so hard against his emotions that Rowan would have sworn she saw them lodge in his throat. 'He told me it sickened him that I'd been allowed to teach the children about religious education and personal and social studies. He said I should be ashamed and the look on his face was one of pure revulsion.'

'There's only one person who should be ashamed and that's him.' Rowan might have a lot of feelings about her estranged husband, anger being right at the top of the list, but she didn't agree with anything that man had said to James. Shame was what had got him into this mess and forced him to hide who he really was. But he was excellent at his job, even if it had sometimes come at the expense of his own children. There was only one way to fight back against people like that man and it was with the truth. 'It was easy for him to make you feel ashamed because you're hiding the truth as if your sexuality really is something to be ashamed of. But it isn't. If you're honest and show the world that it's not something that needs to be hidden, you take away all power from people like that. You can't let him or anyone like him stop you from living the life you want to live.'

'So what, you think I should have stayed at Membory Grange and organised a parade down the high street, waving my rainbow flag as I went?' He gave a brittle laugh that didn't have a trace of genuine humour behind it.

'Maybe one day you should, but for now I think it would be enough to be honest with the people who really matter. Talk to the school and the church before that man does, and tell the kids while you're here.'

James widened his eyes and shook his head. 'You're not serious, are you? I can't tell the children, I wouldn't have any idea where to start and if I get it wrong it'll just make things worse.'

He seemed genuinely shocked that Rowan would suggest honesty, but when lies had caused as much damage as his had it seemed like the only solution. 'Telling the truth won't make things worse, it gives you a starting point for rebuilding your relationship with the children as who you really are. I think you'll get far closer to them that way than you ever will if you keep up a pretence. As for the school and the church, you can't control how they'll react, but they're going to find out anyway and it would be far better coming from you.'

'What if the children hate me? I couldn't stand it if they hated me.' He bit his lip and she forced herself to take a deep breath before responding. True to form, his question wasn't about the impact on them, but how their feelings might affect *him*. When they were together, his inability to put the children first hadn't been nearly so obvious, but since moving back to Port Agnes it was hard to believe she hadn't always seen it.

'They're not going to hate you. They're both good, kind kids and you saw how upset they were at seeing you like this. They just need to know you're okay and how much you love them. It's all kids ever really need to hear.'

'Will you be there with me?' His eyes were pleading and she nodded. Part of her wanted to force him to be the adult in this situation and to find the backbone he suddenly seemed to be completely lacking, but she had no idea if that was the right thing for Theo or Bella.

'I will, but there's someone else you have to tell, now that so many other people already know.' She held his gaze as he shook his head, fresh tears filling his eyes.

'I can't tell my father. I just can't. He'll never speak to me again.' James looked so much like Theo in that moment that her heart softened again and she reached out to take his hand.

'You've got to, because if you don't you're going to lose Euan and that would make everything we went through seem so much more pointless. I know you love him like you've never really loved anyone else.' She held up her hand as he tried to protest; denying it would have been an insult. 'Don't throw that away, because not everyone gets it. If you have to choose between Euan and your father, the way I see it there's only one choice. Euan loves the *real* you, your dad doesn't even know that person, but the least you can do is give him the chance to surprise you and tell you he's willing to try.'

'I wish I could have loved you the way I love Euan.' James looked at her for a moment and she knew he meant it. He'd said it before, when everything had first come to light. She'd known then that a big part of it was because it would have made things much easier for James. But hurting her hadn't been deliberate, she knew that too and now that they were this much further down the line, most of the anger she felt was about the impact on the children, not her. No matter what James's shortcomings might be and no matter how much discovering the truth had hurt, she'd always be grateful that he'd tried to love her, because without that there'd have been no Bella or Theo. That was something she didn't even want to imagine.

18

Leo's sighs since the start of half term had been deep and heartfelt enough to empty all the air out of the room and it was obvious he was missing his best friend like crazy. They might only have known each other for three months, but Leo had been waiting all his life to have a friend who got him in the way that Theo clearly did. Nathan had been lucky to have had that in Will, and he couldn't ever remember feeling bored in the school holidays as a result. Sometimes they'd fought like cat and dog, and taken things further than they would ever have done with someone they weren't related to, but they'd never been bored or lonely. Poor Leo on the other hand couldn't wait for the school holiday to be over.

'I don't understand why we can't meet up, just because Theo's dad has come to see him. Why can't we do stuff together like we do with his mum?' Leo turned what Nathan could only describe as puppy dog eyes in his direction and it was his turn to sigh.

'I'm sorry, Leo, but we can't do that. I know Theo's mum, we went to school together, but I've never even met his dad, so I can't just go round there and ask him if he wants to hang out.' Nathan shook his head when his nephew started to protest. 'Anyway, Theo's dad probably wants to spend time on his own with him and Bella. He hasn't seen them since the summer and he's only here for a week, which is more than halfway over already.'

'A week is ages.' Leo's bottom lip jutted out and Nathan was inclined to agree with him, because a week suddenly felt like a very long time indeed. When Rowan had explained the situation, he'd completely understood why she'd had to cancel getting together on the day James had suddenly turned up, but in the days that followed she'd cancelled more of their plans, even the things that had been arranged for after James had been due to move into the Airbnb.

'He's just not himself and I don't want to leave him on his own with the kids. They've already had to see him turn up here in a terrible state and I know they're worried about him. I'm not sure I trust him not to lean on them for emotional support they're not old enough to give.' Her voice on the phone had been barely more than a whisper, as if she wanted to ensure there was no way of anyone overhearing. 'I'm really sorry, Nathan, and I'd much rather be keeping the plans we made, but you get it, don't you?'

There'd been a note of desperation in her voice that he'd never heard before. He wished he could see her face in that moment, instead of talking on the phone, maybe then he'd have felt reassured that she was okay, but all he could do was ask the question and hope she'd answer him honestly.

'Of course I get it and I'm not here to put any pressure on you, especially as we said we'd keep things between us light for now. I just want to make sure you're all okay. It must be difficult seeing him again, after things ended... the way they did.' He'd wanted to ask her about that more than once, but he had to respect the pace she felt able to move at. He'd told her the truth about the reasons why his marriage to Nicole had ended, but the truth was there were parts of his past he was holding back from Rowan, so he had no right to expect her to tell him everything. He knew that James had been involved with someone else, but that was the extent of the detail. It hurt to think she might not fully trust him yet, but he understood why. Rowan knew only too well that in a village like this gossip could spread like wildfire with plenty of embellishment along the way, and God knows what version Theo and Bella would end up hearing. He just had to respect her privacy until she decided she could trust him and maybe by then he'd be willing to trust her with the unfiltered version of his own story. Maybe.

'I'm okay, but I'm not sure the kids are. Bella is barely talking to anyone because we ruined all the plans she had with Tiffany, and Theo is missing Leo like mad.'

'Leo's the same.' He'd wanted to tell her he was missing her too, but she didn't need any more pressure and he'd already promised himself he wouldn't add to her burden. 'I'm sure Bella will forgive you eventually and we can make it up to the boys once James has gone back to Membory Grange.'

'Yes, he'll be going back soon and then everything can get back to normal.' The way she was saying it was almost as though the words had only just occurred to her.

'If you need anything, you know where I am, and if Theo finds himself at a loose end at any point, all you have to do is give me a call.'

'Okay, I will and thank you for being so understanding, see you soon.'

'Yes, see you soon.' Nathan had managed to stop himself from adding that he'd be ready to drop any plans he had if Rowan suddenly found herself free to meet up. Their plans had only been sidelined for a week and they hadn't made each other any promises. It just felt weird because they'd been spending so much of their free time together, that was all, and because for some reason he couldn't shake the nagging feeling that James's visit was going to change everything. It meant he'd be every bit as glad as his nephew when half term was over, but it the meantime all he could do was try to make it a bit more fun for Leo.

'So if you can't see Theo, what's the next best thing?' Nathan looked across the kitchen. Will was standing behind his son, and he shook his head before Leo could even answer.

'I've told him you can't keep dropping everything to keep him entertained. You worked twelve-hour days most of last week so you could take some time off to make progress on the house this week.' Will ruffled his son's hair. 'You know Mummy's a bit tired at the moment, sweetheart, and that I've got to look after her, but Nanny will be back from her trip to Wales tomorrow and maybe we can go over to Tony and Marion's for a swim later, but Uncle Nathan really needs to get on with his house or it will never get finished.'

'I was planning to spend some time with Leo too, and I've had some of my own plans cancelled, so it'll be good to take a break for a few hours,' Nathan said, looking directly at his brother, who despite his earlier protestations seemed to slump in relief. Nathan might be tired from working long hours and then coming home to focus on the renovations whenever he wasn't with Rowan, but Will looked absolutely wrung out. He'd told Nathan that Heather had started having terrible nightmares about something going wrong with the baby and it was obvious neither of them had been getting anything like the amount of sleep they needed before she arrived. Leo was due a visit to London to see another specialist soon too, where he'd undergo tests that would give them an up-to-date insight on the progress of his condition. The appointment had been weighing heavily on Nathan's mind, so God knows how his brother and sister-in-law felt. He could tell without Will having to say anything when his brother was close to breaking point. He'd seen it before and the one time he hadn't stepped in there'd been catastrophic consequences. Nathan had promised himself he'd never let that happen again. And no matter how hard it was to face it, they didn't have forever with Leo. The only way Nathan could bear to live with that knowledge was to make the most of every opportunity he got. The renovations could definitely wait.

'So where's it going to be, kiddo? What can we do that will make being with me at least half as much fun as hanging out with Theo?'

'Hmm, that's going to be very hard.' Leo grinned for the first time and Nathan felt another rush of love for his nephew. He was the best kid any of them could have asked for and then the thought hit him all over again that one day Leo wouldn't be around. For a moment he forgot how to breathe, but he forced a smile as he waited for the little boy to make a decision. 'Please can we go to the adventure park at Camel Creek?'

'Definitely. Just give me fifteen minutes to grab a shower and we'll get on the road.' He gave his nephew a fist bump and locked eyes with his brother, who silently mouthed the words 'thank you' and Nathan shook his head. He didn't want any thanks for the things he did for Leo, nothing he'd ever done had felt like a sacrifice. This amazing little boy had taught him what love really was, and no price would ever have been too much to pay.

* * *

Three and a half hours later both Nathan and Leo were ready for something to eat. They'd been at the family adventure park for over two hours and thanks to the accessibility arrangements, they'd been able to go on all of Leo's favourite rides at least once.

'What would you like to eat?' Nathan knew what the answer to his question would be, but he asked it anyway.

'Can we go to The Donut Shack?'

'Anything for you.' He smiled at his nephew who looked suddenly serious for a moment.

'You're the best uncle in the world.'

'Is that right?' Raising his eyebrows, he smiled as Leo nodded. 'And why is that?'

'Because you take me to the best places and you let me have whatever I want for lunch, and don't make me eat any yucky vegetables.'

'Maybe I should.' Nathan laughed again at the look of disgust on his nephew's face. 'Okay, maybe not, I don't want to lose my crown as the best uncle in the world. Especially not when I was awarded it by the best boy in the world.'

'I'm not the best boy in the world.' Leo's eyes took on a glassy sheen. 'I can hardly even walk.'

Nathan's breath lodged in his windpipe, liked someone had grabbed him by the throat and tightened their fingers around it. But he had to get the words out, he couldn't let Leo think for one moment that the fact he couldn't walk more than a couple of steps, with the aid of a walker, affected how Nathan thought about him. 'Maybe not, but you can make your wheelchair go so fast that no one can keep up with it. If you beat me to The Donut Shack, not only can you choose whatever you want to eat, you'll officially earn the title of the best boy in the world. Ready, steady, go.'

Nathan shot off first and then slowed down, letting Leo draw level and move past him, before pretending to run as fast as he could but still not catching up. By the time they reached The Donut Shack, Leo was crowing with laughter and teasing Nathan about being so slow.

Nathan was true to his word and let Leo choose exactly what he wanted. It was a far from balanced lunch, but it wouldn't matter this once and he knew Will and Heather wouldn't mind.

'I don't think I can eat any more.' Leo put down his half eaten third doughnut and Nathan grinned, before picking it up and taking a bite.

'Well kiddo, you might be faster than me, but I'm way better at eating doughnut.'

'No you're not, it's only because you're much bigger and... I can see Theo!' Leo suddenly pointed in the direction of a group of people about thirty feet away and, as Nathan turned, he realised Leo was right. Not only that, but Theo was with his sister and both his parents. Nathan recognised James from the wedding photos that until recently had been on display at Tony and Marion's house. No one looking at James now would think he was doing anything other than spending a lovely day out with his wife and their children. Bella and Theo were slightly ahead of their parents, and Rowan and James were walking side by side. For a moment Nathan thought they were holding hands and, when he realised they weren't, he let go of a long breath he hadn't even known he was holding. Rowan had never said they weren't spending family time together, and he had no real right to feel so strange about the fact that they were, but he couldn't help it. They looked so right together, the four of them, like the kind of family the theme park might want to feature on its website.

'Can we go and see them?' Leo's eyes were round with anticipation and Nathan hated the fact that he was going to have to disappoint him.

'Remember what I said this morning, Theo only has this week to see his dad.' He held Leo's gaze until he nodded. 'It's not long at all and I think we should let them have that time together, by themselves.'

He'd been certain that Leo was going to put forward an argument, but to his surprise the little boy nodded again. Nathan had been just as certain that Rowan or one of the others would turn around and spot him and Leo, but they didn't. It was almost as if they were in a bubble of family life that made everything else fade from view. It was how it should be, and it was what Nathan had always hoped he'd have one day, at least before he'd gone to prison. Family should be a rock-solid unit that meant nothing else even came close. The thought that Rowan might want that back made his chest ache and he couldn't deny that his feelings for her had become far deeper than he'd intended to let them. He hated the thought that she might want James back, but if being part of a family was what she really wanted and she had the chance to make that happen, he had no right to raise any objection, no matter how much he might want to. All he could do was focus on the family he did have, one he wouldn't swap for anything.

'You know I said you were the best boy in the world?' He looked at Leo, who nodded for a third time. 'Well you're not, you're the best boy in the universe.'

'What if there are boys on other planets with four eyes and six arms, so they can see behind and in front, and they're strong enough to carry a car?'

Leo furrowed his brow. 'What if they can run faster than a cheetah, or fly, or read people's minds?'

'Even if they can it won't matter, you'd still be the best.' Nathan dropped a kiss on his nephew's head. 'Now if you've finished eating all those doughnuts, how about we try to find a ride that doesn't make us throw up?'

'Okay, but I bet there are some aliens on other planets whose sick glows in the dark. That would be so cool.' Leo started to laugh and Nathan couldn't help joining in. Seeing Rowan playing happy families with James might have felt like a punch to the gut, but this amazing little boy continued to give him a reason to smile, and to be the teacher he'd never even known he needed. Sometimes he had to accept there were things in life that he had no control over and try to find the joy in every moment. Nathan might never be as good as Leo at doing that, but he was determined to try.

19

It was one week into the half term before Christmas and yet it felt like months since Rowan had had a break. Spending most of half term with James had been tricky enough. She'd done it partly because he'd seemed so fragile, and somehow she found herself feeling she still owed him her support, but the biggest motivation for it had been the children. Spending so much time with James had been an attempt to fast forward them to a point where they could have some kind of friendship again, at least enough to co-parent amicably. She didn't want Bella and Theo to experience years of tension, like she had, or ever feel they had to choose a side. There'd been times since he'd arrived that the last thing she wanted to do was to spend another moment in James's company, but she'd pushed through the awkwardness and the sensation that her husband was a stranger she'd never really known at all.

It had undoubtedly been easier to let go of some of her anger towards James because of how she felt about Nathan. She had no idea yet if their fledging relationship would go anywhere. Even so, it had already taught her that what she and James had was just as wrong for her as it had been for him. He might have lied to her about his sexuality, but she'd lied to herself that she was happy with things the way they'd been. James had never made her pulse race the way Nathan did, and he'd never been able to make her laugh in quite the way Nathan did either. More than that, it was Nathan's ability to put Leo's needs above his own that set him apart from James. He was the kind of man she should have children with, and she was more certain than ever that whatever he'd done to land himself in prison, it hadn't been for personal gain.

All of that made it easier to be around James; he hadn't ruined their perfect life together, because they'd never had one. That didn't make everything between them plain sailing and Rowan's biggest concern was giving the children any mixed messages about how things might work out in the future. She didn't want them to be confused and it felt more and more like they needed to know that there was no chance of their parents ever getting back together. She and James had sat up talking until the early hours of the morning, three days after he'd turned up on the doorstep and he'd finally agreed to tell them the truth, before they inevitably heard it from someone else. Now that more people at their old school knew about James and Euan, it was only a matter of time before someone found a way to let them know. He'd promised to tell them before he left, but things hadn't gone the way they'd discussed at all.

'I've decided not to go back to Membory Grange.' James had made the announcement on the last day of the school holiday and Rowan had known that things were about to get even more complicated.

'You can't just quit. Where will you live?'

'I thought I could stay here for a while.'

Rowan was sure her mouth must have dropped open. 'What *here*, here? In this house?'

'Just until I can get things sorted. I promised to tell the children everything, and I will, but I don't want to have to rush it because I'm supposed to be back at school.' James had shifted uncomfortably from foot to foot, staring at the floor for a moment before finally raising his gaze to meet hers again. 'I've been thinking about applying to oversee my own parish eventually, somewhere they can accept my relationship with Euan, but I'll need to tell my father before I can even think about talking to the church.'

'You're going to tell your father that you're gay?' Despite her suggestion that he needed to be honest with the people who mattered, she'd felt certain that he'd back out of talking to his father. The fact that he was actually going to do it had shocked Rowan so much it had stolen the rest of the words she'd been about to say to James, that there was no way he could stay with her and the children at the cottage. She had a strong suspicion he wanted her support when he spoke to Michael, but it wasn't her job to be there when he needed her any more, and James couldn't just lean on her whenever he felt like it. She was glad he was finally showing some signs of doing more than wallowing in his own self-pity, but she needed to be careful that he didn't try to involve her in his problems. They weren't partners any more, except when it came to raising the children.

'I want to tell him, I really do, but I just don't know if I can. First of all, he needs to know we're getting a divorce.'

'He doesn't even know that?' She'd widened her eyes, astonished that James had managed to keep the news from his father for so long.

'He knows we're separated, but I got lecture after lecture from him about the seriousness of the commitment we made and how much damage us splitting up will do to the children.' James had sighed deeply. 'I think if he could just see how well we're managing this and how happy and settled the kids are, he might be able to accept the divorce and then maybe – eventually – he might be able to accept the rest.'

A surge of annoyance had made Rowan's scalp prickle for a moment. James had precisely nothing to do with how well the children were handling the break-up, or settling into their new life in Port Agnes, but that was him all over and he was never going to change. It was far easier to let it go now she knew she'd never have to live with him again, or listen to all the delusions he spouted in an attempt to cover up his inadequacies as a parent. He'd had that expression on his face too, the one that made him look so much like Theo it was impossible to harden her heart towards him as much as she knew she should. 'Do you really think he ever will?'

'Maybe not, but at least this way he'll know the children are okay and even if he decides he never wants to speak to me again, I want him to know that what I've done hasn't ruined their lives.' James had caught hold of her hand. 'Because it hasn't, has it? Please tell me it hasn't?'

'It hasn't.' His shoulders had slumped with relief and it had seemed in that moment as though he was finally able to put the children before himself. She'd been about to hug him, when he'd uttered a sentence that had made her mouth drop open in shock for a second time.

'I just hope my father can see it that way, because he's coming to stay next week.'

'Please tell me you haven't invited him to stay in *my* house.' Her voice had been icy and all the good work they'd done over the past week to forge some kind of new relationship had been perilously close to obliteration. If he'd said yes or even nodded, she wasn't sure she'd have been able to be responsible for her actions. So it was a very good job that James had shaken his head.

'I've booked him a room at the pub by the harbour, but I thought maybe we could invite him to spend a day with us as a family, so that he can see how well we're managing things with the children.'

The thought filled her with dread. Her father-in-law had always been a difficult man and Rowan had never had a close relationship with him, but she figured she could get through one day if it meant James felt ready to leave sooner rather than later. 'Okay, but one day and that's it. Are you going to speak to the children about Euan before your dad comes here?'

'I thought it might be better to wait until he's gone. I don't want them to have to keep it a secret and I'm not ready to tell him yet. If he's ever going to have the slightest chance of accepting this, I need to take it one stage at a time and tell him about the divorce first.'

That was how she'd found herself agreeing to allow James to stay with her and the children for another week, and it was also how she'd ended up agreeing to spend the first Saturday of the new half term with her soon-to-be ex-father-in-law. Michael had been ensconced in the room at the pub since Wednesday evening and James had taken him out for lunch the following day to explain that he and Rowan had decided to formalise the end of their marriage. It was a decision that had apparently been met with another lecture. Between all of that and the usual demands of school restarting, Rowan hadn't been able to spend any time with Nathan. It was something she felt guilty about, but the fact that she missed speaking to him so much worried her too. He was the person she wanted to talk to about everything that was going on more than anyone else.

She could have spoken to Pippa or Odette, but they knew nothing about her life in Port Agnes, or how it had been in the wake of her parents' marriage breaking up. They probably wouldn't have understood her willingness to give James the space to manage this in his own way, so that their children could manage it in theirs. She wanted Bella and Theo to be able to decide how much of their family life they shared with other people. She could probably have spoken to Bex and Toni too, but the children deserved to know the truth about what was going on between their parents before anyone else found out. She couldn't talk to her mother, because it would upset Katrina to know just how much the ending of her parents' marriage had affected her and how very differently she wanted to handle things.

Nathan was the one person she felt would understand the whole picture and who she was certain she'd could trust not to tell another living soul if she asked him not to, but it still felt wrong to tell him everything before the children found out about Euan, and she'd promised James she'd keep the truth to herself until he'd had a chance to tell them. If she saw Nathan she knew she wouldn't be able to keep everything in and the last thing she wanted to do was to lie to him. So for now, she was still keeping her distance, and fobbing him off. He'd seemed to understand when she'd told him that spending time with James was about working in partnership with her soon-to-be ex-husband for the children's sake, but she had to admit that she would have found it difficult if Nathan had suddenly started spending all his time with his ex-wife. Things were just a mess right now and she couldn't wait for this week to be over. Tomorrow she'd be spending the day with her father-in-law, and the day after that James had promised to tell the children and then go back to Membory Grange to sort things out there, before finding himself somewhere else to live. Just another forty-eight hours and it would all be over. That's what she kept telling herself. Then she could stop hiding in the office at pick-up time, to avoid bumping into Nathan.

'Ah, I was hoping I'd find you here.' Keith Hounslow pushed open the door to Rowan's office without knocking and she swallowed against the urge to tell him she had a door for a reason. Bex appeared behind him and mouthed the word sorry, but she knew it wasn't her friend's fault. If Keith wanted to see her, he would, and as chair of governors he seemed to think that gave him unrestricted access to her time *and* her office. Shooting a smile of understanding at Bex, she looked at Keith, trying to determine whether this was an official visit or another excuse to come and grill her about his granddaughter's progress and whether she thought the little girl might be showing exceptional ability in any area of learning. Avery was a lovely child and absolutely nothing like her grandfather, but her favourite part of the school day was undoubtedly spent in the playground rather than the classroom. Rowan had told Keith before that Avery had lots of friends and was very happy, but that didn't seem to be enough to appease him.

'Please, sit down, Keith and tell me to what do I owe the pleasure of a visit?' Rowan painted on a smile and hoped her words sounded far more genuine than they felt, because upsetting the chair of governors was never a good move for any headteacher and she really loved her job. The first time she'd realised it had been about four weeks after she'd started at Port Agnes Primary School. A lot of her friends in the teaching profession had wondered what on earth she was doing taking a job like that and part of her had wondered if it was the end of her career too. She'd never have dreamt of leaving Membory Grange for a job like this if her personal life hadn't caved in. The first couple of weeks had been the trickiest, and the more difficult parents and staff had taken up most of her time in those early days. She'd had to put Sarah Mayhew, the Year 2 teacher, on a written warning after she'd shared inappropriate views about immigration with the children in her class. Thankfully it had happened in front of a teaching assistant and Rowan had implemented an action plan to monitor Sarah's practice, leading her to resign three days later with no notice. It had saved Rowan from having to implement further disciplinary proceedings, but it had been time consuming to arrange initial cover and then set about finding a permanent replacement.

There were also certain parents who came in almost every day to complain about something and pupils whose behaviours had indicated that they needed more support than they were being given, which Rowan had the unenviable task of trying to secure funding for. Coming from the private sector, where money was far less of an issue, it had been challenging to say the least. She hadn't been sure how the staff would respond to her, especially after Sarah's resignation, but they'd pulled together, and the two part-time teachers who usually looked after Year 1 between them, both agreed to go full time temporarily until a replacement could be found. When Rowan had suggested, at a staff meeting, that the school put on a musical at Christmas involving not just the pupils, but the staff too, she'd expected sighs and groans. It was something that had happened at Membory Grange every year and it had helped everyone to really feel part of school life, but it would mean extra work and there was no endless pot of money to fund it. Much to her surprise a couple of the teachers, Lyra and Caden, had taken the idea and run with it, suggesting that they involve the parents as well and enlisting support from several of the teaching assistants.

During Rowan's fourth week as headteacher, Lyra and Caden had invited parents to come in and talk about how staging a very scaled down event might work. Nathan and Will had offered to help with set building and there'd been so much support for the idea that it had suddenly felt as though Rowan had always been a part of the place. That same week they had settled on *The Sound of Music* as the musical they'd be performing, and she'd heard the various classes beginning to practise the songs. Despite the fact that they'd staged a far more ambitious musical every year at Membory Grange, Rowan had never felt so much a part of it – as if she was right at the centre of school life in every sense – and that was when she'd realised just how much she loved her new job. It could only have happened in a school as small as Port Agnes Primary and that understanding had made her realise how wrong her friends had been. This wasn't a step back at all, it was exactly where she was meant to be. This wasn't the stop gap job she'd once considered it might be, it was where she wanted to stay and it was why she couldn't afford to upset Keith, no matter how difficult he might be.

'Did you know I've been chair of governors for seven years now, since long before my granddaughter even started here?' Keith peered over his glasses at her and she wondered how he was expecting her to react. Perhaps he was finally going to stand down, but she doubted it. He liked the sense of power the position gave him far too much.

'It's very generous of you to donate so much of your time to the school.'

'Yes, it has been a huge commitment, but it's worth it when I know the school is benefitting so much from my input.' He preened for a moment, before seeming to remember there was another reason why he was here. 'My point is that I was here for the last Ofsted visit and I met with several of the inspectors.'

'Right.' Rowan still wasn't sure where this was going, so she waited for Keith to elaborate.

'I was having lunch with a friend today at The Sands hotel and I recognised one of the inspectors from the last visit, while he was checking in. Afterwards I spoke to the receptionist, whose husband used to be one of my DCs, and she told me that the guest was staying until Thursday morning and that he'd told her that he was here for work.'

'Leaving on Thursday would fit with us getting the call on Monday and them doing the visit on the Tuesday and Wednesday, except it's very early to be checking in, isn't it?' Rowan didn't want to think that Keith might be right. She absolutely did not need there to be an Ofsted inspection next week. Not with the weekend she had to get through first.

'Exactly, but it makes sense that if the inspectors are coming from outside the area, they might want to come down early to make the most of the chance to do some prep work. It seems a very big coincidence for one of the inspectors to be in Port Agnes for work, and not be coming here next week.'

'It does, doesn't it?' Rowan could almost hear the thud as her heart sank to the floor. Not Ofsted, not now. She just wanted to get through everything with James and Michael, and then have a chance to talk to Nathan, but it seemed fate was determined to get in the way.

'The question is, are you ready?' Keith fixed her with the kind of intense stare she could imagine him using on the suspects he'd interviewed back in the day.

'Of course we are.' Rowan's forced smile was starting to hurt her face now, but she stood up and opened the door to where Bex was working at her desk. 'It looks like we might be getting notification of an Ofsted inspection on Monday, so I'm going to see how many of the staff are still around and do a quick briefing to remind them of the plan, that way we'll be as ready as we can be if the call comes.'

'Can I do anything to help?'

'If you don't mind staying to take some notes of the briefing and sending them out to any of the staff who aren't around, that would be amazing. It won't take long, I promise. I just want to make sure everyone feels confident. This is a great school and all we've got to do is show the inspectors that.'

Rowan said the last part with extra emphasis, to make sure there was no chance of Keith missing it. Even if she hadn't been headteacher for long, she was proud of Port Agnes Primary and she was determined not to let the school down. She just hoped she could find a way of keeping her personal life afloat at the same time, because the timing of the visit really couldn't have been much worse.

20

Rowan grabbed a couple of hours to review some of the school's policies on her laptop, after hosting lunch with her father-in-law. Even preparing for Ofsted felt like fun after spending the best part of half a day with Michael Bellamy. The man loved the sound of his own voice, but the constant droning had added to her tension headache almost as much as being on constant alert not to say the wrong thing. He kept asking questions about how they intended to make things right and end this 'selfish decision to separate' as he put it. When Rowan had brought up the fact that Michael hadn't had such a big issue with his daughter's divorce, it had just seemed to add fuel to the fire and he'd given an exasperated groan.

'Helena had no choice. She tried for two years to make it work, but that idiot she was with was seeing someone else and there were no children involved. There's no comparison to your situation and you two should be putting your family first, instead of giving up on your marriage on a whim.' James had just sat there looking uncomfortable, and in the end she'd had to be very firm with Michael and tell him it wasn't a topic for discussion in front of the children, reassuring Bella and Theo once again how much they were loved and that nothing would ever change that. She shouldn't have been put in that position and the children certainly shouldn't. They might have no idea about Euan yet, but she and James had been clear with them, in all the chats they had over half term week, that their marriage was definitely over. Much to her surprise, the children had seemed more relieved than anything. She'd been so taken aback, that she'd checked in with them again when she'd gone to say goodnight to them the evening after they'd been to Camel Creek.

'You know you can tell me if you're ever worried about anything, don't you? And that even though me and Dad won't be married any more, we both still love you more than anything and we're still going to be family, it'll just look a bit different.' She'd spoken to Bella first, who'd given her one of the slightly condescending looks she often seemed to adopt these days, a certain sign that the teenage years were only just around the corner.

'Yes, I know. There were loads of girls at Membory Grange whose mums and dads weren't together, and Tiffany's dad is really her stepdad. She's never actually met her real dad though, so she says that means he isn't her *real* dad at all and that Brett is.' She'd shrugged and Rowan had caught her breath. Her little girl seemed to have disappeared in front of her eyes and been replaced by someone wise beyond her years.

'Sometimes I forget how grown up you are.' Rowan hugged her for as long as she was permitted, before Bella extracted herself from the embrace.

'Well, I *am* growing up and soon I'm going to need to get a bra. Tiffany's already got her first one. We'll probably need to go somewhere with a lot more shops than Port Agnes. Tiff got hers from somewhere in Truro.'

The swift change of subject had signalled the end of their heart-to-heart about the divorce. Bella had far more important things on her mind and she was inseparable from Tiffany, whose presence in her life had made Port Agnes feel like home far sooner than Rowan had ever dared to hope. It had been a similar conversation with Theo, just without the mention of bras. She'd said the same thing to him about what the divorce meant and how they'd always be a family. The more sensitive and affectionate of her children, he'd reached out to take hold of her hand.

'It's okay, Mama, I'm not sad.' At the grand old age of seven he only ever called her mama these days if the two of them were alone, it would have been far too embarrassing to use the pet name he'd favoured until he'd started school.

'I'm really glad about that.' She'd squeezed his hand in response, but then he'd sighed.

'I'm just worried.'

'What about?' Her heart had hammered in her chest as she looked at him.

'That you might be sad.'

'Oh, darling.' She'd had to blink back tears as she desperately tried to swallow the lump that was attempting to permanently lodge itself in her throat. Not because she was sad, but because of what a wonderful, caring boy she and James had somehow created.

'I'm not sad at all. I really like it here and being close to your grandparents, and some of the friends I first met when I was younger than you are now, and I really like my job at the school too. So as long as you and Bella are happy, then so am I.'

'I am happy.' Theo had given her one of his gap-toothed grins as if to prove he was telling the truth. 'I really like my new teacher and Leo is the best best friend in the world. It's even better that I get to see him all the time because his uncle Nathan is your friend too. It's been nice seeing Dad since he came, but I've really missed them.'

'Me too, we'll see them really soon though and make up for all the plans we had to cancel, I promise. I want you to know how lucky I feel that I get to be your mum.' Rowan had leant forward and hugged her son close to her, hoping she hadn't just made a promise she wouldn't be able to keep. She was sure their new start would get back on track once James left, she just didn't want anything to come along that would stop that happening. They needed to start living their new normal and James staying at the house with them wasn't a part of that, so the sooner he got things straight in his own life the better for all of them. But right now he was looking at her as she shut the laptop lid down, a pensive expression on his face.

'So did you talk to your father about leaving Memory Grange?' Rowan knew the answer as soon as she looked at James's face. He'd been for a walk with his father after lunch, just the two of them, and it had been the opportunity he was supposed to use.

'I tried, but I just couldn't seem to get the words out.' James was wheedling now, wearing the same hangdog expression he'd worn when his father had been berating them both at lunch and he'd sat there and said nothing. She'd have bet that if she'd offered to talk to Michael for him, he'd have taken her up on the offer, but James needed to face up to this himself.

'For God's sake, James. You promised you'd do this if I let you stay and put up with your father for the weekend, so that he can see we're doing this the right way and putting the kids first, but I can't make this any easier for you.

You're the one who needs to have the difficult conversations with him and make it clear there'll be no going back on our decision. If that means telling him about you and Euan, I think you need to do it. He's not going to let this go otherwise. You've got to tell him everything.'

For a long moment James didn't say anything, until finally he nodded, sounding a tiny bit more determined when he spoke. 'I know you're right. He just doesn't seem capable of understanding how a marriage can just come to an end or that it's sometimes the best thing for everyone concerned, even the children, but I'll have to try and find a way of making him listen to me.'

It wasn't the kind of half-hearted determination she wanted him to have. He should have been utterly committed to proving to his father and more importantly to the children themselves that he would be putting Bella and Theo first, regardless of what else was going on in his life, but at least he wasn't making quite so many excuses for not facing up to the situation.

'We both know he's not going to be thrilled, but the kids are happy. I was terrified that they wouldn't be, but you've just got to keep going back to that because nothing else should really matter to him. You and I are adults and we've made all the decisions, the children had no say in any of this and they should be the only ones he's worried about.'

'I'm just worried that all he'll fixate on is my relationship with Euan. What am I going to do if I tell him the truth and he doesn't want anything more to do with me?' He was wearing that expression again, the one that made him look like Theo, almost like he knew the power it had over her, but she wasn't going to give into it this time. Only he could do this. She knew as well as James did that it was going to be tough and she understood why he didn't want to tell his father everything, but Michael was refusing to believe the marriage was over. It was time for the truth to come out. Way past time, in fact.

'If he decides to cut you off, that'll be his choice, but can you imagine ever not loving Theo or Bella because they've made a choice you don't agree with? I know I can't. If he isn't able to love you for who you are, he doesn't deserve to be your dad. Either way, you've got to be honest with your own children before it damages your relationship with them. It's time to put Bella and Theo first and then your dad can decide what's more important to him: a relation-ship with his son and his grandchildren, or his personal prejudice. You can't control that.'

'I know and I promise I'll talk to him tonight, after we've taken the kids to the fireworks.' James locked eyes with her and despite the promises he'd already broken, she could see he meant it. She was only just beginning to see what so many years of lying and living a double life had done to him. He used to be much stronger and more determined than this, she was sure of it, now he was scared and she suddenly felt far sorrier for him than she had before. It was probably why he seemed to have lost interest in the children too. He was so focused on keeping his secret under wraps that he'd lost huge parts of who he'd been in other aspects of his life. 'I know it's asking a lot, but do you think I could have a hug? I need to be fortified with all the strength I can get.'

'In the spirit of us staying friends I think I can spare you one. Just for heaven's sake don't ask me that in front of your father. The last thing we need is him getting any more ideas about how easily we could repair our marriage if only we tried a bit harder.' She laughed and put her arms around James. They might not have quite crossed every hurdle yet, but she was proud of how far they'd come. They just had to get through the next twenty-four hours and one of the most difficult conversations of James's life. Then they could all start to move forward with the clean slate she'd come home to Port Agnes to find.

* * *

The annual fireworks display at Pengarrack Castle, three miles inland from Port Agnes, took place on the weekend closest to bonfire night each year, to raise funds both for the upkeep of the castle and a local good cause. According to Bex, for the last two years that good cause had been the Friends of St Piran's Hospital, but the fundraising was only part of the reason why the event was so popular. The firework display was apparently the best in the area and there was entertainment, including folk music and dancing, as well as a parade of processional giants, with huge papier mâché heads, depicting characters from the gunpowder plot. It sounded like a spectacular event, but what Rowan was most looking forward to was the crowd. All those people would dilute the intensity of being in a room, or even worse in a car, with Michael and James, who was so tightly wound he looked like he might burst into flames long before the bonfire was lit.

'Tiff says I can stay over at hers after, is that okay?' Bella addressed the comment to Rowan, just as she finished parking the car.

'Yes, of course, as long as that's okay with her parents.' As far as Rowan was concerned, her daughter going for a sleepover was a good thing. Bella was far too astute at times and the last thing she wanted was for her to overhear a row between her dad and his own father, something that was almost certain to occur when James finally told Michael the truth. Theo would be easier to distract, he always had been, and the three-year gap between them might as well have been thirty for the difference it made in their awareness of the world around them.

'Don't you think she should ask her father?' Michael, who was sitting in the passenger seat, held Rowan's gaze. She'd always struggled with his barely disguised misogyny, hidden behind a belief that men should be the head of the household, but Rowan didn't need to try to appease him any more.

'No, I don't, because I'm the one who knows Tiffany's family and who's developed a good relationship with them over the past three months, but thanks for your concern.' She didn't even try to disguise the sarcasm in her voice and, as she turned to look at Bella, there was something close to admiration in her daughter's eyes, a look she hadn't seen for quite some time. There was a smile playing around the corners of James's mouth too. 'Right, come on then you lot, let's go and enjoy the evening.'

'Do you think we might see Leo?' There was so much hopefulness in Theo's tone that Rowan found herself crossing her fingers that they would, even though it might make things awkward if Nathan was there too. She was desperate to tell him everything that had been happening, but there was no chance of her being able to do that with Michael watching her every move like a hawk. She had the feeling he'd love to be able to pin the breakdown of the marriage on her. Absolving James of any responsibility would absolve him too, and she wouldn't put it past her husband to let his father come to that conclusion so that he could wriggle out of telling him the truth. They could both come out of this as victims of a woman who was incapable of upholding the principles they'd built their lives around, but she wasn't taking the fall for this one. She didn't care what her father-in-law thought about her, he'd told her more than once that she needed to stop being so opinionated and he clearly thought the opinions she had weren't worth his consideration. But she did care what her children thought and she wanted them to know that they would always come first as far as she was concerned. So, no, she wasn't going to be the fall guy for James or his father.

'I hope you get to see Leo, sweetheart. Did he say anything at school about coming to the fireworks?'

'He wasn't sure, because his mum might have the baby soon.' Theo's eyes were round with wonder at the concept.

'If he isn't here, I promise to set up a get-together soon.' She was sure Nathan would have texted if there was news about the baby, but then again maybe not. She'd told him she needed a bit of space to sort things out with James and he'd given it to her. She couldn't have it both ways. She should be focusing on her own problems and the upcoming Ofsted inspection, but it still hurt to think that something so big could be happening in Nathan's life without him telling her.

'I'm starving. Can we get hotdogs please, Mum?' Bella linked her arm through Rowan's as they got out of the car, but before she could answer Michael cut in.

'If you'd eaten more of the lunch your mother prepared for you, instead of trying to hide the vegetables on one side of your plate, you wouldn't be craving junk like that.'

'It's almost dinner time and we were always planning to eat here tonight, sweetheart, so of course you can have a hotdog.' She shot her father-in-law a look, silently daring him to make another comment, before turning back to Bella. Even if she might normally have made a comment about her leaving so much of her lunch, there was no way in the world that she was giving Michael the satisfaction of thinking she agreed with him about anything. 'I think they might even have candyfloss if you're still hungry after that.'

Rowan linked her other arm through Theo's and left James and his father to trail behind. Maybe they could bond over a discussion about all her short-comings as a mother. James needed all the brownie points he could get before he finally told the truth and she had to get away from Michael, before she tried to prise off one of the giant ornamental swords that were crossed above the main entrance to the castle and turned her father-in-law into the human version of candyfloss on a stick.

It took less than five minutes before Bella met up with Tiffany, dropping her mother's arm and linking it through her best friend's instead, the two of them speeding on ahead with Tiffany's parents, in search of hotdogs. It was the way it should be, Bella beginning to assert snippets of independence, but Rowan couldn't help clinging all the tighter to Theo.

'Don't grow up too quickly will you, sweetheart?'

He looked at her nonplussed for a moment and then broke into a broad smile, craning his neck to see past her. 'Look, it's Leo and Nathan.'

Turning to follow the direction of his gaze, she couldn't stop a smile from spreading over her face too. Within seconds the two boys were deep in conversation, as if they hadn't seen each other in weeks, instead of just the day before at school, and they had absolutely no interest in anything else going on around them now that they had each other. She had a sudden recollection of herself and Bex at school, constantly getting told off for talking in class, only to get home at the end of the day and call each other so they could start chatting again, not stopping until one of their parents roared at them to 'get off the bloody phone'. Having Bex back in her life was something else she was grateful for and, as soon as James had finally told his father about Euan, she was going to confide in her friend too. After all, during their secondary school days, Bex had been the one she'd confessed to about her crush on Nathan. And as cool as she'd been trying to play things, her crush was even more powerful now than it had been back then.

'It's good to see you.' Nathan's voice was low and the boys were far too engrossed in their own conversation to listen to what was being said. He was standing close enough to Rowan for them to be able to touch if they wanted to, and her skin was tingling in anticipation.

'You too, and I'm so sorry again about all the cancelled plans.'

'It's okay, I get it.' There was something in his expression that she couldn't quite read and suddenly the urge to touch him and make a connection was too much.

'I hope so.' She put her hand on his arm; it was a simple gesture but she hoped it conveyed more than her words. She could have told him that she'd really missed him, but it seemed like far too much too soon, even if her feelings were much bigger than they had any right to be. Despite that, she still wanted to be sure he knew the reason she'd pulled away recently. It had nothing to do with him and everything to do with what was going on in her own life. 'James will be gone by next week and even better his father will have left too. We're expecting an Ofsted inspection at school, but after that I'll have a lot more free time.'

'That's good.' Her face flushed with heat in response to his muted reply. She'd made it sound as if he was desperately waiting around for her, as though he had nothing better to do, when in truth their cancelled plans might not even have bothered him. Now she just wanted to backtrack and make it all sound far more casual.

'You've got far more important things to worry about than any of that, what with the baby coming. Theo said it might be any day now, from what Leo told him. So I know you're probably busy anyway and I didn't mean to suggest that—'

This time Nathan was the one to reach out and touch her, stopping her mid-sentence and tucking a hand under her chin to force her to look at him. 'Heather's getting as much rest as she can and there's no sign of the baby yet, but Will is on full alert. Whatever else is happening in my life I've always got time for you. You're the one who's got a lot going on and you've got a long history with James. So I understand if there are things you might want to try and work out.'

'No.' She shook her head vehemently. 'At least not in that way. We *are* trying to work out a way forward, but we definitely aren't getting back together. Absolutely no chance at all.'

'Well, that's good to know.' The clouded look lifted from his face and he smiled. 'It's just that when I took Leo to the Camel Creek adventure park. I saw the four of you together and you looked like every other happy family. If there was a chance you could still have that, I didn't want to be the one to get in the way.'

'There's nothing romantic between me and James and there never will be, but we are still a family. After everything that happened with my parents, it's important to me that we can still do things together occasionally, if that's what the children want. Would that be a dealbreaker for you?'

'Of course not; the children should always come first, but we're not at the stage where what I think really matters are we? No one even knows we've been seeing each other.' The clouded look was back and she wanted to tell him it wouldn't always be that way. She wanted to promise that once they were certain there was something to tell, she'd be open with the people who needed to know. Except she had to be sure she had the courage of her convictions before she made a promise like that. The thought of being anything like her father-in-law – bigoted and judgemental about other people's mistakes – horrified her. But the young girl she'd been was still somewhere inside of her, the one who didn't want to be the topic of everyone else's conversations. That's why she had to be as certain as she could be that things were going to work out between her and Nathan before it became public knowledge, otherwise they'd have to deal with everyone talking about them for no reason. Nathan was right, all of that was a problem for another day and it was easier for now just to change the subject altogether.

'We were going to get something to eat. Can I get something for you and Leo?'

'I'll do it.' Nathan started to step forward, but she held out a hand.

'No let me, please, by way of an apology.'

'Okay, thank you.' He smiled and she wished she could kiss him, but she settled for touching his arm again instead.

Rowan took the boys' requests for food and Nathan told her that anything would do for him. It summed up how easy going he was; a welcome change of pace from life with someone like James. She'd spotted Bex and her family watching the band performing; both sets of her parents were around somewhere too and she wanted to spend time with all of them, as well as Nathan and Leo, before she got consumed by work in the week ahead. Bella and Tiffany had come over to join her in the queue, ready for second helpings, having already worked their way through the hotdogs Tiffany's parents had bought them. Catching up with friends and family would have given her the perfect excuse to stay out of her father-in-law's way too. Unfortunately, Michael seemed to have a sixth sense, not to mention other ideas, and he appeared at her elbow, with James in tow, as she was queuing up at the food truck.

'I take it you've decided to indulge in some junk food after all?' She raised her eyebrows as she looked at Michael, deliberately using his own words against him.

'When in Rome I suppose.' He pulled a face.

'Hi Rowan, any chance you could grab a photo of me and Aidan with the baby.' The man tapped her on the shoulder as he spoke, and when she turned around she realised it was Jase, the headteacher of another primary school in a neighbouring village. They'd met at a training day run by the local authority and had hit it off straight away. Jase was with his husband, who was carrying their baby daughter in a papoose strapped to his chest.

'It's great to see you and of course I will.' She took the mobile phone from his outstretched hand.

'Thanks so much. It's Ellis's first bonfire night party and me and Aidan are the sort of parents who like to document every little moment, even her first bit of hotdog bun.'

'I'm all for capturing as many memories as you can.' Rowan smiled, but she could almost feel Michael vibrating with righteous indignation behind her. Jase and his beautiful little family looked perfect to her, but she knew they represented everything her father-in-law hated. She couldn't bear the idea of him saying anything to spoil Jase and Aidan's memories of their first bonfire night party with their daughter, so she needed to take the photograph as soon as she could. Snapping away as they gave Ellis a little bit of the hotdog bun to try, she held her breath, silently praying that Michael's agitated muttering wouldn't turn into something more. Handing the phone back to Jase, she waited as he looked at the photographs.

'Are they okay?'

'They're brilliant, thanks so much, Rowan. I owe you a coffee at the next training session.' He smiled at her warmly, but she shook her head and leant forward to give him a hug.

'Just save me a seat next to you, so I've got someone fun to chat to.'

'I will, every time! Have a great evening.'

'You too.'

They'd barely turned to walk away before Michael gave an exaggerated tut. When she didn't respond, he did it again and accompanied it with a huge sigh. She still didn't respond, but it was clear he wasn't going to let the moment pass without comment.

'Do you know those people?' It sounded more like an accusation than a question and she was relieved they'd reached the front of the queue, so that she had a moment to think about her response. Her almost overwhelming urge was to tell him that he could take his opinions and leave, but in a far less polite way.

Ignoring him until she'd given the server her order, and then moved to the end of the serving hatch to wait, Rowan took a deep breath and turned back towards Michael.

'So are you going to answer me or not?'

She looked at James, who'd gone back to saying nothing at all, just as he had when his father had been belligerent and rude at lunchtime. If he was going to leave her to it, she'd just have to deal with his father in her own way.

'Yes, I know, Jase, and I met his husband and their baby when they picked him up from a training session we were both attending. Aidan's a nurse at St Piran's and they're both lovely.'

'There's nothing lovely about two men bringing up a child. If they choose to live a life of sin that's up to them, but to bring a baby into it is disgusting.'

Rowan had been about to tell Michael that the only disgusting thing was his attitude, but Tiffany was too quick for her. 'Aidan looked after me when I broke my arm last year and he was so nice, and I bet he's really brilliant at looking after babies too.'

'You don't even know him, Grandpa, and you shouldn't say mean things about people, just because you don't agree with them. The vicar who comes to our school told us that in assembly.' Bella chimed in to back up her friend, folding her arms in front of her chest in an act of undisguised defiance. Rowan had never been more proud of her daughter.

'You've got no idea what you're talking about, but at least you've got an excuse. You're silly little girls who don't know any better.' Michael turned towards his son. 'If your wife isn't going to instil decent morals into your children, you need to double down on making sure that you do. Otherwise who knows what kind of life they'll end up living.'

'I...' James was still just standing there, allowing his father to speak to the children as though they were nothing, and Rowan wanted to shake him and tell him that he needed to stand up to Michael once and for all. Except she was acutely aware of Bella and Tiffany standing right behind her, and she didn't want to upset them more than they already were. She needed to say something, to let the girls know they'd done absolutely nothing wrong. As for what Michael had said about her parenting, she couldn't give in to the rage that was bubbling away just below the surface, otherwise she might have started screaming in his face. There was no way everything could just be left unsaid, though, and James clearly wasn't going to step up and be the father his children needed. Gritting her teeth she turned towards Michael, trying to work out what to say that would leave him in no doubt that he'd crossed a line she wouldn't tolerate but which wouldn't cause the girls any more distress. Just as she opened her mouth to speak, the server called out their order.

'Number eighty-five is ready.' As she collected the order, Rowan allowed herself to take a long steadying breath, before handing the girls what they'd asked for. Her priority was making sure they were okay after what had just happened; her vitriol for her father-in-law could wait.

'I'm really proud of you both for what you said about Aidan and Jase.' Her words were met with a loud snort of derision from Michael, which she chose to ignore, focusing on the girls instead. 'But Dad and I need to talk to Grandpa about something. Why don't you go over to where Bex and her boys are standing, with Tiffany's mum and dad, and I'll come and find you in a little while.' She looked at Bella, who for once didn't debate the decision, seeming to understand. Rowan still had the food she'd ordered for Nathan and the boys, but she wanted to take it to them herself, once she'd finally had the chance to confront Michael about his attitude and give James one last chance to step up.

'Okay, see you in a bit.' Bella planted an unexpected but very welcome kiss on Rowan's cheek and headed off in the direction of her friend's parents.

Moving away from the food stand, she looked at James again. 'Are you going to say something to your father?'

'Of course he isn't because he agrees with me. He knows as well as I do that the Bible says—'

'I don't agree with you.' James cut his father off, but he kept his eyes firmly fixed on the ground.

'You're telling me you think it's okay for two men to live together and raise a child?' Rowan could see the tendons bulging in Michael's neck and she reached out and took James's hand, suddenly nowhere near as certain that now was the right time for him to come clean. She needed to tell him that it was okay if he wanted to wait.

'You don't have to do this—'

This time he cut Rowan off. 'Yes, I do.'

Squeezing her hand once, he let it go and turned towards his father, finally raising his eyes from the ground. When James spoke again, his voice was so low she had to strain to hear. 'The reason I don't agree with you is because the divorce is my fault. Rowan had no choice but to end the marriage when she found out I was in a relationship with someone else. His name is Euan and I love him.'

For a moment Michael didn't speak, his face turning puce and the tendons that had been straining in his neck looking like they might be about to snap.

'Aren't you going to say anything?' There were tears in James's eyes, even before his father finally answered, spittle flying from the corner of his mouth as he fired the words at his son like bullets.

'If that's true, I don't ever want to see you again. No son of mine would choose to live a life as abhorrent and sinful as that.'

'It's not a choice, it's who I am and it's not abhorrent. Euan makes me happier than I ever knew it was possible to be. Please, Dad, just try to understand.' James sounded desperate and a few people standing close to them had already turned to look in their direction. For once Rowan didn't care. She wanted to hug James and tell him how proud she was of him for finally finding his voice with a man who'd bullied him for years. It was suddenly clear why the James she'd known had disappeared more and more over the past few years: he'd been hiding in plain sight. Now he was standing facing his father and his greatest fear.

'How dare you take on the role of chaplain when you were living like that. I'm ashamed to even know you, let alone to be your father.'

'How can you talk to your son like that? You're supposed to love your children unconditionally and if you were any kind of father—'

'Row, don't.' James put out a hand to stop her. His voice was weirdly calm, all of a sudden, as if the realisation had hit him that trying to make his father see sense was pointless. 'Nothing you say will change his mind. Just go, Dad, if that's what you want. Walk out of my life and don't look back.'

If Rowan hadn't already been on her feet she might have stood to applaud James. She'd never have believed he had it in him to stand up to his father like that, but just as James had predicted, Michael was completely unmoved at the prospect of losing his son.

'Oh don't worry, I'm going, and when your sin catches up with you and you realise what you've done, don't expect me to pick up the pieces. You've made your choice and you can live with the consequences.' Michael pushed past James, shoving him hard enough for him to almost lose his footing, before disappearing into the crowd as if he'd never been there. If Rowan hadn't seen the confrontation with her own eyes she wouldn't have believed that James had finally found the strength to be honest.

'I'm so sorry he reacted like that, but you were brilliant.' She tried to hug him, but it felt as though he was made of stone and his voice when he spoke was almost robotic.

'We both knew how he was going to react.'

'It doesn't matter. You heard the way Bella and Tiffany leapt to Jase and Aidan's defence. Bella's a great kid and so is Theo, they won't think any differently of you. You've got them and Euan, and that's all that matters.'

'Except I don't think I have got Euan any more.' The tears that had been threatening to overwhelm James were now falling uncontrollably. 'I didn't leave Membory Grange just because of what that man said to me. When I told Euan about what had happened, I said we needed to double down on making sure that no one ever saw us together. He told me he couldn't keep sneaking around any more and living a lie. He said that he didn't want to be my dirty little secret, and that if I didn't want to tell anyone we were together then maybe we shouldn't be. I couldn't face being honest, so I just left without telling him. Now he won't take my calls, and I've hurt you and the kids. I've messed everything up and everyone would be better off without me. I should just take myself off somewhere and—'

'No.' She put a hand on his chest and then pulled him towards her, holding him tight for a moment. 'Don't you even dare to say those words out loud. The children are happier here than I ever thought they would be, but all of that will change if you do something stupid, and nothing your father says is worth that. Believe me.'

'I just want to go home, but I don't even know where that is any more.'

'Right now it's wherever the kids are, at least until you can get your own place sorted and work out what's going on with Euan. I'm taking you home with me and I'm not leaving you on your own until I can be certain that you're okay. Do you hear me?' She gripped his shoulder until he finally looked at her and nodded. 'Right, wait here, I'll only be a few minutes.'

Rushing over to find Bex, she told her friend that James was really unwell and asked her to take the food she'd bought over to Nathan and the boys and explain what had happened. She also asked Bex if she could keep an eye on Theo until one of her parents came to collect him, before letting Tiffany's parents know she had to leave and checking that they really had offered to let Bella stay over. After that she rang her mum asking if Theo could have a sleepover at her place, using the same excuse about James being ill and telling Katrina that she didn't want Theo to catch whatever his dad had got. No one had better organisational skills than a headteacher in a crisis and, just as she'd promised, she was back at her husband's side within five minutes.

James hadn't moved from the spot where she'd left him and she had to put her arm around his waist to usher him back to their car. She had no idea how Michael had got back to Port Agnes, and she didn't care. Her only concern right now was stopping James from doing something that would hurt their children a million times more than the break-up could ever do. She just couldn't allow herself to think about Nathan, or how he might react to what Bex told him about why Rowan had needed to leave. Spending time with Nathan was the only time in years she could remember putting herself first, but right now her happiness had slipped back down to the bottom of her priorities. All she could do was hope it didn't slip off the list altogether.

21

Nathan had seen Rowan embrace her husband from where he'd been standing waiting with the boys. It was obvious James had been upset, he'd been gesticulating wildly at one point and had slapped the palm of his hand against his forehead several times, before Rowan had pulled him towards her. He couldn't hear what they were saying, but that didn't stop him creating his own subtitles for the conversation. James must have been saying what an idiot he'd been, and how he'd do anything to win her back. Rowan would have told him at first that there were no second chances, but then James would have played his trump card and reminded her that being together was best for the kids.

The children were everything to her, that much was obvious, and it was one of the many reasons why he liked Rowan as much as he did. She put children at the centre of every single decision she made. Not just her own children, but all of her pupils too. That was why, when Will had asked Nathan if he had time to fill in the questionnaire that the inspectors had sent out, three days after the firework party, he'd written down every wonderful thing he could think of about Rowan's leadership and the ethos she was working so hard to embed. He couldn't allow how hurt he'd been, when she'd sent Bex to talk to him, to affect how he felt about the good things she'd done. None of that changed the fact that Rowan was an excellent headteacher, who had worked tirelessly to make Leo's transition to using a wheelchair at school as seamless as possible.

When he'd got home on the night of the fireworks party, he'd resisted the urge to text her and ask how her husband was, and he'd refused to allow his thoughts to drift to what Rowan and James might have been doing at that point, or the promises they might be making one another about giving things another try. His prison sentence had taught him some lessons he wanted to forget, but it had also taught him some useful skills that he was determined to hold on to. One of them was the ability to shut down his thoughts if he needed to. When the cell door had first closed behind him, he'd realised that this awful place, filled with desperate screaming voices, would be his home for a minimum of six months. His breath had quickened and he'd wanted to claw at the door, and at his throat. He wasn't sure how he'd lasted that first night, or the next, but over time he'd learned to send his mind somewhere else, back home to Cornwall and the big skies that seemed to stretch on forever. He'd picture Leo's laugh, or his mother in the kitchen cooking up a storm, the way she always did when she needed to relieve some stress.

Ever since the fireworks he'd been using that same technique to avoid thinking about Rowan, to stop himself imagining her telling James that she was willing to go back to Membory Grange and give things another try. Her relationship with Nathan had barely begun, and he didn't really expect to be able to compete with what she and James had. He wished there'd been an opportunity to find out where things might have gone, but what he'd regret even more, if she left Port Agnes, was losing her friendship. Losing Theo would break Leo's heart too, and he didn't want to face that possibility until he had to. Eventually, just before midnight, a text message had finally come through from Rowan.

> I'm so sorry I had to run out on you and the boys and I know I've been doing a lot of that lately. James isn't in a good place and he needs to stay with me for a bit longer. Can we meet after the inspection is over and James has gone back to Membory Grange to sort things out? I'm not sure how long that will be, but I'll explain everything properly then. Sorry again and thanks for being so understanding xx

He'd stared at the message for a moment, wondering how to respond. In the end he kept it simple.

Don't worry about me. You've got more than enough
to think about right now xx

He turned his phone off after that and tried to sleep, but his ability to force
the images of Rowan and James out of his head didn't extend to his dreams
and it had been a relief to wake up from another fitful sleep and see sunlight
streaming through the window.

The next day he'd worked flat out on the renovation, before starting work
at 6 a.m. on Monday on the internal fixings of a holiday cottage that he and
Will had been building for one of their clients, so that he could finish in time
to pick up Leo from school. The playground was abuzz with parents talking
about the inspection and discussing what they'd put on the questionnaires
circulated on behalf of the inspectors. One woman said she was being interviewed the next day, which seemed to give her minor celebrity status amongst
some of the other parents, and Nathan tried to suppress a smile. This was how
life worked in Port Agnes, small things became big news and he'd had his own
unwanted brush with infamy as a result. He was far happier blending into the
background these days, but people still remembered what had happened.

'Ah, Mr Lark, Leo said it was you who'd be picking him up today.' Lyra
Blythe, Leo's class teacher, looked disappointed to discover that the information he'd given her was spot on.

'Is there a problem?' Everyone at the school knew they could share any
information about Leo with both Nathan and his mother, even things that
would normally be reserved for a child's parents. It was in Leo's care plan,
because they did so much to support Will and Heather, and it meant Nathan
was finding it hard to imagine a scenario where his presence at pick-up would
cause an issue.

'No, it's just that one of the Ofsted inspectors asked if they might be able to
speak to Leo's parents about how well they feel the school meets his needs.'

'My brother was snowed under today, so he asked me to fill in their questionnaire earlier and I sent it back in. But if they still need to speak to someone, I'd be happy to talk to them, if they're okay with it being me?'

'I can't see why not, you're here at least as much as his parents and Leo is
lucky to have such a loving family.' Lyra's smile was genuine and it crossed his
mind for the first time how attractive she was, and how often she shot a smile
in his direction, or let her hand linger on his arm for just a bit longer than was

necessary. He'd been so closed down to the idea of being involved with anyone again that he hadn't even noticed, but Rowan had woken him up. The trouble was now no one else could compare to her and, if she left, he'd be back to closing off that part of himself again.

'I'll let the inspectors know you're happy to have a chat, if you don't mind waiting?' Lyra smiled again and he nodded.

'Of course not, but what about Leo? Can I just take him into the meeting with me?'

'There are a few other parents meeting with inspectors, so Mr Pengelly is doing an arts and crafts workshop in the Year 6 classroom until the meeting is over. Theo is already in there, so I'm sure Leo will be happy to go along too.'

'He's always happy when he's with his best friend.' Nathan smiled, pushing the thought of what it might do to Leo if Theo disappeared out of his mind. Those were worries for another day. Right now he had one job to do and that was to get Rowan the recognition she deserved. Maybe if she saw how much her work was appreciated, even after such a short time, it would give her more motivation to stay. If that happened, neither he nor Leo would have to face up to the prospect of losing Rowan and her son.

* * *

The meeting with the inspector, a warm and friendly man, had gone really well. He'd been nothing like the kind of inspectors – of the income tax and VAT variety – who Nathan had encountered on far too many occasions in the run up to his prosecution. He'd talked to him about how Rowan was helping to create a culture of inclusion at the school, securing funding to make the green area accessible immediately after her appointment, and before she was even officially due to start. He talked about how she'd supported other fundraising initiatives and secured support from the governors and PTA to get more sensory equipment for the playground, including a wooden archway with stained-glass-style plastic panels, wide enough to be wheelchair accessible, and an area for water play. There were also plans to develop a sensory garden, all of which allowed Leo to play outside and feel included, even though he wasn't able to join in with many of the more traditional playground games.

Rowan and Lyra had also arranged for a guest speaker, who was part of the UK paralympic swimming team, to come and talk to the whole school about her experiences. Practical adaptations had been made for Leo too and it was clear, as Nathan had told the inspector, that none of those things were an afterthought that had to be requested by the family, or done just to tick a box. He and the inspector had been laughing together like old friends by the end, and he'd even given the man some advice on how to deal with the crumbling render on the back wall of his house. He hadn't realised quite how long the meeting had gone on for, until he went through to the Year 6 classroom to find Leo and had discovered that the only other child left there with him was Theo. Mr Pengelly looked delighted to see Nathan, shooting him almost as warm a smile as Leo's class teacher had done an hour earlier.

'Oh brilliant, you're all done. How was it?' Mr Pengelly lowered his voice as he asked the question, casting his eyes around the room as though he expected one of the Ofsted inspectors to spring out from underneath a desk at any moment.

'Very well. I told them how great you all are with Leo.'

'He's the great one. I wish all the kids were as much of a joy to be around as he and Theo are. It's been heaven for the last twenty minutes, just the three of us.' Mr Pengelly looked over his shoulder again, laughing as he did. 'Yeah, I probably shouldn't say things like that out loud at the moment, should I?'

'Maybe not.' Nathan laughed too, before giving the teacher a more serious look. 'How do you think the inspection is going overall? Have you got any idea yet?'

Nathan wanted to ask how Rowan was holding up too, but it might have seemed overly familiar and made Mr Pengelly question just how close Rowan and Nathan's relationship had become. It wouldn't take much to trigger the kind of gossip he knew she was desperately trying to avoid, especially now that James was back on the scene.

'Mrs Bellamy has just been in to give a briefing to the rest of the staff, mostly about the outcomes of the teaching observations, but the two of us are catching up once I'm done here. As head and deputy, it's probably our necks on the line more than anyone else's if we don't get the outcome everyone is expecting. If it's anything less than the good grading we got last time we could get the chop.' He'd lowered his voice again, shooting a glance towards the two boys this time, but they were far too busy splashing brightly coloured paint onto a huge piece of paper.

'It sounds like you're both really busy and if it's okay with Mrs Bellamy...' Nathan paused for a moment, something about using her married name feeling far more poignant since James's arrival. 'I could take Theo back to our place so that he can hang out with Leo, until she finishes work.'

'I'm sure she'd really appreciate that and I know I would, because it means we can get stuck straight in to reviewing what's happened today. Bella's already gone home with one of her friends, so that would mean poor old Theo being left here on his own otherwise.' Mr Pengelly smiled again. 'Can you keep an eye on the boys for two minutes and I'll go and see what she says?'

'Of course.' Nathan watched the deputy head disappear, and wondered if he could get away with asking Mr Pengelly if he knew why Theo hadn't been picked up by his father. But that would definitely have been overstepping the mark.

'She said you're an absolute lifesaver and that she'll come and pick Theo up from your place. She won't be any later than seven, even if I have to shove her out of the door at half past six myself!'

'Great. Can you let her know I'll make sure the boys have dinner by then too. I really hope the rest of the inspection goes well for you all.'

After a bit of negotiation with Leo about bringing their part completed painting home to finish, the three of them headed off. They were two minutes away from the house when Nathan's phone started to ring. It was Will.

'Are you still at the school?' His brother's voice sounded strained and Nathan's scalp prickled in response.

'We're just on our way back now. Did you get my text saying I had to speak to one of the inspectors?' He felt guilty that his late arrival home with Leo might have made his brother or Heather worried, but he'd checked that the WhatsApp message he'd sent had been read before he'd gone into the meeting.

'Yes, and I'm glad you got the chance to talk to them about how great the school is. It's just...' Will hesitated for a moment. 'Are you on speaker phone?'

'Yes, and I've Theo with me too. Rowan's working late.'

'Okay. Well, we're off to see if we can find a stork in Port Kara, if you know what I mean.' Will might have been talking in riddles, but Nathan knew exactly what his brother meant and he also knew why he hadn't just come out and said that Heather was in labour. Leo could be a worrier, especially when it came to his mum or anything to do with hospitals. So they'd agreed it would be better not to let him know that the baby was on her way until she'd arrived safely. Port Kara was code for St Piran's, the hospital that was located there, and the stork was code for the midwives who'd be bringing the baby into the world.

'Amazing. Has Mum gone with you?'

'Do you seriously think I could do anything to stop her?' Will laughed.

'Not a chance. Take care and good luck. Love you all.' The words caught in Nathan's throat as he thought about how scared his sister-in-law probably was. She'd been paranoid the whole way through the pregnancy that, despite the frequent scans, there'd be something that had been missed. Nathan had seen her crying in Will's arms, not long after they'd discovered they were having another baby, and telling him she couldn't cope if she had another child with a life-limiting condition, because she couldn't face the prospect of losing them both. He'd watched as his brother had reassured his wife, but he'd seen on Will's face that he was every bit as scared as she was. All he could do now was silently pray that their fears would be unfounded.

'Love you too, bro, and give Leo a big hug from me.' Will hung up the phone, as Nathan pulled into the driveway and stopped outside the main house, turning to look at his nephew who had a quizzical expression on his face.

'What's a stork?'

'It's a big white bird.'

'Why are Mum, Dad and Nanny going to look for one in Port Kara?'

'Because looking at beautiful birds is a nice relaxing thing for your mum to do before she has the baby.'

'I suppose so.' Leo wrinkled his nose. 'But I'd much rather look for dolphins or seals, if I was in Port Kara.'

'Me too, but do you know what would be even better?' Theo nudged Leo's arm. 'Imagine if you saw a shark, or a killer whale. That would be so cool.'

They were off then, the boys, talking about all the animals it would be way cooler to spot than a stork. It was a brilliant distraction from worrying about Heather. Nathan took the boys up to the main house, and set about making their dinner as they continued with the artwork they'd started with Mr Pengelly, adding in some of the animals they'd decided might one day grace the beach at Port Kara. They'd wanted to carry on with it after dinner and, by the time there was a knock on the door, just before 7 p.m., there'd been a hippo and a giraffe added to the picture which could now give the passenger list on Noah's ark a run for its money.

'Hey.' Nathan kept his greeting casual when he opened the door to Rowan, but the sight of her still made him catch his breath. She was beautiful, despite the dark circles under her eyes that indicated a run of sleepless nights. He'd texted to let her know he was up at the main house and what was happening with the baby, and the concern was evident on her face, despite the brevity of her response.

'Any news?'

'No, and I check my phone at least twenty times a minute.' He laughed as her eyebrows shot up behind her fringe, and he stood back to let her in to the house. 'You might think I'm joking, but I'm really not.'

'I'd be doing that too. I can't wait to be an auntie one day, but with Charlie living his best life travelling around the world I could be a very old lady before that happens.'

'Maybe another baby first instead.' Nathan hadn't meant for the words to come out of his mouth, but she and James wouldn't be the first reunited couple to have a 'sticking plaster baby' in an attempt to get their marriage back on track.

'Another baby?' She blinked a few times in quick succession, as if she was trying to make sense of a far more complex sentence and then she laughed. 'For a moment there I thought you were making me an offer.'

He wanted to laugh too, but he couldn't. He seemed incapable of playing it cool any more and waiting for her to tell him what was going on with James, because not knowing what was happening was almost as torturous as waiting for news about the baby, and suddenly he wasn't capable of doing both things at the same time. 'I don't think James would be very amused by me even joking about that. Not if you two are trying to make a go of things.'

'We're not. Oh God, Nathan, I'm so sorry, I've messed you about so much and I know that it must be what this looks like, but I promise you I've got no intention of giving things another go with James.' She took a step towards him and he wanted to kiss her so much that he had no idea how he stopped himself, but somehow he did.

'Does James know that?'

'Of course he does and even if I desperately wanted to get back with him, which I absolutely do not, I know without a shadow of a doubt that it isn't what he wants either.'

'Look, it's none of my business and I've got no right to even ask you any of this really, it's not like we made each other any promises. But I really like you and I hope at the very least that we've become good friends again over these past few months.' He waited as she nodded. 'Okay, so as your friend, I hope you won't mind me saying this, but I think you're wrong. When I saw you all at Camel Creek you looked like the perfect family and then at the fireworks it was obvious how devastated James is by everything that happened. He still loves you and I can't blame him for that for one second.'

'Even if that's true, you think that means I should just give him a second chance?' There was an edge to Rowan's voice now, but they were still in the hallway, far enough away from where the boys were sitting not to be overheard. Nathan had no idea why he was pushing it the way he was, because the last thing he wanted was for Rowan to give James another shot, but it would have made him a hypocrite if he completely closed down the idea of second chances.

'Only you can decide if you think he's worth that, but I have to believe that second chances can work out, or I shouldn't even be back living in Port Agnes.' Nathan sighed. 'I think any man who would risk losing you is an absolute idiot, but we've all done stupid things in our lives and if there's even a chance that James is the person who can make you as happy as you deserve to be, I want you to take the chance. As your friend.'

'What about if we're more than friends?' She held his gaze and the air between them seemed to fizz as she waited for him to respond.

'If we're more than friends, then of course I don't want you to go back to James, but I don't know that we are. It doesn't matter how much I want us to be a proper couple, it doesn't mean anything unless you feel the same way.' He could so easily had taken a step forward and kissed her, but he kept his feet rooted to the same spot on the ground. 'We've seen each other a handful of times without the children and it's been great, but it's also been a secret and I'm not sure why that is. Not if you're really certain there's no chance for you and James.'

'I told you before, it's because of the children and...' She hesitated for just a moment too long, a look flickering across her eyes that seemed to confirm all his worst fears.

'Because you'd be embarrassed if people knew you were with someone like me. Someone who's been to prison. What on earth would they make of you then?' His tone was more resigned than bitter, because he'd been here before, and he didn't wait for her to answer. 'Nicole couldn't live with the prospect of me having a criminal record and we were married, so I don't expect you to risk your reputation in a village like this, where gossip is the lifeblood that seems to keep half the population going.'

'That's not true, Nathan. There might be a handful of people who think like that, but that's on them. The vast majority of people can see all the good you do for the community and they like you for who you are. They don't care about one mistake that you more than paid the price for.'

'So why the insistence on sneaking around then? I get that you don't want the children to know, when we're still not sure what this is, but why the insistence on being so secretive with absolutely everyone? Just be honest with me, I can take it.'

Rowan signed. 'Okay, maybe at first there was a part of me that didn't want to be the person everyone was talking about again, just like they were after my parents' messy divorce, but I'm over that now.'

It was his turn to raise his eyebrows. 'In that case you'd have no problem with us going out for dinner this week, down by the harbour, where anybody could see us.'

'I...' She was hesitating again and he knew the answer before she even gave it. 'I can't yet. It's James. If people saw us out together, there'd be even more speculation about why my marriage is over. I'm not ready for that question to be on everyone's lips yet. There are things that need to be worked through and sorted out first, and conversations that need to be had with people who deserve to hear the truth from me and James. You and I being openly together would complicate that, but I just need a little bit more time.'

'I wish I could believe you and I know you aren't deliberately lying to me, but you are lying to yourself. Even if there is some reason tied up with James that means you can't be open about being with me, you don't trust me enough to tell me what it is. And the reason you don't trust me is because of what I've done in the past. You don't want the complication of being with someone like me and I don't blame you, but I don't want to wait around until you realise that, or pressure you to do something I know you don't really want to do. Whatever is happening with James doesn't matter, because there can't ever really be anything between you and me. I wanted there to be, but I promised myself that when things ended with Nicole, I'd never put myself through something like that again. I don't want to try and force a relationship with someone who doesn't think I can move on from being the person who went to prison. I'm not the man who committed that crime, not any more, but I understand why sometimes I still have to pay for it.'

'Nathan, please, it isn't that, and if I could tell you everything and make you understand, I would, but I promised James that I'd wait until he's ready.' She couldn't meet his eye for a moment and he felt like she was desperately trying to find some excuse for why they couldn't take the next step. 'There are things even the kids don't know yet and it just feels wrong for me to share that with anyone outside the family until they do.'

Nathan sighed, trying not to feel envious of the fact she still considered James to be a part of her family. Of course he was and he always would be, because it was best for the children. Nathan understood that and it was something he completely supported, but he couldn't have any kind of future with Rowan unless he thought there was a chance there might one day be space for him in that family too and now he knew there never would be. 'Even if James is eventually ready for everything to be out in the open, I don't think you ever really will be, not when it comes to being with me. But can we at least do the friends thing? Because I'd really hate to lose that, and for the boys to lose it too.'

'That's not what I want, it's just the timing of all of this is...'

'Off?' He forced a smile that made his face ache. 'We seem to specialise in our timing being off, and maybe it is the universe telling us that this is what we were supposed to be, just friends. I think that's what we're best at.'

'Do you? Is that really what you want?' She searched his face and it was his turn to lie.

'Absolutely. So let's do what friends do: have a cup of coffee in the kitchen and talk about our days. You can tell me how the Ofsted thing is going and I can tell you about how difficult it's been to source the right shade of flooring for my client's holiday cottage. Then you can look at the boys' glorious artwork; it's got aspects of Salvador Dali with a fair bit of David Attenborough thrown in.'

His laughter felt fractionally more genuine than his smile had been, as he turned and led the way down the hallway. It was a tiny step towards a future where he might really be able to think of Rowan as just a friend and to feel okay about that, and for now tiny steps were the best that he could hope for because this was not what he wanted. When he was with Rowan, it was as if he could see the future he'd always longed for and he couldn't imagine ever finding that with someone else, mostly because he didn't even want to try. He'd got through the toughest of times before and he'd have to find a way of doing it again; he had no choice but to try and get over her for a second time, no matter how impossible that might seem.

22

'She's beautiful, Will.' Nathan didn't even try to blink back the tears as he looked at his brother, before pulling him into a hug. 'Absolutely beautiful.'

'She is.' When they eventually moved apart, Will had the same mixture of relief and joy on his face as Nathan felt. They were standing outside the hospital room where he'd just met his new niece, and where Heather was recovering from the C-section she'd ended up needing. 'She's absolutely perfect and when I held her in my arms for the first time, it made it feel like everything we've been through and all of the pain that caused won't be for nothing any more. I love Leo with all my heart and I'd give anything to know he was going to be okay, but the chances are we're going to lose him. It feels like the baby gives us something solid to hold on to, not just the hope of a miracle that probably won't happen. Does that make me a terrible person?'

'Of course it doesn't.' Nathan shook his head, his heart somehow breaking and flooding with happiness all at the same time. 'It makes me feel like every-thing we've been through was all worth it too, but I'd have done it a hundred times over just to have whatever time we can with Leo, and I know you would too.'

'I would, but I'm his father and it should have been me who made all the sacrifices. You've had to give up far more than I ever have.'

'You can't measure that sacrifice when it comes to Leo, because there's nothing we wouldn't do for him. All of that's in the past anyway; today is for celebrating and we don't need to keep going over old ground.'

'We do when it affects the here and now.' Will put a hand on his shoulder. 'And don't even try to tell me that it doesn't, or that you don't have feelings for Rowan Adams.'

'Bellamy.'

'She'll always be Adams to me and I know she will to you too. She needs to know the truth. And so does Mum, and everyone else who matters to us. I can't carry it any more, it feels like a burden that I'll have to pay the price for eventually and I can't risk karma. Not now the baby is here.'

'Everyone knowing won't change anything, except for the worst. Mum will still have a son who committed a crime, two if you count perjury and perverting the course of justice. And while Heather will almost certainly forgive you, do you really want to risk ending up in prison and leaving her and the baby? Or missing valuable time with Leo? That's why we decided to do what we did in the first place. It was far better for me to say that I falsified the paperwork, I had much less to lose.'

'That's what I thought back then, but you had a lot more to lose than we thought: six months of your life, your reputation, and your wife.'

'If Nicole had really loved me, she wouldn't have left and the impact of you being locked up for six months would have been far greater. As for my reputation, what makes you think I don't like being the bad boy?'

'Because it cost you the person who might well have been the love of your life.'

'I've already said that it proved Nicole didn't really love me. She knew what the money that was taken was used for. It wasn't like anyone jetted off on some fancy five-star holiday, even the judge said he wished he didn't have to impose a custodial sentence.'

'I'm not talking about Nicole, I'm talking about Rowan. And I don't think I can live with myself knowing this has probably taken her from you too.'

'You've got to.' Nathan's jaw was set in a firm line. 'That's your punishment; having to live with the consequences of what happened and that's more than enough. If you suddenly confess now, all you're going to do is hurt Heather, Leo, the baby and Mum, and we might both end up in prison this time.'

'Nath—'

'No, I mean it.' He cut his brother off, his tone sharp. 'If you do this, I might never be able to forgive you. It's done, I served the time and that's all that was needed, one of us had to take the punishment for the crime and we did.'

'But it should have been me, you didn't know anything about it until after it was already done.'

'It doesn't matter and it was my choice. We both agreed it was for the best and nothing's changed, except that you've got the baby to think about now too. So just live with your guilty conscience if you have to, and suck it up.'

'Maybe I could just tell Rowan.'

'No!' Nathan's response was forceful, but he needed to make sure Will got the message. 'Telling just one person could make the whole thing unravel. This was our secret and if you tell anyone else we've lost control of it.'

For a moment Rowan's words about James came back to him; maybe there was justification for her refusing to tell Nathan everything that was going on, but it was a very different situation and he couldn't think about that now. All that mattered was stopping Will from doing something stupid and making sure he stayed with the family who needed him. As he locked eyes with Will, his brother finally seemed to realise that nothing had changed and they had to keep this to themselves, otherwise all of the sacrifices that had been made might really end up having been in vain.

'Okay, it'll stay our secret until the end, just like we promised, but I need you to know how much what you did means to me.'

'I already know and I've told you before, there's no need to thank me any more. It's over and we can all move on.'

Will looked doubtful for a moment, and Nathan knew he couldn't let his mask slip and allow his brother to see that his doubts were valid when it came to some people, because there were those who would never allow him to truly move on. It was a relief when Will finally nodded. 'Okay I know you're right, but I think I might have found a way of showing you how much what you did means to me.'

'You've bought me a sports car?' Nathan grinned, glad of the light relief after such an intense conversation.

'No, but Heather and I have agreed to call your new niece Nathalia, after the uncle who made her existence possible.'

'Is Heather really up for that?' There was a lump in his throat as his brother nodded.

'It was her suggestion and she doesn't even know the half of what you've done for us, but she still thinks you're amazing and absolutely the best person for our children to look up to.'

'Are you sure that's not the drugs from her op talking?' Nathan grinned again and Will hit him playfully on the arm.

'Shut up and take the compliment for once in your life.'

'Thank you.' He put his arms around his brother one more time and tears blurred his eyes. They held on to one another until they both regained control of their emotions. Things might not have worked out with Rowan and that had affected Nathan far more than it ought to have done. But for the first time in a long time it felt as if they could look forward to the future with hope, and he'd have repeated every sacrifice he'd made a hundred times over just to hold on to that possibility.

* * *

Rowan hadn't felt the way she had for the past two days since she was a teenager, when she'd been pining over Nathan the first time around. Even the news that the Ofsted inspectors would be grading the school as outstanding hadn't lifted her spirits the way it should have done, because she knew how much she'd hurt Nathan. She woke up thinking about him and went to bed thinking about him, going over the conversations they'd had and trying to work out if there was a way she could have handled things differently and not made such a terrible mess of everything.

She'd wanted to be honest and admit that when they'd moved beyond friendship there *had* been a part of her that didn't want anyone to know, because of how they might view the headteacher dating someone with a criminal record. But she'd got past that recently, she really had, because she knew just what an amazing person Nathan was. She hated the fact that he might doubt how she saw him, but she couldn't tell him the whole story until the children had been told as much as they needed to hear. It wasn't even that she didn't trust Nathan to keep whatever she said to himself, but she'd promised James when he'd been on the verge of doing something stupid that she'd support him through the process of talking to the children. The trouble was James was still putting it off. After the way his father had reacted, he'd been even more certain that they should handpick the people who were told, even once the children knew. That was something they'd have to work through eventually, but for now her priority was getting James to face up to his responsibilities to Bella and Theo.

Discovering that her husband was cheating on her would have been a huge knock to her self-esteem regardless of who his affair partner had been, but finding out that he'd fallen in love with another man had been a body blow she hadn't been sure she could get up from at first. Logically, she knew that some of the feelings she had made no sense. It wasn't 'her fault' that he'd fallen in love with a man. It was no one's 'fault', it was just the way James had always felt but had never been able to admit. That made the feeling that she was somehow less of a woman, because he'd rather be with a man, completely illogical. She knew that, but it didn't stop that feeling coming to her in waves over the weeks and months after the discovery. Embarrassment had mixed in with those feelings too. What would people say about a woman whose husband preferred another man to his wife? It was another ridiculous thought. James had finally been true to himself, that was all, and he hadn't had the strength to tell her. Being the last to know that her marriage was over and that her husband loved someone else was humiliating. It shouldn't have been, because there was nothing she could have done differently to change that, but feelings and logic often didn't go hand in hand.

When Nathan had said they should just be friends, she should have told him she didn't want that, because she liked him in a way that went far beyond friendship and that she'd never felt the kind of attraction to James that she felt to him. But that was difficult to admit even to herself, because in a way it made her just as complicit as James in the death of their marriage. She might never have cheated, but she'd gone into it knowing she didn't feel the kind of explosive attraction to him that she'd felt to Nathan. She'd put that down to being a teenager when she'd fallen for Nathan first time around, with the kind of big all-encompassing feelings that couldn't be replicated as an adult. Only suddenly it felt like they could. She'd loved James, he'd been there for her in the wake of her parents' marriage falling apart when she'd moved to London, and he was always there to listen to her problems and offer a shoulder to cry on. James was the one she should have stayed just friends with. They both knew that now, but she couldn't regret it, even for a second, because of Theo and Bella.

What she did regret was not proving she trusted Nathan by telling him the truth about James from the start. She was sure he'd have kept the secret if she'd asked him to. It was too late for all of that now and he'd never believe that one of the reasons she still didn't want to go public was to protect him. There'd been the inevitable talk of affairs when she'd come back to Port Agnes without her husband, and she knew from Bex that a lot of people seemed to think it must have been her who'd slept with someone else. After all, a chaplain would never do that kind of thing. The people closest to Rowan knew that it was James who'd met someone else, but only her mother knew about Euan. If people found out about her and Nathan, he was bound to be painted as the man who'd ruined her marriage. It was easy to sling mud at someone like him, but he didn't deserve it and she didn't want her children to ever believe it was true, and to start hating the man who'd been nothing but kind to them. She couldn't think about Nathan any more, because all she was doing was going around and around in circles. She'd just have to try and learn to live with the knowledge that she'd blown it and accept that all they could ever be was friends. For now she was focusing on getting James to face up to his own mistakes, so that there was a chance of them one day going back to being friends too.

'What did your uncle say? Has Stephen spoken to your father?' Rowan looked up as James came back downstairs after making a call to his father's twin brother. Michael hadn't returned any of his son's calls or answered his messages, and James had been beside himself with worry. It had made it very difficult for her to push him to speak to the children, even though the conversation was long overdue, because he was still reeling from his father's reaction.

'Dad's okay.' James looked deathly pale and his hands were visibly shaking as he sat down with a thud on the armchair in the corner of the kitchen.

'You're not though, are you? You look terrible. What else did Stephen say?'

'I'm just trying to process it all. It was such a shock and I still can't believe it.' James shook his head, staring straight ahead, but without seeming to see anything at all.

'You're scaring me now, just tell me what it was so that I know how I can help.' Rowan had no idea what she could do if Michael had decided to cut James out of his life forever, but she didn't want any more secrets.

'Stephen told me he knew why my father reacted as badly as he did and why his homophobia goes far beyond anything his faith dictates.' James locked eyes with her for the first time. 'When the two of them were at boarding school, something happened with one of the housemasters. They weren't the only ones it happened to, Stephen doesn't think, but it was awful. They were only twelve years old.'

'Oh my God.' Rowan's hand flew to her mouth.

'He's convinced that's why Dad's the way he is. He can't separate out what happened to him from sex in consenting relationships between gay men. He's tried speaking to Dad, and telling him that it doesn't make any more sense than it would to despise heterosexual relationships if they'd been abused by a woman instead of a man. But he thinks the reason Dad can't accept that is because he's never dealt with the trauma. Stephen's had counselling, but Dad buried himself in the church and, until the last couple of days, he refused to even talk about it or acknowledge that it happened.'

'But he is now?' Rowan's heartbeat was thudding in her ears; this was all so much to take in and it was no wonder James looked so shell-shocked.

'A bit, but Stephen has made a big decision that he thinks will be the only way Dad will finally face up to what happened and accept that it was abuse and nothing to do with what happens between consenting adults.' James let out a long breath. 'Stephen's going to tell the police. The housemaster is still alive, but he's in his eighties and he might die before it ever comes to court, even if the police think there's enough evidence. Stephen said it doesn't matter, and that he and Dad need to let go of the secret to stop it having any more power over them. I told him it's like what you said to me, about keeping my sexuality hidden. Secrets just make everything toxic. Stephen said a counsellor told him that a long time ago, which was why he sat Auntie Jane down and told her everything that had happened. He's almost certain that Dad has never told anyone, though, and that it's eaten away at him as a result. He's never been able to make the housemaster accountable for what he did, so he directed all his hatred to the wrong place instead.'

'That's...' Rowan could hardly catch her breath. 'Your poor dad has been through hell, and Stephen too. I can't bear to think about it, but it's true, secrets can be toxic.'

'I think we know that better than anyone.' James got to his feet and took her hand. 'I'm so sorry, Row, I wish I'd known how to be honest with you sooner and never put you through a marriage my heart wasn't in.'

'I don't, because it gave me Bella and Theo, and for a long time it gave me my best friend. Who knows, maybe one day we can go back to that, especially now that you're no longer having to keep things hidden that stopped you from really being there.'

'I hope so and I know I need to start by being honest with the children.'

'Right now?'

'Yes, right now. I've put it off for far too long and if Stephen can face going to the police, talking to our wonderful kids, who we both know probably won't even be fazed, is nothing in comparison.'

'They won't, because they're brilliant and they love you, and all they'll care about is that you're happy.'

'They want you to be happy too and so do I, more than anything. It's the only way I'll ever have a chance of forgiving myself.' James squeezed her hand again.

'You telling the kids will be a good start to that. Do you want me to be there with you?'

'No, it's okay, I want them to be able to come to you and ask any questions without feeling like they need to protect my feelings.' James smiled. 'What is it they say? Teamwork makes the dream work, and we can still be a team, can't we? When it comes to the kids?'

'I'd really like that.' She leant forward and gave him a kiss on the cheek. Whatever happened with Michael, and even with Nathan, she was glad that she and James had reached this point in their relationship as quickly as they had. As long as the kids were okay, that was all that mattered and she could find a way to be happy too, she was almost sure of it.

23

Just as Rowan had expected, the children took the revelation that their father was gay really well.

'I actually think it's quite cool.' Bella had shrugged when Rowan had asked her if she was okay. 'I think I'd rather have a stepdad than a stepmum, anyway. None of the stories about stepmothers are good.'

Rowan had laughed. 'Maybe not, but Marion is lovely and she's my stepmum.'

'I forget about that sometimes.' Bella had wrinkled her nose. 'I can't imagine Nanny Kat being married to Grandad Tony. It seems like it should always have been the way it is now.'

'I think it probably should have, and sometimes people are much happier after a divorce than they were before. But just because they aren't married, it doesn't mean they can't be friends, and me and Dad intend to keep being very good friends.'

'Okay, great.' Bella had shrugged again. 'Can I open the chocolate biscuits please?'

That had been the end of the conversation as far as her daughter was concerned, but Theo had always been the more thoughtful and reflective of the two, and Rowan had waited until they were alone together to speak to him about everything.

'Is there anything you're worried about, you know about what Dad told you? Or anything you want to ask?' They'd been walking her mother's dog on the beach when she asked him the question, and Theo had looked thoughtful for a moment.

'You know Dad has a boyfriend?' Theo screwed up his face as she nodded and she'd braced herself for what he might be about to ask, hoping that her little boy's innocence hadn't been corrupted by conversations in the playground far sooner than it should have been. 'Do you think he's going to be nice?'

'I'm sure he is and I know he works for a charity, helping get food to people who don't have enough to eat. That sounds like something only a really nice person would do, doesn't it?'

'Uh huh.' Theo had looked thoughtful again. 'Do you know who else is really nice?'

'Who?'

'Nathan.' He turned to look at his mother. 'I hope Dad's boyfriend is as nice as Nathan, then I'll definitely like him.'

Rowan had caught her breath, Theo's words taking her by surprise. She'd known how much he liked Nathan, but suddenly he'd become the benchmark by which all other men were judged. It was a legacy she'd been aware she'd have to carry into the future, but she hadn't realised just how big an impact Nathan had had on her son. 'I'm sure he will be, but if you've got any worries at any point, you can always talk to me. You know that, don't you?' Theo had nodded then and gone off in hot pursuit of Bluey, sending a spray of sand shooting up into the air in his wake and she suddenly felt a bit worried for Euan. Having to live up to being as nice as Nathan, in Theo's eyes, was going to be a very tough call.

However nice Nathan was, Rowan knew for certain now that her chance with him had passed. He responded to her messages when she texted him, but the replies were guarded, and they were no longer signed off with two kisses. Even when James had headed back to Membory Grange, to try and patch things up with Euan, and she'd texted Nathan to let him know he'd gone, asking if he was free to meet up, his response had been non-committal.

> I hope that makes life easier for you all and we'll all see each other at Leo's party, so we can have a chat then. He really misses seeing Theo outside of school, hopefully we can start to do that again soon.

She didn't need to read between the lines to know it was a brush off and that he only intended seeing her for the boys' sake. She only had herself to blame, because she'd been the one who'd set those boundaries when it came to meeting up in Port Agnes. It must have made Nathan feel like a dirty secret and she hated herself for that. What worried her most was that he might hate her for it too and that they wouldn't even be able to salvage a friendship out of the mess she'd made of everything. She missed just spending time with him and talking, but she had to accept she might have a long road to travel before she could start to regain his trust. Now that the day of Leo's party had finally arrived, she just hoped she wasn't about to discover that it was already too late.

'Is it time to go?' Bella came into the room wearing her new pink dress and a headband made from a ring of pink silk roses.

'In about five minutes, sweetheart, you look beautiful by the way.'

'Thanks.' Bella narrowed her eyes. 'You look sad. Is it because of what happened with Dad?'

'Oh no, darling.' She shook her head, looking at her daughter. Bella might seem far older than her years, but she didn't want her little girl growing up too soon, or worrying about Rowan, even for a moment. 'I promise I'm not unhappy, I was just thinking.'

'What about?'

'Nothing in particular.' She smiled, but Bella narrowed her eyes.

'I'm sure you could find a boyfriend too if you wanted one. You're much prettier than all of my friends' mums, even though you are quite old.' Bella shrugged and Rowan couldn't help laughing.

'Well thank you, I think. But I'm not in the market for a boyfriend right now. I've got everything I need with you and Theo.'

'I'm just saying, that's all.' Bella's tone was the epitome of casual. 'And me and Theo wouldn't mind, as long as he's nice. Like Nathan.'

Rowan tried to keep her face neutral but inside she was screaming. She knew as well as her children did how wonderful Nathan was, and that there was no one 'like Nathan' because he was a one-off. Hearing how much Bella and Theo loved him was a kick in the teeth, because she wasn't the only one missing out as a result of the decisions she'd made. Somehow, she managed to keep her tone light when she answered her daughter. 'Good to know. Can you tell Theo it's time to go now please? We're meeting Bex and the boys on the way up to Leo's house and I don't want to keep them waiting.'

'Okay.' Bella walked back through the kitchen door and hollered her brother's name. Both of her children had used Nathan as a benchmark to measure anyone new against, but she had a feeling he'd be impossible to live up to and she had no intention of even trying to find someone who could.

* * *

'So, look, I'm sorry I didn't tell you all of this before, when I first came home and we reconnected, but I don't think I'd even fully processed how I felt about it all at that stage.' Rowan was walking in step with Bex, along the lane that led to where Leo and his family lived. The children were running on ahead of them and she'd used the opportunity to fill Bex in on everything that had happened since James had arrived in Port Agnes. The only part she'd left out was how spectacularly she'd messed things up with Nathan.

'You don't have to tell me or anyone else anything you don't feel comfortable sharing, and I get why you wanted to keep your private life to yourself. We both know what this village can be like only too well.'

'We do.' Rowan shot her a conspiratorial look. 'God, do you remember what it was like when Mum and Dad split up, and some people seemed determined to believe that it was a wife-swapping ring gone wrong? I just didn't want Theo and Bella to have to overhear gossip about me and their father, but getting it out in the open means everyone knows the truth and that makes the gossips far easier to ignore. I should probably have done it from the start, but I didn't want to be the main topic of conversation again. And I suppose if I'm completely honest, part of me was embarrassed about what people might think of my husband leaving me for another man.'

'What they think says far more about them than it does about you, and it will be old news as soon as the next bit of village gossip comes along anyway.' Bex rolled her eyes. 'But I know it doesn't feel like that when you're the one everyone is talking about. I thought there'd never be a time when I wasn't remembered as the woman whose fiancé dumped her because he was in love with her sister.'

'What?' Rowan stopped in her tracks. 'That really happened? I can't believe I didn't know. I'm so sorry.'

'I'm not, not any more. I was young and stupid and thank God I wasn't the sort to plaster everything over social media back then. He did me the biggest favour ever by showing me who he was before I married him and as for my sister...' She trailed off for a moment, then seemed to shake herself back to the present. 'Regardless of what they did, it proves my point perfectly. All of that happened more than fifteen years ago, although you'd think in a small place like this it might have lived on in the memory, but it hasn't, not really. I'm not poor little Bex any more, the girl who'd saved for two years straight for a big white wedding and had nothing to show for it. Now I'm Bex, the best school secretary in Cornwall, the wife of an overworked farmer, and a harassed and worn-out mother of three.'

'You're definitely the best school secretary in Cornwall or anywhere else for that matter.' Rowan squeezed her waist for a moment, before letting her go again. 'And I'm glad I'll eventually be able to look forward to the gossip dying down. How long did it take for you to stop being the centre of attention?'

'Did you ever hear about it, on any of your visits back here to see your dad and Marion?'

'No, never.'

'Exactly. Three weeks after it happened the man who was the verger at St Jude's at the time was caught trying to feed rat poison to his next-door neighbour's cat, because it kept pooing in his garden, and me being jilted became ancient history overnight. No one even batted an eyelid when I met Matt within three months of when I should have been getting married. Or when just six months later we flew out to Las Vegas and got married. After more than thirteen years together and three boys, I can barely remember my ex-fiancé's name. None of it matters any more, not even to the most vicious of gossips, because I really don't care. As soon as you truly don't care, nothing anyone else says can touch you.'

'I think I'm nearly there, already.' Rowan smiled and Bex mirrored her expression.

'Good, because the men who didn't appreciate how lucky they were to have us, don't deserve to have us waste a single second of our time on them. So if you end up jetting off to Vegas in three months' time, I promise I won't judge and I'll even give you the name of a very good Elvis impersonator who can officiate at the ceremony!'

'I'll bear that in mind.' Rowan laughed. 'But for now I'm happy as I am, I promise you. I feel so much better for having everything out in the open and the last thing on my mind is trying to find someone else.'

Almost unconsciously, Rowan crossed two of the fingers on her right hand over each other, despite the fact that it wasn't a lie. She didn't want to find anyone else, but it wasn't because she'd written off the possibility of finding someone she liked enough to take a risk on. It was because she'd already found him. That was one secret she couldn't share, even with Bex. If she did, she'd have to admit how badly she'd messed up and just how shallow she'd been, and she still hadn't fully come to terms with that herself.

* * *

As Rowan walked inside the beautiful Georgian house that Leo and his family shared with Nathan's mother, she tried not to think about the last time she'd been there. Thankfully there was no mistaking that this time she was there for a birthday party. There were banners, bunting and balloons, including a huge silver one in the shape of an eight, so that no one could forget the birthday boy's age. A veritable banquet had been laid out on the table and the party games were ready to get underway. The only things that seemed to be missing were the birthday cake and Leo's uncle.

'Have you seen Nathan?' Rowan turned to her father, as they stood on the far side of the room, watching the children's entertainer make a sculpture out of giant bubbles. Both her parents and stepparents had been invited to the party and there were probably more adults than children there. Half the village seemed to be in attendance, and she completely understood why every birthday Leo had would feel like a landmark one that deserved to be cele-brated. He was such a great kid, who'd brought more joy into Theo's life than any other friendship he'd ever had. It seemed as if that feeling was mutual, because Leo appeared completely unaware of the fact that quite a lot of the other children had gone outside to play hide-and-seek in the back garden, despite the crisp mid-November weather. It clearly didn't matter to him where the others were, as long as he had Theo by his side. The two of them were giggling with one another as the entertainer invited them to try and pop the bubbles, using a remote-control device that made a sound like a whoopee cushion every time they managed to pop one. It was the perfect entertainment for boys their age.

'Apparently there was a mix up with the cake delivery. When Irene opened the box, the piping said "Happy 40th Anniversary Bill and Diane", so Nathan went off to sort it out.' Rowan's dad put his arm around her shoulder and gave her a squeeze. 'Heather and Irene were just going to scrape the piping off, and stick some of Leo's Lego figures on top, but you know what Nathan is like when it comes to that boy. Nothing is too much trouble. Truth be told, it's what Nathan's like when it comes to helping anyone out really. I could probably tell you a hundred stories about that lad stepping in to help someone. He had a client whose husband died just after he'd finished their extension and the last part of the bill was still outstanding. She was beside herself because paying the bill would have meant she wouldn't have had enough money left for the funeral, so he told her there'd been a mistake in the paperwork and that she'd already paid everything that was owed. He's one of the good guys, maybe even the best.'

'I know. He's helped loads up at the school too, with all the stuff we've been working on, not just for Leo, but putting up playground equipment for the other children too. He's a pretty special person.' Rowan tried once again to keep her expression neutral, but her father didn't miss the look that must have crossed her face.

'I knew it!' He wagged a finger at her. 'I told Marion there was something going on between you two, but she kept telling me that I was wrong and that you and James might still make a go of things. I'm glad that's not true, because he's not right for you, he never was and life is too short not to give yourself a second chance to find the person you're supposed to do life with. But maybe you already have.'

'Now you really are getting carried away, Dad.' She laughed, leaning in to his shoulder for a moment. The weird thing was she could picture herself with Nathan, but it was probably because she'd spent half her teens doing just that. It was ridiculous to think it might actually happen, especially when Nathan had made it clear that they were better off as friends. She hadn't had the chance to tell him the full story about James yet; her dad and stepparents still didn't even know. Marion had invited everyone to Sunday lunch and she was intending to explain everything then, so it wouldn't be a shock the next time James came up for a visit and hopefully, if Euan could forgive him, brought his new partner to meet them all. Either way, James had decided not to retract his resignation at Membory Grange. He was still considering the possibility of becoming a parish priest, but he'd told Rowan, after everything they'd gone through, that he needed to be able to be completely true to himself and not hide who he was just to get a job.

'I owe you that,' he'd said, hugging her tightly when they'd been saying their goodbyes. It meant he was considering other options, one of which was to do a master's degree in social work or counselling, so he could help young people who might be going through something similar to what his father and uncle had faced. Rowan was sure he'd make the right choice, because he was finally able to be himself and he already seemed lighter for it. She hoped he might make the decision to move to Cornwall too, so that the children could see him whenever they wanted, but she wasn't going to try to influence him. James had been constrained for so long and he deserved this second chance to discover what he wanted without anyone else telling him what to do.

'Oh, here's Nathan now.' Rowan's dad nudged her and she wanted to blame her sharp intake of breath on the elbow she'd just got in the ribs, but it had been far too gentle to provoke that kind of reaction. It was Nathan who'd taken her breath away. He was smiling as he showed Leo the cake, his blue eyes lighting up at his nephew's excited reaction. Nathan's dark hair looked slightly windswept, but in a very attractive sort of way, like Heathcliff striding across the moors. *Oh my God.* She tried to shake the thought out of her head the moment it arrived, but she couldn't. He was a beautiful man, inside and out.

'Can you get some more people to come and play hide-and-seek with us, please, Nathan?' Bella, who'd been outside with Tiffany and some of the others, had shot back into the house, clearly having seen him arrive. 'The little kids are rubbish at finding us and none of the other adults would come outside when you weren't here, but I bet you can get them to do it because you managed to get loads of them to do the race. Even Mr Phipps and he never runs, even when he's supposed to be teaching us how to play football.'

Nathan was obviously trying to suppress a smile at the mention of Mr Phipps, who came in to run some of the sports' sessions at the school. He was a good teacher and popular with the children, but Rowan had been warned by Bex that he had a reputation for doing anything he could to avoid physical assertion, which even included wearing the type of trainers that had elasticated laces so that they didn't have to be undone. It had been nothing short of a miracle to see him panting to the finish line, among the last of the stragglers, on the day of the half marathon.

'I promise I'll round some of them up, as soon as we've cut the cake. Do you think you could be an absolute star and get everyone who's outside to come in and sing happy birthday to Leo?'

'Yes, you're the best!' Bella grinned, unknowingly echoing her grandfather's words as she dashed back outside to round the other children up.

Within a couple of minutes everyone was assembled for Leo's big moment. Will and Heather were standing to one side of their son, with their gorgeous baby daughter, Nathalia, cradled in Heather's arms. Irene was on the other side with Nathan, and because Rowan wasn't sure if anyone was capturing the moment for the family, she'd reached down into her bag, which was on one of the chairs, and pulled out her mobile phone.

'Are you ready, Leo?' Nathan looked at his nephew who nodded, before lighting the candles on the cake, as a rousing rendition of happy birthday began.

'Now you just need to blow out your candles, darling,' Heather instructed. 'And don't forget to make a wish.'

Everyone cheered as Leo managed the feat with a single breath and then screwed up his eyes to make a wish. Ending the recording, Rowan was about to pick up her handbag, so that she could drop the phone back into it, when Louise Duffy, one of the parents at the school, suddenly hissed in her ear.

'Best to keep your handbag close to you in this house. You never know when your purse might get nicked with someone like Nathan around.'

'What did you say?' Rowan's tone was icy cold as she turned to look at the woman who'd made regular appointments to see her to complain about one thing or another. Last time it had been the fact that her daughter had supposedly received fewer house points than she should have done, and to share her opinion that the system was rigged so that certain children were guaranteed to come out on top. In her words, it was *clear to anyone with eyes in their head that my Ellie-Mae should be top of the class*. Louise Duffy was a thorn in Rowan's side that her job forced her to put up with, but she wasn't at work now and a line had been crossed that Rowan just couldn't ignore.

'I'm just saying, everyone knows what he did, and a leopard never really changes its spots, does it? I know your boy is friends with his nephew, but you wouldn't want to leave your purse unattended around him, would you?'

'Oh, I'd do a whole lot more than that.' Dropping her bag back on the chair, Rowan turned away from Louise Duffy and crossed the room to where Nathan was now standing. Blood was whooshing in her ears and her heart was racing with the adrenaline that was pulsing through her veins, but she couldn't have stopped herself even if she'd wanted to.

'Nathan.' Her eyes met his as he turned to look at her and she reached up, putting a hand on either side of his face and pulling it towards hers before kissing him, not with the kind of passion she would have if they'd been by themselves, but in a way that would leave no one in any doubt that she saw him as far more than a friend.

The room seemed to go deathly silent for a second or two as she pulled away again, before another massive cheer erupted. The only problem was that the expression on Nathan's face was completely blank, and Rowan had absolutely no idea how he felt about what had just happened. Whatever it was, it didn't look good.

24

'You told her, didn't you?' Nathan had all but dragged Will upstairs by his arm, when the cheering had finally died down after Rowan had kissed him. He felt awful for just leaving her there, batting away all the questions he could hear coming thick and fast from the other guests, about how long all of this had been going on, and what dark horses they were. He had no idea what the kiss meant, or what was happening with James, but before he did anything – before he even spoke to Rowan – he needed to know one thing and he was still waiting for his brother's answer, but Will looked completely nonplussed.

'Told her what?'

'That the VAT fraud...' Nathan lowered his voice to almost a whisper. 'Was you and not me.'

'No, I didn't. I swear.' Will locked eyes with him and he knew his brother was telling the truth. 'But I think you should. She needs to know it was me who took the money, I was the idiot who risked everything and you were the one who paid the price.'

'You weren't an idiot, you were desperate. I might well have done the same thing in those circumstances.'

'No, you wouldn't have, because you're a better man than me. You took my sentence to protect my family, that's something I'll never forget. But you deserve people to know that, especially Rowan, if you like her even half as much as I think you do.'

'I don't like her.' Will raised his eyebrows in disbelief as Nathan paused for a moment. 'I love her. I did when we were younger, but I was too slow off the mark and I missed the chance. Now, I don't know what to do. It's all so much more complicated, she's got her position in the community, and then there's the situation with James.'

'You're an amazing person, Nath, but sometimes you can be as thick as a brick.' Will grinned. 'Don't you see that none of that matters? Rowan couldn't have made that more obvious by kissing you in front of everyone, although maybe she actually needs to hit you over the head with a brick if you still don't get it. She. Feels. The. Same.'

He said the last four words incredibly slowly and then pretended to knock on the side of Nathan's head. 'Please tell me you get it now?'

'Do you really think so, even though she has no idea what happened before I went to prison?'

'Yep, she *lurves* you!' Will mimed cuddling himself and making kissing sounds. Suddenly it was like they were teenagers again and he was teasing Nathan about how much he'd liked Rowan back then.

'Will you shut up?' Nathan laughed despite his words.

'I will if you go down there and tell her how you feel, because if you don't, I will.'

'Okay, but I'm not going to tell her about the VAT stuff. Maybe one day, but not yet.'

'Why not?' Will narrowed his eyes. 'I can't imagine Rowan wanting to go to the police or HMRC, and tell them what really happened. She'll understand why we both did what we did. She might not condone it, but it's obvious how fond she is of Leo, and she'd never do anything to hurt him.'

'I know that, but it matters to me that she likes me enough for none of that to be a dealbreaker for her.' Nathan shrugged. 'Maybe it's a twisted way of thinking, but after the way some people have treated me over the years, the fact that she thinks I'm worth a second chance is everything.'

'It's okay, I get it. Now for God's sake just go and talk to her, and whatever you do don't blow it this time, because I'll think you're a bloody idiot forever if you do.'

'Thanks for the pep talk.' Nathan grinned again before heading out of the door and taking the stairs two at a time. Second chances really were priceless and he'd never wanted one more than he did right now.

* * *

'Have you seen your mum anywhere, Theo?' Nathan's voice filtered through to where Rowan was standing, crouched behind a Red Robin bush in the back garden. She'd thrown herself into playing hide-and-seek with the children, to get away from all the questions after she'd kissed Nathan and he'd immediately disappeared.

Hiding seemed like a good idea given that her cheeks still felt as though they were on fire. There was every chance she'd given the village gossips the best fodder they'd had in years for absolutely no reason, and embarrassed Nathan into the bargain. He'd told her he only wanted to be friends and she'd been arrogant enough – certain enough of the attraction and feelings between them – to think it had been his way of letting her off the hook, because of everything that had been going on with James. Except he'd stood there after the kiss, looking as if he'd forgotten how to speak. She'd turned away for less than a couple of seconds when Bex had let out a delighted whoop and, by the time she'd turned back, Nathan was gone. As much as hiding out was a good way to stop the rest of the guests from seeing how embarrassed she was, it was also giving her far too much time to wonder just how horrified Nathan might be about what she'd done. But she was about to find out.

'She's hiding somewhere, but she's really good at it and we can't find her.'

'Shall I give you a hand?' Nathan's tone was conspiratorial and she could hear the grin in Theo's voice as he replied.

'Yes please, she'll never be able to hide from you.' Rowan had a horrible feeling that her son was right and she knew she couldn't hide forever either way. She'd have to face Nathan sooner or later, but she still tried to hold her breath as she heard footsteps growing closer and then suddenly there was a hand on her arm.

'Found you.' Nathan's tone was warm, but as she forced herself to turn and look at him, she still couldn't read his expression.

'You were the one who disappeared first.' She wanted to drop her gaze so that she didn't see a look of pity cross his face, but she made herself hold eye contact and then he took hold of her hand.

'I'm so sorry, it was just... It was the last thing I ever expected you to do, especially in front of a room full of people and I didn't know what it meant.'

There was a smile tugging at the corners of his mouth, but she was done with trying to read his emotions. She needed to know.

'What does it usually mean when a woman kisses you? I know we've probably lived very different kinds of lives but when I kiss someone like that, it means I like them. A lot. And when I kiss someone in public, it means I'm happy for the world to know that I like that person. A lot.' Rowan was aware that there was an edge to her voice now, but she didn't want any more half measures. They were either in this for real, or they were out. 'There's a lot I need to tell you about what happened with James, but I can do that now the children know everything. I also know how much Bella and Theo like you, so there's only one barrier stopping us from taking this any further. There aren't any cast-iron guarantees in life, I understand that, but I've got to be as sure as I can that we're on the same page. I'm not about to let myself or my kids fall any more in love with you than we already are, if you're not sure how you feel.'

'You're in love with me? I think that might be the best thing I've ever heard.'

'I didn't say that, I said—'

'You more or less did.' He grinned, cutting her off and she pretended to push him, trying not to laugh, all of the tension she'd felt slowly diffusing. He was infuriating and gorgeous and a big part of her just wanted to kiss him again, but she needed more than that. She needed to hear him say how he felt.

'Oh for God's sake okay, maybe I did say that, but you still haven't told me how you feel and whether you're as sure as you can be that we aren't making a huge mistake by giving this a try.'

'I've never once doubted how I feel, from the moment I saw you again. It was exactly how I felt more than twenty years ago, but then it got even bigger. The only doubt I had was how you felt about me and the person I'd been in the time we were apart. Then you kissed me and I wanted it to mean everything I thought it might mean, but I couldn't believe it did. That's why I disappeared and asked Will what he thought; he told me I was an idiot and to get myself down here before I ended up blowing my second chance with the most beautiful woman I've ever met.'

'You are an idiot, but after that comment, I might just let you off.' She dropped Nathan's hand and stepped back, his face falling in response.

'What's the matter?'

'Nothing. I'm just waiting for you to kiss me this time.'

'Oh.' When he smiled again, she couldn't help mirroring his expression, her whole body tingling as he pulled her towards him. The kiss, had anyone been there to witness it, would have left no one in any doubt how Nathan felt about her, least of all Rowan, but this kiss definitely wasn't for public consumption.

* * *

By the time the last of the other party guests had gone, Rowan had been able to fill Nathan in on what had happened with James and how much she wished she hadn't tied herself up in knots trying to keep things secret from him. He'd kissed her again and told her she was just doing what she thought was best for the children and that he'd probably have done exactly the same thing. It was yet more proof that Nathan understood the most important thing about her, that the children would always come first, and that it wasn't just something he'd be able to tolerate, it was the way he lived his life too. Back in the days when she used to practise a signature that said Rowan Lark, she'd pictured what it might be like to have a family with Nathan. It hadn't looked anything like her life did now, but just like a patchwork quilt could be far more beautiful than a blanket made from one neat piece of material, the family they might one day become felt like a beautiful possibility.

All of that was a long way off, but it didn't feel like it as she sat in Will and Heather's kitchen, holding baby Nathalia in her arms. All four of her parents and Irene were playing Monopoly in the living room with Bella and Tiffany, while Leo and Theo sat at the kitchen table eating what was quite possibly their third slice of cake.

'This is so yummy,' Theo announced as he swallowed another bite. 'Please can I have a cake like this for my birthday, Mum?'

'Of course you can, sweetheart.' Rowan stroked Nathalia's cheek as she spoke, the baby's eyelids flickering in response.

'And I already know exactly what I'm going to wish for.' Theo speared another piece of cake with his fork.

'Don't tell us what it is, or it won't come true.' Heather smiled at the boys. 'That's what I told you, wasn't it, Leo?'

'Yes, and that definitely works, 'cos I think my wish has already come true.'

He shot a look towards where Rowan was sitting, with Nathan's arm draped around her shoulders.

'Already?' Will tilted his head to one side. 'That is impressive. So are you going to tell us what it was now then?'

'When you said I was getting a sister, it wasn't really what I wanted.' Leo wrinkled his nose.

'But she's so cute.' Heather looked a little bit crestfallen, but then Leo nodded.

'She is and I'm really glad we've got her now, but I still kind of wanted a brother. But then I thought if I can't have a brother, maybe I could have a cousin.' Leo shot another look at his uncle. 'Except a baby wouldn't be that much fun to play with, not like Theo and I thought maybe he could be my cousin, if Uncle Nathan marries his mum. So that's what I wished for.'

Everyone laughed and Will ruffled his son's hair. 'Well, I wouldn't say that's quite come true yet, but there's definitely progress. Good work, buddy.'

'I think I might change what I'm going to wish for.' Theo exchanged a knowing look with his best friend, making them all laugh again.

'As it happens, it's my birthday next month too.' Nathan trailed his fingers down Rowan's arm and she let out a small sigh of contentment. Sitting in the heart of this cosy kitchen, amongst so many people she cared about, she suddenly felt enveloped in love. It might be far too soon to be thinking about forever, but she knew without a shadow of a doubt that this was the best second chance any of them could have asked for and she couldn't wait to find out just how many wishes might come true.

* * *

MORE FROM JO BARTLETT

Another book from Jo Bartlett, the latest instalment in the Cornish Country Hospital series, is available to order now here:

https://mybook.to/CornishHospitalBook7

ACKNOWLEDGEMENTS

As always, I want to start by thanking my wonderful readers. I'm so grateful to you for choosing my books and I will never take that for granted. It means so much to receive your messages of support and they really help keep me going when I'm struggling with a plot point, or another deadline is looming. Thank you all so much.

I really hope you've enjoyed the first instalment in *The Cornish Bay Collection*. Although this is a brand-new series, returning to the setting of Port Agnes and including some cameos from the characters in my other two Cornish series has made it feel like coming home.

This book is centred around the village school and as someone who taught for over twenty-five years before becoming a full-time author, there's a lot in this story that feels familiar to me, especially as my own children attended a very similar village school. One of the most heartfelt aspects of the novel is Leo's story. I chose to write about muscular dystrophy as one of my best friends has the condition. Although she doesn't have the same form as the Duchenne's muscular dystrophy Leo has, it's something that is very close to my heart and, as ever, I hope I have done the subject justice. If you are someone with personal experience of muscular dystrophy, I hope you feel that there are aspects of this story you can relate to. If you want to find out more about the condition, this website is a very good starting point: www.-musculardystrophyuk.org.

This is the point where I begin to thank all the other people who have helped get this book to publication. At the end of the books in my other series, I write a long list of book reviewers and social media superheroes, who have played such a big part in bringing my books to new readers by spreading the word to others, including by regularly commenting on and sharing my posts. As this is a brand-new series, I am going to list the top fans on my Facebook page, who always do so much to celebrate my success and share my books with others. As well as the reviewers who were involved in promoting my most recent release via the blog tour, which, at the time of writing these acknowledgements was *A Cornish Winter's Kiss*:

Book Escapes with Barbara Wilkie, Kirsty's Book Buying Addiction, Kirsty Reviews Books, The Witchy Storyteller, Little Miss Book Lover 87, Leanne Bookstagram, Sapphyria's Books, The Eclectic Review, Books, Life and Everything, Wendy Reads Books, Jen Loves Reading. Two Ladies and a Book, Splashes into Books, MrsLJGibbs, TBHonest, Eatwell2015, Being Anne, Annette Reads Daily, Staceywh_17, Tizi's Book Review, Isabell from @dwoe.reviews, @maries_world_in_books, @decantingbooks *Adventures in Reading, Running, and Working from Home. As well as @a_coffee_and_a_book, who has said such lovely things about the Cornish Country Hospital Series.*

Sam Clarke, Tracey Miller, Lesley Riches, Maria Lemmon, Cindy Dodd, Bookstagramshaz, Sarah Louise, Donna Pritchard, Gail Stokes, Luna Hayes, Jessica Benge, Lucy McDonagh, Jan Whaites MacMillan, Diane Devison, Mary Grand, Deirdre Palmer, Leanne Reads and Reviews, Helen Rachel, Vicky Trotter, Emma Messenger, Shreena Morjaria, Pamela Spearing, Joanne Edwards, Tea Books, Jo Bowman, Jane Ward, Elizabeth Marshall, Tina Pearson, Laura McKay, Katherine Jane, Rayo Reads, Jane Woodcock, Dawn Warren, Lesley Brett, Tris Ashe, Mo Hardy, Sarah Lizziebeth, Margaret Hardman, Vikki Thomson, Mary Brock, Suzanne Cowen, Debbie Marie Sleigh, Kathryn Paddock, Jean Norris, Sally Starley, Michelle Hallowes, Jackie Bruce, Stacie Elizabeth, Hayley Marsland, Kerry Coltham, Meena Kumari, Emma Stokes, May Miller, Gillian Ives, Grace Power, Carrie Cox, Elspeth Pyper, Lauren Hewitt, Beverley Ann Hopper, Wendy Neels, Bex Hiley, Kay Love, Julie Foster, Ros Carling, Miehele Hoskin, Christine Spiers, Maureen Bell, Caroline Day, Tanya Goodsell, Teg Elizabeth, Kate O'Neill, Janet Wolstenholme, Lin West, Isabella Tartaruga, Judit Howe, Audrey Galloway, Hayley Elizabeth, Helen Phifer, Nicla Clough and Johanne Thompson.

I'm so thankful to everyone who takes the time to review or share my books and, as this series progresses, I promise to continue adding names to the list, starting with all those who are involved with reviewing and promoting this first book in the series.

My thanks as ever go to the team at Boldwood Books, especially my amazing editor, Emily Ruston, and my brilliant copy editor, Candida Bradford, and fantastic proofreader, Rachel Sargeant, all of whom helped so much in shaping this story into something I can be proud of. I also want to thank my good friend Jennie Dunn, for providing such wonderful support with final checks on the novel.

In addition, I'm hugely grateful to the rest of the team at Boldwood Books, who are now too numerous to list, but special mention must go to my marketing lead, Marcela Torres, and the Directors of Sales and Marketing, Nia Beynon and Wendy Neale, as well as to the inimitable Amanda Ridout, for having the foresight to create such an amazing company to be published by.

I'm also very thankful to have such a great partnership with Emma Powell, who has expertly narrated all my novels for Boldwood Books, and who always does an amazing job.

As ever, I can't sign off without thanking my writing tribe, The Write Romantics, including my fellow Boldies Sharon Booth, Jessica Redland, Helen Rolfe, and Alex Weston, and to all the other authors I am lucky enough to call friends, especially Gemma Rogers, who is another fellow Boldie.

Finally, as it forever will do, my most heartfelt thank you goes to my husband, children and grandchildren. Every story I write is for you.

ABOUT THE AUTHOR

Jo Bartlett is the bestselling author of over nineteen women's fiction titles. She fits her writing in between her two day jobs as an educational consultant and university lecturer and lives with her family and three dogs on the Kent coast.

Download your exclusive bonus content from Jo Bartlett here:

Follow Jo on social media here:

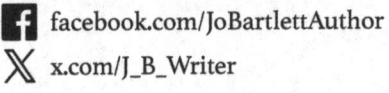

facebook.com/JoBartlettAuthor
x.com/J_B_Writer

ALSO BY JO BARTLETT

The Cornish Midwife Series

The Cornish Midwife

A Summer Wedding For The Cornish Midwife

A Winter's Wish For The Cornish Midwife

A Spring Surprise For The Cornish Midwife

A Leap of Faith For The Cornish Midwife

Mistletoe and Magic for the Cornish Midwife

A Change of Heart for the Cornish Midwife

Happy Ever After for the Cornish Midwife

Seabreeze Farm

Welcome to Seabreeze Farm

Finding Family at Seabreeze Farm

One Last Summer at Seabreeze Farm

Cornish Country Hospital Series

Welcome to the Cornish Country Hospital

Finding Friends at the Cornish Country Hospital

A Found Family at the Cornish Country Hospital

Lessons in Love at the Cornish Country Hospital

Together Again at the Cornish Country Hospital

Mending Hearts at the Cornish Country Hospital

The Cornish Bay Collection

Letting Go of Yesterday

Standalone Novels

Second Changes at Cherry Tree Cottage

A Cornish Summer's Kiss

Meet Me in Central Park

The Girl She Left Behind

A Mother's Last Wish

A Cornish Winter's Kiss

BECOME A MEMBER OF

THE SHELF CARE CLUB

The home of Boldwood's
book club reads.

Find uplifting reads,
sunny escapes, cosy romances,
family dramas and more!

Sign up to the newsletter
https://bit.ly/theshelfcareclub

Boldwood

Boldwood Books is an award-winning fiction publishing company seeking out the best stories from around the world.

Find out more at www.boldwoodbooks.com

Join our reader community for brilliant books, competitions and offers!

Follow us
@BoldwoodBooks
@TheBoldBookClub

Sign up to our weekly deals newsletter

https://bit.ly/BoldwoodBNewsletter

www.ingramcontent.com/pod-product-compliance
Lightning Source LLC
Chambersburg PA
CBHW011800010726
47497CB00012B/3214